The World Without Mirrors

Confessions of a Peace Terrorist

Connect with the author:
www.nickbruechle.com
nick@nickbruechle.com
facebook.com/nickbruechlebooks
@nick_bruechle

ISBN 978-0-6450839-1-0

Set in Adobe Garamond

For my darling wife, Rachel.

1. Moving in

It began with a two-line ad on Craigslist: 'Wanted: room-mates to share laid-back rental in Brooklyn. Suit students or similar.'

I'd had enough of campus life over the previous two years, and I knew that if I moved out of the dorm at NYU, where Abby and I both studied history, she'd keep our room but would spend almost all of her time wherever I was. So going home was out of the question; not that I would ever have dreamed of doing so anyway.

Nevin and Bevan, whose names were on the lease, were very welcoming, especially when I paid a security deposit and six months' rent in advance (thanks, Daddy). I moved off Manhattan for the first time in my life.

Brooklyn was bigger, flatter and dirtier than I'd imagined. I had of course been through it many times before – how else are you going to get to Coney Island and Rockaway Beach? But when you don't live in a place, you don't see it for what it really is. Or at least you don't pick up the gritty detail.

The house, in Devoe Street, was probably very nice when it was built a couple of world wars or more ago. And it was probably nice again when it was last renovated, thirty or more years ago. But it hadn't seen a hair of a paintbrush since then, and some of the timber had a mouldy, rotting look and smell. Sturdy, but senile and wrinkled, the weatherboard exterior was painted pale blue, the shingles on the roof were ancient and grimy, and the small, sparse backyard held, wonder of wonders, a cherry tree, as well as an old outhouse, which was now jammed with flotsam from the house. And there was a huge, dank basement, complete with radon detector and scant, spooky lighting. When I moved in, it just held broken-down furniture and other junk that never made it to the kerb.

Still, the house was comfortable and secure, and my room on the ground floor at the back was large and airy. It was all a bit expensive for what it was, but in a fabulous location: being close to shopping and the subway made it easy to get to college, and I was a long, long way (in New York terms) from my family home.

The best room went to Nevin, who was top dog, at least in the beginning. He had a good job as a video editor at a local television news station and, although he was tall and gangly and had bad skin, and quite often his breath smelled as though he'd just eaten some roadkill, he could be charming and likeable – not what you'd expect from a techno-geek who immersed himself in darkness all day, pushing buttons or twiddling knobs or whatever it was he did. Perhaps I'm being unkind. He wasn't my type and I couldn't understand the girls who did like him, either. Bimbos.

Nevin was in charge because he and Bevan had found the house and Bevan never asserted himself if he could avoid it. So Nevin had the prime, second floor bedroom at the front of the house, as far away from me as could be. This was a good thing, because in addition to being the first personable nerd I'd ever spent any time with, he was also very successful in enticing comely, stupid young women back to our place for random sex, and according to Lucas, whose room was closest to Nevin's, he was very noisy at it.

Mind you, Lucas, who'd answered the ad and was a newcomer like me, was one of those self-obsessed pretty boys for whom everyone else's life and actual being was at best a nuisance. He thought he was much smarter than he was, so he would make pronouncements rather than have conversations.

These pronouncements were rarely well thought out, and it was amusing to see him tie himself up in logical knots or end up defending a position he'd recently denounced. But often he was just hard work. On the other hand, late at night, drunk and/or stoned, he could be sweet and self-effacing. He just wouldn't remember it in the morning.

Lucas was studying some hipster shit at Columbia – literature or feelings or something equally useless; he never paid attention anyway – and drew endlessly on a fat trust fund his grandfather had set up. His clothes were always new, his hair was always carefully coiffed, and his room was always an obscene mess, because he didn't have the slightest clue how to clean up. True to his personality and his privileged upbringing, Lucas loved the idea of action and intensity, but hated dirt, blood and hard work.

The last full-fledged member of the house was Bevan. Dear, unobtrusive, but ultimately bold and bloody Bevan. When I first met him, he was a bit of a blob, shy and lacking confidence. He'd always been overweight, and in his younger days, his hair had been an even more alarming carroty red, so people had instantly classified him as a fat, dumb ginger, and that stayed with him. All his life, he never got credit for being as smart and emotionally deep as he was. He was difficult to read and hard to excite, but he could be maddeningly logical and wonderfully warm. Later, his focus, his physical strength and his tenacity lent a powerful force to our group.

Bev was capable of remarkable insight, and I think he saw more clearly than any of us what was happening. He just didn't care to stop it. He enjoyed the ride too much.

When I moved in, Bev had just started a security-work training course, while working irregular nights and weekends stocking supermarket shelves. Once he got his first security job, his confidence and sense of authority, not to mention his capacity for menace, grew as quickly as his muscles.

I was drawn to Bevan first, maybe because he was Nevin's understudy the way I was Abby's, and he remained my best friend and closest ally among the housemates. Sure, I grew to like, even love, Lucas and Nevin. But I was always happy to see big Bev. Even when he'd turned into a fierce warrior, he was cuddly, and it helped that he was endearingly protective of me and Abby. He never once tried to put any moves on either of us. Abby, on the other hand, entertained herself with him a few times.

Abby and I loved my room. The walls were the same sky blue as the house's exterior, with a beautifully profiled white timber shelf running around the perimeter, about three feet below the high ceiling. The window onto the yard was tall and wide. The ceiling had lovely cornices and there was a huge, elaborate ceiling rose in the middle, from which hung the ugliest light fixture I have ever seen. The floorboards were dark, and although they were free of major scratches and gouges, my mother, who inspected the house with me, rushed out and bought a huge Persian rug to cover them.

In fact, we went on a bit of a shopping spree, Mother and Abby and me. Having tradesmen tramp through her precious Manhattan pile to remove the furniture I'd grown up with would be far too much of a drag, Mother said, so why not just get everything new? I certainly wasn't of a mind to object: I was bored with everything about my previous existence.

The only thing we disagreed on was buying a lounge that would function as a sofa bed – for Abby's exclusive use, of course. It was the best sofa bed money could buy, but Mother objected. It was such a banal, utilitarian item. Why not an elegant, if uncomfortable, chaise? What was I thinking?

I was thinking that it would be the best piece of furniture I ever bought, because it made my room into Abby's room as well. She stayed over between three and seven nights a week, and nobody ever minded. I probably didn't need the sofa in the end, anyway; we were usually too tired to bother unfolding the bed, and shared mine, which was plenty big enough.

Lucas tried to bed Abby very early in their acquaintance, which was a spectacular failure. Nevin never really tried, but I often caught him looking lustfully at Abby when he thought no one was watching. Otherwise, he opened doors, carried things and generally acted as her personal doormat. Abby laughed it off.

And you can take your dirty minds out of the gutter, because nothing ever happened between us girls, either. No pillow fights, no sly touch-ups, no friendly massages that got out of hand. We loved each other deeply and at times wildly, but never physically. So get over it.

2. Common vices

Waiting for furniture to be delivered delayed my moving in for a week, and by the time it happened I was like a cat sitting at a window watching the birds outside. I was itching to get the fuck out of that dorm and tear my freedom to pieces.

Abby came with me, and we spent the afternoon arranging and rearranging the room – well, directing Bevan and Lucas (Nevin was, luckily for him, at work). We had them dragging drag heavy pieces of furniture here and there while we put pictures (mostly selfies) on the new corkboard, and otherwise messed about in our new playground. The feeling of freshness, adventure and unlimited expectations was incredible. I could barely contain my anticipation.

Then Abby said she was going home. Talk about instant deflation.

'What?' I bleated in disbelief. 'You can't go.'

'You don't expect me to stay, do you Jayney?' Her golden hair bobbed and her eyes laughed. 'Not on your first night? Your roomies will think they'll never get rid of me. And they'll be right. They'll hate me if I stay.'

'I'll hate you if you go.'

She put her arms around me and squeezed tight, her breath hot in my ear and her hair tumbling over my shoulder and tickling my neck.

'You know you have to do this on your own, darling. Don't worry; I'll be back tomorrow. It won't be too long before you're sick of the sight of me.'

I pushed her face away from mine so I could look her in the eye, but immediately put my arms back around her waist.

'You know I never could be.' She laughed again and stepped away from me, looking around for her bag. Her mood was light, and my distress at her leaving didn't seem to touch her at all. I was suddenly petrified.

'Please Abby, just stay for dinner?'

'Uh-uh,' she shook her head. 'You need to get to know your delightful boys.'

I knew she was right, and I had known all that day that the moment would come sooner or later, but I didn't want it to. Perhaps the psychologists who will inevitably study us will make a big deal of that moment – one may even earn a PhD on the question of why I was so eager to abandon my family but couldn't bear to see Abby go.

Whatever the source of my dependence on Abby, no matter how much I needed her to get me through that scary first night at home with the boys, there she was, heading for the bedroom door. I could see that in her mind she was already back across the East River, stalking an unsuspecting tourist in Times Square, or browbeating some poor boy from the neighbourhood into taking her out for a drink. Her ability to drop one thing and move onto the next with total disregard was, frankly, disheartening. I wondered if she cared for me at all, or if I was just another plaything.

Just as she reached the door, she stopped and flung herself back across the room with typical theatricality, and for a moment I thought she'd changed her mind. But she thrust her hand into her handbag and pulled out a small but fat bag of weed.

'Here you go, sweetie. This should get you through the night.'

And then the wispy golden phantom vanished from my door, leaving me to stare at the buds in my hand. At least it was something, I guess.

She ran down the long hallway of the house, her footsteps echoing lightly on the timber floors, yelling, 'Bye Jayney, bye Nevin, bye Bevan, bye Luke.' I bet Lucas hated that. He always went on about first impressions and how his one objective in life was to make a good one. But Abby didn't even remember his name. Then again, maybe she did it because she knew it would wound him, and make him redouble his efforts to impress her.

For a long while after Abby had left, I pottered around folding clothes, positioning pictures and knickknacks, and straightening the bedspread like a weird anal person, which I usually am not. After a while I realised I couldn't spend my life in my room, but I still wasn't ready to interact with my housemates. When I emerged at last, I stopped in the hallway, listening. I knew that Lucas, at any rate, was locked away in his room – apparently studying but probably watching porn. Bevan was napping because he had to work that night. Nevin, whose early shift at the TV station had finished mid-afternoon, was in the living room at the front of the house, watching *Rambo*. I could hear him reciting the dialogue.

'Live for nothing, or die for something. Your call.' He did a good impression of Stallone's thick, barely intelligible voice.

I'd never lived with any young men – my little brother was too pubescent, nerdy and in touch with his feminine side to qualify – so I was offended by how many horrible movies and television shows the boys watched. They simply could not get enough of blood-soaked, explosion-ridden, expletive-laden, high-body-count movies and shows.

They didn't discriminate when it came to the politics, either. The *Rambo* series was a favourite, but they also loved a lot of post-Vietnam antiwar movies: *Deer Hunter, Apocalypse Now, Born on the Fourth of July and Full Metal Jacket*. They didn't care which of our many wars it was: celebrations of Iraq and Afghanistan like *Jarhead* and its Iraq III sequel, *Bonehead;*

The Hurt Locker; American Sniper; Fallujah – No Questions Asked; Death and Freedom in Kabul; and *Zero Dark Thirty.* Then there were all the television series that normalised torture, illegal search and interrogation, the harassment of innocent people, and blatant discrimination. None of that mattered, as long as there were loud bangs, billows of flame, showers of gore, harrowing screams and twisted, burned and mangled dead bodies. Every time the television was on, my boys were exposing themselves to some new form of murder and mayhem, with ever increasing volumes of gore and splatter.

The worst part of it was, when Abby and I hassled them about it, they didn't see any contradiction in loving violent stories but hating violence. Violence on the screen wasn't war, it was entertainment. A character torturing someone they suspected of a crime – to elicit a confession that would never be admissible in any court – was as unreal, or so they claimed, as a cartoon. No matter how realistic the cruelty, or how authentic the shrieks of the victim. It was weird.

'One of these days I'll put you all in a real war; then we'll see how entertaining you find it,' Abby used to say to them.

It occurred to me later that a lot of those old movies, like the Rambo series, while bloody and horrifying in the way they glorified violence, were in some ways less insidious than the later ones. Back in the day, those movies were about wonderful, upright, staunch American heroes. The enemies were one-dimensional, and incidental to the story – they were just there to provide a backdrop for our boys' spine-tingling heroics and unblemished honour. Sure, there were rivers of blood and it was self-evident that all those gooks and reds were shitty second-raters and they all deserved to be killed, 'because freedom'. But at least the focus was on how good our boys were, not how bad other people were.

But the more recent movies changed all that. *Zero Dark Thirty* and *American Sniper*, and *Father of Terror, Death*

Prayer and *Guilt Nation* were about how hateful, debased and inhuman the people we killed were. From being one-dimensional targets, our enemies became the embodiment of evil, irretrievably steeped in bestial hatred and soulless immorality, worthy only of destruction. They killed Americans because we were free and wonderful and exceptional, not because they were defending the countries we had invaded and whose resources we were stealing as we destroyed their lives. Those movies convinced you that everyone beyond our borders had an unfounded urge to brutalise and terrify us, and the only just thing to do was to kill them all as quickly and grotesquely as possible. Luckily, our magnificent heroes could do just that.

My reaction to those movies was the kind of thinking that got me, and my friends, into trouble. I was disgusted by the blatantly one-sided, propagandistic, psychologically manipulative 'entertainment', and I wanted to put a stop to it.

It didn't hurt that I had seen firsthand the effects of actual war. After graduating high school, Abby and I had spent a year 'plush-packing' around the world – roughing it by staying in hotels and motels as low as three stars, and occasionally even youth hostels. We'd seen the damage American bombs had done to the ancient temples at Angkor Wat in Cambodia, skirted fields still strewn with cluster-bomb bomblets in Laos, shared tamales with Nicaraguans and Salvadorans whose families and friends had been murdered by CIA-supported death squads, and walked the streets of Hiroshima and Dresden, where our forces had deliberately targeted civilians to maximise the pain their countrymen felt. We'd talked a lot about it and were both, even before we started college, vehemently antiwar.

On my first afternoon in the house, though, I wasn't thinking about any of that. I came out of my room and laughed at Nevin, his t-shirt tied around his head, bandana-style, emulating the great John Rambo, grunting 'Go home' every few minutes. I couldn't face that, so I took a walk.

Aimless and blank-minded, I enjoyed the smells, colours and personality of my new neighbourhood. On Graham Avenue, I came across the local war memorial, a sad little triangle of green, fenced-in and bounded on all sides by streaming traffic. On the plinth sat a white globe, straddled by a white eagle, and a flagpole with yardarms displaying four flags. I guessed the three that flew subservient to the Stars and Stripes were local veterans' associations. It was all very well kept, respectfully free of litter and the daubs that disaffected youths had splashed on so many other surfaces. But it was wretched. Did those brave young men invade so many other countries and die for this? A tiny oasis in a desert of hot paving, unnoticed and unremarked except for a couple of outrageously emotive days a year?

As night fell and more people came out onto the streets, I picked up a six-pack of beers and went home to Devoe Street. On the way in the front door, I met Bevan, who was tucking his blue shirt into dark blue pants, on his way to his night work.

'O God!' he said, with exaggerated horror. 'The new roomie and beers! How can I be working tonight?'

I laughed and brushed past him.

'Don't worry. On the nights when you don't work, whoop! We'll party.'

He grinned with enthusiasm and anticipation, and ran down the steps. I took the beers inside, where I found Lucas and Nevin sprawled in front of the television.

'Drink, boys?' I didn't wait for an answer, grabbing out two cans and throwing them across the room to them.

Starting something new with people you don't know is always a process of discovery, trial and error and, a lot of the time, compromise. Remember when you started a new class or a new job, and you were nervous and cautious, trying to project confidence without putting your new colleagues or classmates off? Wanting to be liked but not wanting to appear either pushy or a pushover, hoping that others shared your prejudices and attitudes so there wouldn't be conflict? That's what that night was about for Lucas, Nevin and me. Testing each other's views and understanding across a wide range of subjects, tentatively putting forth beliefs and seeing if there was support for them in the room, and, if not, resolving to skirt that subject where possible, or to at least try to accommodate the others' perspectives.

It turned out that the three of us were on common ground in almost all the important areas. This was good. I am guessing the booze helped.

By 10 p.m., we'd been back to the bodega for more booze and were on the tequila, and blithering. Lucas sang Taylor Swift songs, and I teased Nevin by asking him to name just one AC/DC hit, then put on one of my playlists to educate the boys.

Inspiration hit me after my third tequila shot.

'Hey!' I hate it when I sound girly, but it sometimes happens when I'm properly gassed. 'Shall I roll a joint?' I produced the weed that Abby had left me.

Lucas scowled and shook his head, and Nevin looked positively horrified.

'Oh my God, no! In this house? Never!'

I had expected a very different reaction.

A chill spun through me and the blood rushed to my face. I'd overstepped the mark. Lulled by their voracious appetite for booze, I'd assumed, wrongly, it appeared, that they would be stoners too. I was devastated, but not overly surprised. Even though there had been a general trend towards tolerance when I was a kid, in the last few years there'd been a marked shift in the other direction. The conservatives had taken power in 2017 and never let it go, and many people believed we were living in a proto-fascist state. The police had continued to become ever more militarised, their application of the drug laws much more diligent, and the courts much less lenient. I should have realised that the boys were probably a product of that environment.

'Never, ever—' Nevin walked past me, and reached into the cupboard next to the cellar door below the stairs '—as long as the bong is clean.' My cold sweat evaporated and I giggled and threw the bag at him.

We were huddled around the bong, turning solidly sauced into completely cabbaged, when a crash and a bang at the front door were followed by a terrifying roar. It's a miracle that none of us screamed, though Lucas, who'd been holding the bong, threw himself at the basement door, disappearing over the edge of the couch in tangle of arms, legs and empty beer cans.

I stared at the apparition that had blasted into the room, and my dread dissolved instantly into uncontrollable laughter: it was Bevan, holding a six-pack and three large pizza boxes, chortling like a maniac.

'You're busted!' he yelled.

'You motherfucker,' said Nevin. 'I should have known.'

Lucas re-emerged, trying not to look as pissed off as he obviously was.

'Fuck, man, don't ever do that again,' he said. 'You frightened the shit out of me.'

Then, noticing that I was still chuckling and Nevin was doing the same, he tried to make light of it.

'I nearly dropped the bong.'

Bevan looked at Nevin with a smirk. 'Dude, you knew I was coming. You messaged me about the pizzas.'

'Yeah, I know. But I forgot, okay? I had other things on my mind.'

'Yeah, right,' said Bevan, eyeing the bong. 'How about you get one of those things on my mind?'

Nevin looked at me and I nodded, impressed that he thought to check with me before sharing my weed with our housemate. Bev, for his part, opened the pizza boxes and spread them around the floor – there was no room on the coffee table strewn with empties – and we all dived in like starving dogs, sloppily chomping molten cheese and sludgy pastry, crunching crispy crusts, and listening to Bevan bubble as he wrenched several catch-up cones in a row.

At last, sated, smashed and slit-eyed, we were all sitting or lying where we'd dropped, practically panting. Every now and then, one of us would raise a head long enough to slurp on a drink, but for a long while nothing was said. Eventually, I felt as though I would fall asleep where I sat, or more accurately, slouched, so I shook myself awake.

'You know, I think I'm going to like it here with you boys,' I said as I headed down the hallway to my room.

Bevan was the only one awake enough to have noticed. 'I think we're going to love having you here, Jayney.'

3. Finding Jihad

A broiling Thursday afternoon was drifting into searing evening, just a few weeks after I'd moved in. Abby and I were in our third year at NYU, and the initial novelty had long since worn off. For all the money they charge and the prestige one gets from being there, college was nowhere near as stimulating or socially enchanting as I'd expected. The students were mostly glum, dressed even less fashionably than I did – and that's saying something – and walked around looking tired and stressed or bored and out of it. Presumably the tired and stressed ones were thinking about the debt they were running up learning a bunch of useless facts (sprinkled like rare jewels amongst the bushels of worthless opinions spouted by pretentious professors), while the bored and out of it were squandering their parent's money and their own time in an effort to avoid eviction into the real world. Abby and I were definitely part of the latter crowd, but at least we were having fun.

Anyway, by late that week, which had been exceptionally hot, and which I'd spent actually applying myself to my studies, we all had a thirst on. Bevan had the night off, Nevin would be home early, and Lucas was, as usual, doing nothing but hanging around looking slightly uptight. So Abby and I went out to get some booze. As we walked out the door, Abby called over her shoulder, 'While we're away, Lucas, for Christ's sake get that stick out of your ass!' and he thought she was joking, so he laughed. So did we, all the way down Devoe Street.

The pavement was sticky and the air had a tightness that implied imminent violence. Sullen, brooding men sat on stoops drinking liquor from brown paper bags, whining and snarling at each other. They stared at Abby and me with untrammelled lust, tainted with the contempt that came from knowing we'd never deign to talk to them. For once, I was glad to see an NYPD cruiser drifting slowly down Graham, the sweaty cops ogling the stoop boozers with the same intensity as the boozers were ogling us.

We'd had a joint before we left the house, so we were both feeling joyful and mischievous. I guess our satirical mood had made Abby throw that insult at Lucas. I was saying to her, as we approached the bodega (named 'Ye Olde Bottle Shoppe' in a misguided attempt to appear authentic in a tragically hipster way) that she shouldn't be so mean to him, because he really wasn't as awful as he seemed, but I was giggling as I spoke, and so wasn't very convincing.

'Bah!' she barked. 'He laps it up. He's like a puppy dog. If I asked him to, he'd lick his own balls to please me.'

'True. But I have to live with him, so if you could just back off a little bit, that would be great.'

'Are you saying I'm a bitch?' Abby rounded on me with a wild grin.

'You know you are, bitch,' I said. 'And a slut.'

'You'd know, Slutty McSlutface,' she said.

'Buttfucker.'

And so on. Hardly edifying discourse, I'll grant you, but to us, at that time, hysterically funny. Our noisiness attracted more stares from the old locals, and sneers from the hipsters who slouched next to walls looking about as 'authentic' as the bodega, but we didn't care.

We stopped to finalise our purchasing plans and divvy up the in-shoppe tasks.

'I'll get the brews, you get the bourbon.'

'Done.'

As we turned to *ye olde doorwaye*, I noticed that we were being watched by a slight individual with soft brown skin and long, straight black hair parted acutely at the side. He seemed to be there almost all the time, like a piece of street furniture. Usually, I swept past, but this time I couldn't help but throw a glance at him, and somehow ended up looking deeply into his mellow, bronze eyes.

He flashed two rows of perfect white teeth, and said, with a solicitous air, 'A bit windy out, is it?'

'Huh?' I was confused. 'No, why?'

'I thought it must be, because your eyes are so red.' He smirked.

'Ah, that. No, I've been crying. Thanks for noticing, though.'

For a brief moment, a cloud of remorse scudded across his sunny expression. Then he realised I was biting back.

'I, too, weep for the world.' He closed his eyes as if in pain. 'And yet there is, it seems, a dim sliver of hope.' He smiled again.

Abby elbowed me lightly and said, 'I'll get the drinks, Jayne,' leaning on my name to make sure my interlocutor caught it, before dashing inside.

He looked at me for a little longer. When he spoke again, with a soft, charming lilt, he almost sounded English.

'I'm not at all sure you have been crying,' he said. 'I think you've been laughing. Perhaps chuckling. Most definitely tittering. Possibly even cackling. There's a remote chance you've even been roaring. Regardless, there has been some rowdy humour about you, and that is what has made your eyes red. Or—' He paused dramatically, holding his hand under his chin and letting his curled finger cross his fleshy, pink lips for a moment. 'Or, someone has introduced, possibly without your knowledge, some tetrahydrocannabinols into your bloodstream.'

I was happy to buy into it. 'I think you're Sherlock Holmes,' I said, gently prodding his chest.

He held up a finger. 'No, not quite. I'm Doctor Watson. And as a doctor, I prescribe more of the same.'

He dug his left hand into the pocket of that huge, suspect coat, and pulled out the corner of a bag of weed, which he then pushed back into the depths. I loved his velvety skin and his pinky-white nails, the richness of his voice and the dazzle of his smile. And most of all, the humour in his mind. I could see he was not unimpressed by me, either.

'Hmm, interesting proposition, Watson. And timely, I'll allow you that. We have this very afternoon found ourselves in a predicament, source-wise.'

'I am nothing if not convenient,' he replied with an almost imperceptible bow.

'How much?'

He looked offended. Hurt, even; in a bogus, put-on kind of way.

'Heavens! You're like a bull at a gate. Would you not rather observe some niceties? You know, introductions, perhaps some small talk and an exchange of views to ensure that we under-stand each other before we descend into a merely commercial relationship, regardless of how satisfying we may find it?'

I nodded at every clause, but went on the offensive anyway.

'That would be nice, but my friend will no doubt complete her transaction in Ye Olde Bottle Shoppe at any moment, and I'm in a bit of a hurry. Besides, I already know your name; you're Doctor Watson.'

'Alas, that was a subterfuge, and a poor one at that,' he said with bowed head, although I could still see his eyes and they were shining. 'Employed to further a delightful conversation with a stranger I hoped would become a friend. My name, in truth, is Jihad.'

He eyed me frankly as he said this, and I could see instantly that this was no further jape, his name really was Jihad. But I couldn't help myself; the words were out before I could rein them in. I hoped they didn't sound too derisive. 'You're joking.'

'Regrettably, no,' he said, without a trace of regret. 'Although I would point out to you that my parents, whose hearts were in the right place at the time, named me in honour of the traditional use of the term, which relates not to armed assault, but to the struggle daily to improve oneself. True *jihad* is the battle against sin and immorality. A battle I must confess to be losing in many respects – at least as far as sin is defined by the legislature of our fine nation, state and city.'

He certainly was an interesting, forthright and erudite individual. I enjoyed his elocution, and I was entranced by his smile. But I couldn't let him know that.

'Still, it must be awkward, being saddled with a handle like that.' I felt dirty, having used such an unrefined term as 'handle'. Why, oh why didn't I say 'appellation'? And what the fuck was with 'saddled', for that matter? Why not 'burdened' or 'encumbered'?

Jihad affected not to notice my shame. 'Let's just say that interactions with officialdom can be interesting.'

'Anyway, enough of the trials of being me,' he continued. 'I gather from your friend's subtle deployment of the appellation that your name is Jayne?'

'It is.' Appellation? Damn him! 'Jayne Silver.'

'Long Jayne Silver, eh?'

I didn't have the heart to tell him I'd heard that one about a million times before.

'Arrrr.' I nodded.

He was kind enough to chuckle. 'You know, there's a story that the famous pirate, Edward Teach – nicknamed Blackbeard – was actually quite a scholarly and intellectual chap, and whenever his minions said something like "We be pirates," he would say "are", obliquely instructing them that the correct articulation is, "We are pirates," and that's why people think pirates make that noise.'

I was kind enough to return the favour, chuckling politely. Just then Abby emerged from the shop, weighed down by beer and bourbon. Jihad rushed to help her, and as she offloaded it all into his arms, she raised her eyebrows at me.

'I'll take that, Jihad.' I held out my arms.

Abby cast a second, bemused glance at me, and I gave her a sly, pleased look.

Peeking over the beer box crowned with not one but two bottles of bourbon on top of it – Abby was always generous, and hated to run out of alcohol on a Friday night – Jihad shook his head.

'I have a proposal. No, wait,' he corrected himself, 'it's a bit early in our relationship for that. Better make that a proposition. Ooh. Err,' he amended again, shyly, 'I have an offer. Allow me to convey this precious cargo to your place of abode, and when we get there, we can conclude our business.'

Behind him, Abby's mouth was working comically, and her astonishingly blue eyes were starting out of her head. She gave me an energetic two thumbs up sign.

'Well. We've only just met, but that is a generous *proposal*. As long as my friend Abby agrees.'

Jihad turned to look at Abby, regarding her with the kind of casual affability that said he was interested in her only as a friend of mine. He rose again in my estimation.

'Jihad may be able to help us out in our horticultural quest,' I said.

'Well, then. Any friend of yours is a friend of mine, Jayney. Here, let me help.' She took the two bourbon bottles so Jihad could see. Then she examined him more closely.

'Abby, Jihad; Jihad, Abby.'

We walked home in raucous good humour.

When we got there, Jihad carried the beer through the living room – where the boys were watching yet another war film, the brutal black comedy of *Inglorious Basterds* – and upstairs into the kitchen. My housemates were disconcerted to see a stranger waltzing through the house with a case of beer, and even more so when I introduced him to them.

Nevin and Lucas both looked wounded and betrayed that this young man was hanging out with us.

Upstairs, as Abby put the beer cans in the fridge, Jihad and I exchanged cash and grass, our hands lightly brushing each other's, exchanging warmth and pheromones. I asked if Jihad would stay for a drink and a smoke. He shook his head.

'Technically, I should be back at my station. My shift has a couple of hours to go, and the boss doesn't like it when the shop window isn't open. He calls it opportunity cost.'

I walked him out the front door while Abby distributed beers to my sullen, sulky housemates. Jihad closed the door behind us and kissed me languorously on the lips, right there on the dusky street, two feet from our front door. He was confident and forward, and his lips had a warm, arousing, honeyed softness. I kissed back with gentle urgency, and my blood heated up as our bodies pressed together.

But then he broke away, apologising, and ran off down the street. I called after him that he should come around tomorrow so I could cook for him. He turned, nodded and grinned, then scuttled off like a good employee, back to his retail post.

Jihad's departure improved the boys' moods instantly, and they were further cheered by the news that he had provided a good-sized bag of weed. I could see both Lucas and Nevin were dying to ask questions, but refused to do so on the grounds that it might incriminate them.

It's interesting, the proprietary attitude toward me that Nev and Lucas shared. It always amuses me that men assume ownership over women, and think, unconsciously, that they can decide who a girl hangs out with and sleeps with. After all, it wasn't as though either of them was inflamed with an unquenchable passion for me. But there was still this weird expectation that if I slept with anyone, it should be one of them. Indeed, there seemed to be an unspoken competition to see who would be the first to nail me or Abby, not so much out of actual desire, but as a result of that sense of entitlement that men should be able to fuck whoever they want. In fact, often they don't even really want to have sex; what they really want is the right of refusal. Power.

Bevan alone seemed genuinely pleased that I had found a new friend. But then, he was always supportive, and never had the fits of jealousy and petulance that the others went through.

4. The world without mirrors

By the start of my third year, I'd accepted that college life would be satisfactory but disagreeable. I'd chosen history as my major because I thought it would help me find insights into what motivates people to do great things, good or evil. More than anything, I wanted to know the *why* of the Holocaust.

I knew a lot of Jewish people, and many of them carried the anger and horror of a people that had been monstrously persecuted. So, on behalf of my Jewish friends, I was desperate to know: how could sixty five million Germans, many of whom must have known at least a little about what was going on and likely suspected more, let that happen? They'd seen their fellow Germans who were Jewish, and many others, rounded up and herded into rail cattle cars for unimaginably horrific trips to mysterious camps "in the east", or simply shot on the street for not complying fast enough; they were married or related to the men who designed, operated and ran those trains; they knew the guards and SS men who brutalised the prisoners at every turn; and there were so many more unavoidable clues to what was going on. How could those people watch their former neighbours, friends, bus drivers, bakers, dressmakers, babysitters, and yes, bankers, bosses and professors, endure such degradation and disdain? How could the Jews go so obligingly to their deaths? How could they suffer so much on the way to their deaths, yet barely whimper with each fresh new imposition, indignity and injury?

I wanted to know what drove some people to carry out acts of despicable evil, and what led others to just stand by and watch with ghastly passivity. I wanted to know how the very same circumstances inspired some people to acts of incredible courage and profound humanity, displaying almost saintly levels of selflessness and morality, while others who were in almost every way just like them went precisely the other way, and still others remained in a state of moribund stasis, unable to do or apparently even to feel anything.

But studying history only taught me that the world is a much more cynical place than I had thought. Even when the primary actors left copious notes, records and correspondence, they were almost always dishonest and self-serving. Those at the heart of great events almost without exception shrouded them in a fog of ego and conceit.

So, if anything, history taught me that men are liars. Women can be awful too, especially more recently – Clinton, Nuland, Haley, Power, Harris and so on. But the great mass of history has been created, contrived, fabricated and distorted by men.

After two years of study, I was no closer to understanding how the Holocaust – which my Jewish friends called the Shoah – had come about, which suggested that it could happen again. In fact, I grew certain that it would, because of that old cliché about learning from history or being doomed to repeat it. Still, I persevered, less in the hope that my studies would answer my questions and more in the knowledge that continuing at NYU would keep me insulated from the real world for at least one more year.

Then there was the solace and escape I found in drugs and alcohol, shared with my housemates and friends. We followed a strict schedule of indulgence. It began on Tuesday night, peaked on Friday and Saturday nights, and tailed off to a sodden conclusion early on Sunday nights. Only Monday nights were 'dry', reserved for the in-house preparation and consumption of a healthy, balanced meal.

By fall, the heat had gone out of my relationship with Jihad. We'd tried passion; it wasn't really for us. We were too good as friends, too addicted to verbal jousting and baiting banter to drop the pretence and share our vulnerabilities. We liked each other, we respected each other's intelligence and we shared a cynical, wilfully distorted view of the world. But we weren't cut out to be lovers.

Besides, there was Abby. Oh, she was happy to fade away and let us be a couple. She would make her own way home at night, and if Jihad and I were going to have a date night, she wouldn't come over at all. That was okay with her. But it wasn't with me. The bottom line was that I preferred to share my room with her each night, rather than Jihad. What really got between us was me, and my devotion to Abby.

Meanwhile, Devoe Street remained a hive of hedonism, for everyone except Bevan. He was deep into healthy living and bodybuilding to remain fit for his security work, and had drifted away from our indulgent lifestyle. He'd transformed from a soft, ginger jellyfish into a delectably well-defined dreamboat. Whether it was his new, improved appearance or the job, which taught him to handle all kinds of difficult situations with authority, his confidence grew markedly. He was still quiet, tolerant and good-natured, but now he backed it up with the knowledge that, should diplomacy fail, he could resort to force. This gave him a powerful if understated presence. Despite his newfound sobriety and his growing sense of self, Bev never passed judgement on our continuing debauchery. He watched with interest, a sly, knowing smirk on his face, when we began with boozy bravado, progressed into potty humour, slipped into wildly speculative stupidity, and ultimately collapsed into flaccid catatonia.

Nevin and Lucas seemed to have accepted that neither of them would be bedding me any time soon, which made our interactions more affable. The competition was replaced by a mutual enjoyment of intoxicants and the lazy, contemplative lifestyle. Abby had slept with Nevin once, which made for some awkwardness between them (and also between her and Lucas, who resented his own failure). But she was such a bundle of infectious fun that she soon had them both back at ease and under her subtle command.

If they had been honest with their feelings – they are genetically incapable of that, being men – both would have realised that they were already deeply in love with Abby, and would have done anything she asked in a heartbeat. The most compelling evidence of this was that Nevin stopped going out to find himself floozies, and stayed at home with us.

Beautiful autumn took over our streets, dressing the trees in earth tones and cooling our air so that it was once again a pleasure to wear clothes. There was still sunshine and clarity, and the atmosphere was infused with that primeval scent of decay from fallen leaves and steaming sewers. One balmy Wednesday evening, Lucas, Abby and I trooped off to the bodega for yet more supplies. The sky was deepening orange and brisk gusts sent brown and red leaves scurrying along sidewalks to gather in the gutters. We were anxious to get our booze and our bag and retire to our cosy lounge room. Jihad was ready, as always, with wit and a bag of impressive dope. I asked him to join us for a few beverages and some dirty air; he agreed to come as soon as his shift finished. I pocketed the gear, Abby and Lucas carried the drinks, and we marched home to get stuck into it.

A couple of hours later, it was done. Except for Bevan, we were all fairly roasted, lounging rubber-limbed around the television set. The program was one of those travelogue things where improbably beautiful presenters take holidays to improbably beautiful locations. They are fêted and pampered before the cameras, and gush about the companies who sponsor their trips. At least it was a pleasant change from the endless diet of murder and war: a refreshing lack of screams, sirens, gunshots and bombs, even if the bubbling enthusiasm of the hosts and the effusive, cliché-laden commentary were difficult to swallow.

The presenter, just your average six foot four, blonde-haired supermodel in a flowing flower dress, with over-augmented boobs busting out of her plunging neckline, was aboard a ninety-foot yacht anchored in the azure Aegean Sea off a rugged Greek Island. Greece had been the flavour of the month for some time; the new drachma was still chronically under-valued, and tourists flocked to take advantage of the desperate, anxious and underfed locals. The talking head was saying that the value of holidays in Greece was unmatched, but it wasn't as though she appeared to need to practice thrift, as the yacht she was standing on charged passengers several thousand dollars a day. How the producers ever thought that average Americans might afford such getaways was beyond all of us. And yet the ratings for this advertising of wildly expensive holidays to places no American could ever find on a map were phenomenal.

Mercifully, there were ad breaks. Normally we all dozed through them, but there was something in the weed that made us talkative and stimulated our imaginations. Abby, curled up like a queenly cat in her armchair, posed one of her thought experiments. It happened every now and then. She would ask, 'If you could be the child of any president, which would it be?' or 'You're on a desert island and you can get one monthly air-drop of either booze or pot for the rest of your life: which one do you choose?' Then she would nominate the person who had to answer first.

'If you could live anywhere in the world, where would it be? Lucas?' She pointed with her elbow – if you pointed with your finger you had to finish your drink in one mouthful.

Lucas didn't hesitate. 'Upper West Side Manhattan.'

The rest of us groaned.

'Jesus, Lucas,' said Abby. 'You've spent your whole life there. Couldn't you choose somewhere different?'

As he so often was, Lucas was defensive but unrepentant. He usually maintained the courage of his absurd, sanctimonious convictions for at least three minutes, defending them smugly until he folded under a particularly cutting comment from Abby.

'It's the best part of the most exciting city in the greatest country the world has ever known,' he said. 'Why shouldn't I choose it?'

'The greatest country the world has ever known?' Nevin was incredulous. 'Tell that to the people in the dozens of nations we've invaded, interfered with, overthrown or corrupted in the last hundred years or so.'

'It's our responsibility to keep the world at peace,' said Lucas. 'Can we help it if those other countries present a security threat that we have to deal with?' Even though he was often critical of our country's record of military meddling, Lucas sometimes felt the need to adopt the patriot's stance when others condemned that same record.

Abby, who had posed her question as a lighthearted way of waking us up during the ads, wasn't about to allow this to descend into a standard Lucas-versus-the-rest debacle.

'Okay. Lucas chooses to live with his parents. And that's his choice. Bevan?'

Bev, who'd been focused on his tablet through most of the evening, studying something, looked up and smiled. His blue eyes were clear and the lower regions of his newly thin, muscular face were dusted with a coating of ginger stubble.

'As much as I'd like to live in the penthouse next door to Lucas, I'd rather live in China. I'd become a Shaolin monk, a master of kung fu.'

Abby was impressed. She sometimes only saw the best in people. The rest of us could be too cynical for our own good.

'You'd be the biggest, whitest, pinkest, Shaolin monk that ever lived,' said Nevin.

Bevan was unabashed. 'And I would use my powers only for good. What about you, Jayne?'

I was startled.

'Me?' I stared at the ceiling for a couple of moments. 'Italy. All that pizza and pasta; all that art and history.'

'All those Italians.' Jihad smiled at me.

'Mmm, I'm hungry,' said Abby. 'Anyone else want pizza?'

But I wasn't about to let Jihad off the hook for what I construed as a racist remark.

'What's wrong with Italians?'

'Oh,' he said, still smiling. 'They're passionate, informed, eloquent, artistic, sociable and interesting. Sort of anti-Americans.'

'Hey,' said Nevin, 'you can only say that sort of stuff if you were born here.' He, too, was grinning.

'You mean America? Or New York? Or Brooklyn?' Jihad spread his pale, pinkish palms before him. 'Either way, that's me.'

'Okay then smarty-pants,' Abby said. 'If you could live anywhere at all, where would it be?'

Jihad's eyes got that wicked, mischievous look. He was about to challenge us all, again. He could turn any conversation into a kind of existential investigation.

'If I could,' he said, slowly, looking at each of us in turn, 'I'd live in a world without mirrors.'

He scanned our faces again, to check whose minds he had just blown, and who was still trying to understand what he had said. Abby and I fell into the former camp. Bevan was chuckling softly to himself. Lucas and Nevin seemed to belong in the latter.

'Huh?' asked Nevin.

'If you think about it, it's only really been the last few hundred years that most people have had mirrors. Before then, we didn't know, or really care too much, what we looked like. We took care of our bodies not so much for appearance's sake but for our health. There were times when we wanted to look our best, naturally, but we were much more concerned about how we acted towards others than the way we looked. We were much less self-conscious and ego-driven, and much more altruistic and community-minded. Now we're all self-obsessed. There's a reflective surface everywhere we look, and we spend our whole lives peacocking in front of mirrors. It's become all about how we look, and very little about what we do. We don't look inside anymore, because we're too busy admiring our out-sides. Just ask yourself, when was the last time you saw someone on TV who wasn't utterly gorgeous, even if it took them years of surgery to get that way? When was the last time you listened to the opinion of someone who wasn't at least passably good-looking? Never. Ugly people hardly exist anymore, except as part of the invisible majority. But even ugly people look at themselves approvingly in the mirror all the time now. We're bred that way. And I think a world without mirrors would help us see ourselves more clearly because the real us would be reflected in the way people interacted with us.'

'That took the experiment to a whole new place.' Bevan smiled. 'How stoned are you guys?'

'Pretty stoned', I said. And I was. 'But I like the idea. I think in a world without mirrors, fashion would be more functional and less onerous. We would value the way things work rather than the way they look. Too much emphasis is put on appearances.'

Abby, who'd been staring wistfully off into space while this was going on, her eyes almost glassy, spoke in a soft, trance-like voice that came from far away – or from deep inside.

'The world without mirrors is dangerous. If you don't have mirrors, you can't see what you've become.'

Jihad shook his head vigorously. 'In the old world, before everyone had them, the only people who had mirrors were the people in charge. The kings and the rich.'

I guess he'd been thinking about this for a while.

'They saw themselves getting fat on the lives of their vassals and slaves. They watched the lines of hardness creeping across their faces as they became more callous and less concerned with the fates and futures of their subjects, and more addicted to the lives of comfort and indulgence that the suffering of others bought them. They saw what they were becoming and they didn't care. They embraced it, even when the mirror showed them that they had become wicked and unscrupulous.

'Nowadays, in a sense, we're all kings: slaves to our mirrors and our ambitions, not caring what we're becoming because we're consumed with how we appear.'

'But without mirrors, we can't see how we're changing. That we choose to ignore it isn't the mirror's fault.' Abby was still a bit glazed and distant.

'You're saying that the mirror feeds our self-deception?' asked Lucas. It was good to see him sincerely involved in the conversation; he was capable of insight, but too often he ignored his mind and gave voice to his prejudices instead.

'Yes,' agreed Jihad. 'Having mirrors everywhere, whether physical or metaphorical, helps to reinforce our biases. We see only what we want to see. But in my world without mirrors, we'd go back to being what we were born to be – less egotistical and more socially aware, more interested in real relationships than mutual admiration.'

'We're a generation that is all self-image and no self-awareness,' said Abby. The idea seemed to make her sad. 'We see everything and understand nothing, and we just become what we are to become, blindly.'

The program restarted, and the woman on the yacht was wearing a bikini, so the conversation fell away in a wail of boyish hoots and groans. We all forgot it. Well, I assume the others did. I never did.

5. POW

It was a Thursday morning early in November, and we were all up and ready. The previous night, Abby had instructed us to be dressed warmly and prepared for a 'family outing', so we were. No one knew what it was about – even me – so there was an air of excitement.

We caught the subway across to Manhattan and followed Abby to a diner in Greenwich Village, where she treated us all to a big breakfast. There were lots of people around, quite a lot of them in uniform. Of course: Veterans Day. I wondered what she had in mind.

After breakfast, we took a walk up Fifth Avenue, up around the Sex Museum on the corner of Twenty-Eighth, and squeezed into a space on the sidewalk to await the parade.

The crowd was respectfully festive, trying not to talk too loudly, and looking with dewy-eyed gratitude at the uniformed men and women threading their way back downtown to the starting line. After an excruciating hour and a half hemmed in by obnoxious New Yorkers from all the boroughs, listening to pointless arguments and tedious conversations, the rumble of the Harley Davidsons leading the parade rolled like muted thunder up the avenue. The parade was on – a celebration of the many wars the United States had started, finished, fomented, planned, encouraged, abetted, participated in, lost, abandoned or was still prosecuting, since the end of the First World War over a hundred years ago.

How gaily the Stars and Stripes waved! How solemnly the good burghers of New York saluted the soldiers, sailors, air warriors and marines. How crisp the uniforms were, and how upright the men and women wearing them, how heartfelt the homemade signs saying 'Thank You' and 'God Bless You' were. How often and how emotionally the national anthem was played, while the gathered faithful sang those blood-soaked words over and over again, hands on hearts.

It was sickening, to be honest. As long as a society treats war as something to be exalted, that society is inescapably a combative culture. It can't be anything else, because the most anyone can aspire to is to be a part of, to win, or better yet to lose and die in, the battle. The talk of sacrifice, selflessness, service and honour was endless and alarming. If we, as a people, did away with that bullshit and held the same parades, gave the same misty-eyed thanks, and threw the same kind of funding to teachers, philosophers, artists and scientists as we do to soldiers, we would be a much greater, more centred and enlightened community than we are. Who knows, we might even begin to earn the title of 'exceptional, indispensable nation', which we have so humbly bestowed on ourselves and repeat manically every time war is mentioned, as if to convince ourselves that international law could, like our own elastic 'rules' of morality, admit exceptions for we 'indispensable' people.

Abby and I maintained an air of sombre propriety, even though I knew she was thinking exactly what I was, and the boys of course thought it all a fine and uplifting spectacle.

'These people,' Abby whispered to me, 'they're so deadly serious about this, Jayney. It's beyond reverence; it's worship. It's obeisance. They're believers and war is their religion.'

I nodded, and looked nervously around me. I didn't want any of these earnest believers to hear such a seditious thought being uttered out loud.

'We need to shock them out of their automatic acceptance of this loathsome cult of death and conquest.'

I nodded again, and my heart beat a little faster. She was definitely up to something.

But then the parade was over and the people shuffled off to get home, get warm and watch the build-up to the next war on cable TV. The street was empty save for the flags fluttering impotently in the cold breeze, and the debris of devotion and xenophobia: coffee cups decorated with the Stars and Stripes; red, white and blue streamers; and cheap, homemade confetti gathering in clumps in the gutter.

Abby shepherded the boys back down Fifth to our favourite rooftop bar, and we got ourselves a table over on the west side, under a heater. It was fresh and our cheeks were rosy, especially once we started sipping on the spicy Bloody Marys Abby ordered for us.

'So. How did we enjoy the parade?' She was too solicitous; it had to be a trick question.

'Yeah, great,' said Nevin tentatively. He knew something was up, too.

'Anything missing, do you think?'

Uncertain looks, hesitant shakes of the head.

'How about the dead? The crippled, the blinded, shattered and broken? The down-and-out drunks who live on the street because they weren't lucky enough to come home all shiny and well pressed? How about the families of all those broken soldiers? How about the blood and the screams and the victims in every hemisphere?' Abby was angry.

'Do you know, our soldiers have invaded or bombed at least twenty countries since the end of World War II? Some of them multiple times and for years and years on end, like Iraq and Afghanistan, Vietnam, Laos, Cambodia, Bosnia, Kosovo, Korea, Somalia, Grenada and Libya and so many more. It's almost shorter to list the countries that have not in some way been brutalised by the United States. And in every one of those wars and invasions, our soldiers have killed and been killed: terrible, horrifying deaths. But we didn't see that today. We saw the sanitised, brass bands and grateful citizens version of war. Even those idiotic movies you boys watch so obsessively on television have more truth in them than what we've just seen.'

The boys were shocked. The parade had stoked their patriotic fervour, and Abby's sacrilegious rant was in danger of shattering their nationalistic dreams. It was clear to me that Abby had been working up to this for a long time. We had of course talked about the futility and horror of war ourselves quite often, but I had never heard her get so heated about it.

'But we have to honour the troops who defend our freedoms,' ventured Lucas. Was he brave or stupid? It was hard to tell.

'Oh really?' Abby turned her most venomous look on him, and he literally shrank away from her. 'So, when was the last time the United States was actually "defended" by its troops? Pearl Harbour, you say? An attack that took place on a bunch of islands in the middle of the Pacific that we stole from the Polynesians, where our venerated troops actually failed to mount any sort of credible defence.'

'What about 9/11?' said Bevan.

'Well, that wasn't an army; it was a group of allegedly freelance Saudi Arabians in hijacked commercial jets,' Nevin chimed in. He wanted to be on Abby's side. 'And they didn't meet with a lot of resistance, from what I gather.'

'Quite right, Nev,' said Abby. 'The air force, which might have repelled the attack of those hijacked planes, was otherwise occupied at the time. So, in other words, the two times we have been attacked in the last eighty years – the first time by the Japanese and the second time by a bunch of Arabs – the people whose job it was to protect and defend us did neither. I'd like to know why we are honouring those people. And what the hell are the current troops doing with their time that puts us so deeply in their debt?'

'They're fighting terrorists.' Lucas's tone suggested that he was serious about defending the defenders, but he also looked as though he could abandon his position at any moment if the majority went the other way. 'Taking defence offshore, to the places where the threat begins, and fighting the good fight there.' This was a bit more flippant. He was having a bet each way.

'Invading other countries, you mean,' said Nevin.

'Well, yeah. When you put it like that, yeah,' agreed Lucas.

'And the sad, undeniable truth is that all that bombing and killing is super-effective at creating exactly the kinds of threats we need to counter with more bombing and killing. It's like a great big happy circle of death and destruction,' said Abby, grimly triumphant.

'So, what can we do about it, Abs?' asked Bevan. His eyes were beginning to shine, but whether it was the cold, the conversation or the Bloody Mary, I couldn't tell.

'We can stop it. We can wake up the sheeple and expose the truth about war. It's a small start, but it's a start – we'll form a group.'

'Ooooh, a group,' said Lucas. 'That sounds heavy.'

'Fuck you, Lucas.' She kicked him swiftly in the shins under the table. 'I'm serious. I'm not talking about a discussion group, you fucking pussy; I'm talking about an action group. We tag recruitment offices and billboards; we organise peace marches and sit-ins; Jayne and I write witty but deeply insightful antiwar blogs that capture and galvanise the imaginations of millions of young people like us who've never known anything but war. We go on talk shows and become famous and influential.' If anyone could carry it off, it would be Abby.

Inspiration struck her like a rubber bullet. 'We'll call it POW! People Opposed to War.'

'Good name.' Bevan was always going to be on-board with anything Abby suggested.

A strange kind of transformation was coming over the boys. Only a short while ago, they'd been tearing up over the veterans, and now I could see that they were starting to believe in what Abby was saying. She'd long been carping at them about their violent movie addiction, including some lengthy lectures about the real effects of war, but I'd always assumed that they just weren't listening. Maybe they had been. Or maybe they were just prepared to go along with whatever Abby said because … well, Abby.

Abby looked at Lucas with scorn. 'I know you'll go along with whatever, dick.' She nudged Nevin with her foot. 'What about you, mister? What do you think?'

'I like it. I'm in. Look out world, here come the People who're Over War.'

'People Opposed to War, dummy.'

She turned to me, and I couldn't keep the sly, smug grin off my face.

'Sorry,' I said. 'That's lame.'

I could see the consternation on her face.

'Nobody listens to people. You want something a bit more attention grabbing. Because, I mean, we're Patriots. Patriots Opposed to War.'

'POW!' she said. Then, more loudly, 'Patriots Opposed to War,' with her right fist clenched above her head. 'The legend has begun!'

'POW!' we screamed. And just like that, we were a group.

'Let's have another Bloody Mary,' said Nevin.

6. PIVOT

Let me tell you a little about how *USA-Brand War*™ works. There's a process that's been refined to a high degree of efficiency over the last forty or so years, particularly since the beginning of the twenty-first century.

Ninety-nine times out of a hundred, the objective is going to be to take control of a piece of land because you want to run an oil or gas pipeline over it, or get at the resources underneath it, and for some reason the existing government is unfriendly to your aims. Sometimes, the country in question stubbornly pursues an independent foreign policy (independent of yours, that is), and may even refuse to participate in the global economic miracle of international government borrowing. They just don't carry enough debt, and that leaves them disappointingly immune to the kind of financial pressure that could get them to fall into line with your requirements. Quite often, the target government is guilty of all three of these sins.

Before you can embark on a little constructive regime change, you need to create a narrative, because the first rule of *USA-Brand War*™ is never to be upfront about your objectives. You need to sell a story about how one particular person ('the enemy') is offending your sense of moral justice, standing in the way of freedom and democracy, and oppressing their very own people in the most brutal manner.

In crafting your enemy, it's important to ascribe the most bizarre and diabolical crimes to them. It doesn't matter if there isn't so much as a grain of truth in the accusations, because your compliant media will print them regardless, and your audience won't consider applying any critical thinking to the matter. After all, if the media says it's true, who are they to argue?

Hammer the accusations and demonise the nominated enemy for a good long while, and gradually expand the scope of their evil until it's accepted as a 'flat fact' that they are the most despicable person on the planet. In the meantime, to punish the people for supporting the enemy, start applying sanctions that can be used to strangle their country's economy. The idea is that if you can halt trade, stop the flow of medicines, foods and other goods into the country, when people start to die of starvation and treatable illnesses, they will blame the enemy. Keep piling the sanctions on until the entire population is screaming, and get your willing press to write about how terrible things are in the target country, emphasising that it's all the enemy's fault.

While this is happening, your NGOs – non-government organisations – should be active. Their role is to train locals or exiles who oppose the government – you'll always find plenty of them, anywhere – to become fighters, martyrs if necessary, and to arm and fund their fight. You get the loyalty of this opposition by promising them pallets of greenbacks, palaces and power when the enemy has been defeated. Your NGOs will also need to arrange buses for paid demonstrators, banners, flags, rifles and ammunition, flare guns, gas masks and a million other things that make 'spontaneous, peaceful protests' the well-planned bloodbaths you always 'feared'. It's a busy time.

When all of that is cooking along, you can take the next step – announce that the enemy is planning, or has even carried out, a particularly vile offence. Something so unbeliev-ably revolting that it simply must be true, because no one would make something like that up. Your preconditioned audience will not only buy your story, they will practically beg you to take any steps necessary to stop that bastard. That's your cue to invade the country in question, effect regime change no matter how much blood must be spilled to do so, and announce success. If the country is, unfortunately, wrecked in the process – an unavoidable consequence of saving it, you say – then while you're quietly implementing your original objectives: signing pipeline agreements and mining leases, you can make a few bucks on the side rebuilding it.

If the new, US-friendly government needs to borrow a few billion dollars from the IMF to pay for all that rebuilding, so much the better. Everybody wins. Well, except for the dead and maimed, the dispossessed and displaced, and all those other bit players in your grand victory.

That, as a general rule, is how we start a *USA-Brand War*^{TM} these days, and the formula's efficacy has been demonstrated regularly over the last few decades. There may be variations to the way it plays out, but the basics are usually present.

The process had been in play for quite some time as regards Venezuela, and was reaching its peak intensity at around the time we formed POW.

Aside from sitting on the largest proven oil reserves in the world, Venezuela had the temerity to achieve some success with socialistic policies during the Bolivarian Revolution started by Hugo Chávez. For a few short years, the Venezuelan people had enjoyed significant elevation in their standards of living, with indicators like health, education and poverty reduction all heading in the right direction.

A dramatic drop in the price of oil in 2014 quickly wiped out those gains. Sanctions were applied, the currency went berserk, and the opposition started getting very active, with lots of demonstrators mysteriously furnished with flags, weapons and banners turning up all over the place. In 2019 the United States unilaterally announced that a fellow named Juan Guaido, a product of CIA education, of course, had become 'interim president', because President Nicolas Maduro

— Chavez's successor (after that gentleman had conveniently died of cancer) had won another election in spite of all that hard NGO work. Guaido became something of a comical figure, perennially unable to assume the office he had been bestowed by his friends, and after a couple of bungled coup attempts and a great deal of corruption, he apparently outlived his purpose, and died in the inevitable plane crash.

By the time we started POW, the thing was approaching its climax, and leading the charge was a non-government organisation called PIVOT, or the Project for an Independent Venezuelan Oil Trade. Allegedly a private organisation put together by Venezuelan 'patriots', PIVOT bore all the hallmarks of being a gloriously inept, but no less deadly, CIA front.

The problems in Venezuela were featuring ever more heavily in the news, and PIVOT was ramping up its activities. They launched a new campaign of subway posters and billboards, including a giant animated billboard in Times Square, suggesting that the re-nationalisation of the oil industry in 1976 had been just the Venezuelan socialists' first step in a plan to conquer the world – starting with the good ol' USA of course. The Venezuelan government was a bloodthirsty vampire who, once it had finished torturing, starving and murdering its own people, would be coming to slay innocent Americans in their beds. The only solution, according to PIVOT, was a humanitarian intervention, that is, dropping huge quantities of incendiaries and explosives on the Venezuelan people who so desperately needed our protection.

The new campaign featured posters that were all variations on the same theme – a word, framed in the cross hairs of a rifle sight, with an outline of the United States behind both.

There were variations, using all the buzzwords we love and depend on: Democracy, Freedom, Liberty, Profits, Happiness, Your Rights, Family, God, Jesus and Faith. The Times Square billboard rotated through all of them.

There was also a radio commercial, which was played ad nauseam on all the local stations, voiced by the gloomiest, most threatening voice you can imagine. *'They won't stop at blowing up democracy for communism. They won't stop at stealing American property. They won't stop at dismantling your family, crucifying your god or trampling your rights. Make no mistake: the nationalised Venezuelan oil industry is a threat to every American. And they won't stop at Miami... Stop the dictators and save the people of Venezuela now – say yes to humanitarian intervention. Sponsored by the Project for an Independent Venezuelan Oil Trade.'* Of course, as the call to action came on, so did the martial music that sounded more than a little like the 'Star-Spangled Banner'.

Right-wing commentators on all the major television networks gave plenty of airtime to enlarging upon the threat that was, supposedly, so clearly expressed by a South American country taking charge of its own destiny. There was much talk of the moral threat and, yes, even the phrase 'domino effect' was deployed with no trace of irony. One United States congressman, appearing on a tried-and-true reactionary, hawkish talk show, said, 'You know what stops commies? Bombies.' Again, no irony.

It was all very crude and depressingly effective – polls showed that a growing minority of people supported the idea of bombing Venezuela, and that the minority could soon tip over to become a majority. Every time we saw a poster, heard a radio commercial or watched a blatantly biased news report, Abby seethed.

'Every time I see one of those fucking posters, it makes my blood boil. It's just promoting murder. We have to put a stop to it, because without people like us, it will happen.'

7. Subway fun

Monday morning the week after we agreed to become POW, Abby and I cut class and took the subway up to the Bronx, then tramped the cold, ugly streets in search of thrift shops. We bought bags of unsightly items, the rejects of people who had worn them for too long and possibly never once washed them correctly. Our haul included reversible overcoats in styles and colours we'd never ordinarily wear; horrible wigs in a rainbow of putrid colours; disgracefully ugly hats; several pairs of broad, old-man-style sunglasses; and five umbrellas. We paid for this fashion and sanitation tragedy in cash and took it home in several big bags. When we took it to my room and emptied the bags out onto the bed, it looked like we were planning to open a rag shop, and a particularly gruesome one at that.

Having sorted these disguises into five piles – one each for Nevin, Bevan, Lucas, Abby and me – we got back on the subway to spend a delightful hour on trains and in stations, travelling to Newark, and bought cans of spray paint that we could have bought around the corner.

'Did we have to go all the way to New Jersey just to buy paint, Abby?'

She gave me that look. 'No Jayne, we didn't. We didn't have to pay cash, either. And we didn't have to leave our phones at home all day, but we did. Because if we are successful in either stopping or at least slowing down the war on Venezuela, there will be a lot of powerful people very angry with us. And whether we like it or not, our government is collecting data on every single thing we do: every phone tower we ping, every web search we make, every phone call, email, facebook, tweet and instagram, and every electronic transaction. Every. Single. One. For most people, they're just holding junk, and even most of our stuff is junk too. But if at some stage we do start making a difference, they'll be very keen to stop us, and it's piss-easy for them to comb the data they already have to connect us with our activities. I'm not saying they won't find us if we muddy the trail, but let's not make it too easy for them.'

I might have called it paranoia, but I couldn't argue that the government really was collecting all that information, and I could see that Abby was deadly serious. That attitude was behind a lot of what she called 'hygiene' but the rest of us thought was just a waste of time and energy.

That evening, we had a house meeting. Bevan was already at the gym, but he would be working on the night of our first action anyway.

Abby addressed the three of us. 'Okay, this is the plan, POWers. Those fuckers at PIVOT are spending millions to start a war in Venezuela. Every fucking subway station. Times Square. The radio. They're everywhere. So we need to give them a kick. Push back with a little POW power. You've all heard that old saying about the only thing evil needs to triumph is for good men to do nothing? Well, in this case I won't allow you good men to do nothing. P Day is Thursday, Thanksgiving Day.'

I'm not kidding – she really said 'P Day' and she was in earnest. The only thing that kept me from popping out a loud guffaw was the knowledge that she would cut me dead with a look, and that I would really hurt her by letting slip a chuckle at that point. A change really had come over her.

'The Black Friday sales start at six in a lot of stores, so the subway will be madness from five onwards. At six, we strike, using the crowds and some especially heinous costumes Jayney and I have cooked up as cover. Lucas, you're with me. Nevin, you're with Jayne.'

Lucas grinned broadly as though he'd just won a contest. I'm sure she knew exactly what she was doing.

Nevin pouted, miffed at being relegated to Team Jayne. 'But I need to have Thanksgiving dinner with my parents,' he protested.

'Cancel it,' said Abby. 'You're having lunch with them; you don't need to be there for dinner as well. We need you, and you're not getting out of it.'

He shrank a little and nodded dumbly.

'We travel in pairs, and we work quickly,' she continued. 'One on a spray can, one holding an open umbrella to keep prying eyes and snooping cameras away. Take turns at each. As usual, we take the L from Lorimer Street, all together and dressed normally. Carry a bag with your disguises in it, have your overcoats reversed. Lucas, you and I will transfer to the 1 line via Fourteenth Street. Jayney and Nevin, you stay on till Fourteenth and Eighth, then take the A or C, whichever comes first. Before we get on these next trains, we change into our costumes – reverse overcoats and button them up, put on our silly wigs and grandpa sunglasses. We travel up the line as fast as possible, and at every stop we jump off, one of us scrawls our message on the nearest PIVOT poster while the other one screens them, and get back on before the train leaves the station, or get the next one. We meet on the street outside Washington Heights, casually discard our costumes, turn our coats inside out again, and catch the subway home together looking for all the world as if we've just had an early dinner in our favourite Harlem diner. Got it?'

'What's the message?'

'The important thing is to scrub out the call to war.' She held up an example – she'd stolen a poster already and marked it up to show us what she meant. She had scrawled, 'Invasion is not an expression of' over the headline word 'Freedom', turning their own word back on them. Below that, there was type saying, 'They won't stop at Freedom. So we have to stop them. Humanitarian air strikes in Venezuela now!' and Abby had scribbled out several words so the sentence now read, 'we have to stop Air strikes in Venezuela now!'

At the bottom she'd scrubbed over the PIVOT address and written 'POW!' above it, and put the word 'STOP' over the PIVOT logo. The message was inescapable.

'Be creative, but be fast, and make sure you leave "we have to stop" on every poster,' she said. 'Tag it POW too. We want to get credit for this. It's a lot to ask, but we can do it.'

Abby's military precision was admirable, and we all felt as though we had no choice but to agree. For the next three nights, Abby drilled us again and again; she took on the role of commandant with relish. And although she was fairly intense about it, she tried to talk it up as though it would be fun, and even threw in a few forced laughs. We all played along, because it was distracting and different to be planning something so rebellious, and because, well, it was Abby.

On Thanksgiving, we all spent the afternoons with our families, but under strict instructions not to drink too much or get so full we'd be drowsy. Abby and I shared a town car back to the 'Burg, and were gratified to see that the traffic was picking up everywhere. I was getting nervous, but also excited – I thought Abby's plan was practical and smart.

That evening at 5.30 on the dot, we marched out of the house. The mood on the train to Manhattan was one of tense expectation. I could see that Lucas and Nevin were going over the plan again and again in their minds, anxious not to screw it up and earn Abby's displeasure. Only Abby was buoyant, happy, smiling and laughing. She could have been going to a party, and of course she looked magical in her thrift shop coat, while the rest of us looked awful and smelled worse.

At Sixth Avenue, Abby and Lucas left the train, and Nevin and I were on our own. Abby had gently patted Nevin on the cheek as she'd gone past him, whispering something in his ear that lit up his face with a smile, so he was suddenly keener than ever to do a terrific job.

As it turned out, the plan worked handsomely. Nevin and I were a good team. We were fast, effective and fluid. We ditched the umbrella pretty early on in the piece – that just made us more conspicuous, not less – but otherwise it all went almost exactly according to the strategy. We did have to go off the platform to find the PIVOT propaganda at a couple of stations, so the whole operation took a solid couple of hours. At 50th Street, we saw MTA security for the first time, one apparently guarding the PIVOT poster on the platform, and a couple more waiting to get on to the train. Paranoia kicked in and we decided they were on to us. We quickly took our wigs and glasses off, and removed our overcoats and sat on them as the guards moved through the train, and of course didn't dare get off to hit any posters.

'We should make out,' said Nevin with a hopeful smirk. 'It's the perfect disguise.'

I couldn't help but admire his chutzpah.

'Not going to happen. Just move on, soldier.'

He grinned and looked mildly chagrined, but I could see he was pleased with himself. He'd seen the humour in my eyes and knew he'd scored a point. The guards didn't glance at us as they walked through the train, but we were convinced they were after us. They might even be waiting for us at the next few stations, and there was a remote possibility they would start searching the trains in earnest. Looking back, that was pretty naive, but we were full of adrenaline and it was the first time in my life I'd done something like that, so I was petrified of being caught. I should have had more confidence in their incompetence.

Just to be sure, we got off at Columbus Circle, carrying our disguises, and went into the Time Warner Center for a quick coffee. We gave it ten minutes, then went back down to the subway station to continue the journey.

'You know what they'd never expect?' said Nevin. 'That we go back to 50th Street.'

I laughed and agreed, so that's what we did. We caught a train back down there, jumped out and headed for the uptown platform. The guards were long gone, so we ducked into a dark corner, donned our coats and wigs, and hit the posters. We had to wait a few minutes for the next train, but we hid in the thick throng of stressed shoppers and got on without seeing any more MTA personnel. There was a security team at 135th Street, so we stayed on the train and hit 155th Street instead, before getting off at 168th Street to meet Lucas and Abby.

They looked anxious – they had been waiting almost an hour and were beginning to suspect that we'd been busted. They were delighted when they saw us walking up, and we all high-fived like idiots.

We had a new sense of fellowship and mutual accomplishment; we laughed explosively at anything and everything, and got a thrill out of seeing the results in so many of the stations on the way home – we were on Abby and Lucas's line. Nevin and I had done a great job, and we were proud, but what they had done was spectacular. Their graffiti was bold, hilarious, profane and wickedly on target.

The only moment of strain came when Lucas pulled out his phone and began manically prodding at the screen.

'What are you doing?' asked Abby, her voice laden with viciously sudden suspicion.

Lucas glanced up innocently, his glee fading when he saw Abby's face.

'Just checking Twitter…' he said. 'I want to see if we've got any traction.'

'You're not searching POW, are you?' said Nevin. His eyes were boring holes into Lucas's head as well. I thought I could see where this was going.

Lucas swallowed and said, 'Um, no. Well I was going to—'

'You fucking idiot,' Abby hissed. 'You'll get us all arrested.'

Lucas was confused. 'What?'

Her expression softened, and Abby went through her hygiene and data collection spiel. Nevin backed her up, with references to Ed Snowden and William Binney and the NSA's Utah Data Center, saying, 'They aren't collecting twenty terabytes of data a minute because they're looking for new meatloaf recipes.'

'But I thought we were going to have a Twitter account and a Facebook page and all that?'

'We are,' replied Nevin. 'But leave that to me. For the time being, let's not link ourselves to this in any way if we can avoid it.' He and Abby appeared to have discussed all this at some other time, because they were both on the same page.

'Sorry,' muttered Lucas. 'I just thought—'

'You weren't to know, Lucas,' Abby said. 'We didn't explain that to you. So, to be clear: what we have just done is a criminal act, and we will be committing more and more serious offences as we go on. We need to be absolutely serious about protecting our identities. That means taking extra care online, and telling no one – absolutely no one – about our involvement, no matter how much we want to take credit, big note ourselves or use it to get girls into bed.'

She sent a searching gaze around each of our faces, lingering on Lucas's and Nevin's, although she then looked at me and winked.

'This wasn't just a one-off, guys. We need to keep going until our message gets out. If you're not up for that, speak now and you're out.' She was looking unflinchingly at Lucas. To his credit, he held her gaze and, swallowing, nodded.

'I'm in.' Abby leaped up, jumped across the carriage, and threw her arms around him.

'I knew I could count on you.'

Lucas was in heaven, but Nevin looked like a kid whose ice cream has just fallen out of its cone; why was Lucas getting all the sugar when he was the one who'd transgressed the rules? Abby gave me another sly wink.

At home, we drank and smoked ourselves into absolute oblivion, toasting Abby for her brilliant scheme, cheering ourselves for carrying it off so professionally, and rejoicing in the new political force, POW. We couldn't wait to plan another job, and we all, of course, looked to Abby for leadership in this. She was radiant: proud and exquisitely affectionate with each of us, and as eager as we were to go again, only bigger, better and harder.

Bevan came home some time after two and found us still congratulating each other, raving about what we had done to stick it up PIVOT's ass, and revelling in our fellowship. He tried to join in, but clearly was not part of it. I could see that it hurt him a little to have missed out. He would move heaven and earth to be involved in the next job.

8. Winning and losing

Black Friday, the day after Thanksgiving, is always a sluggish, flattish kind of day. The entire country has a hangover, and in New York – the fairy-tale centre of Thanksgiving thanks to the marketing phenomenon we know as the Macy's Parade – the hangover effect is even more pronounced. Devoe Street was a microcosm of the nation that Friday morning, but with an added spritz of joy thrown in. We were still basking in the glow of what was, to us, a revolutionary act, and dying to know its effect.

When Abby and I emerged from our comas sometime after ten, we found Bevan working out with his giant weights in the lounge room, and Lucas fiddling with his tablet on the couch, trying to ignore big Bev's clanking and grunts. Looking up from the glowing screen, he was immediately defensive.

'I wasn't searching for POW, Abby, I swear,' he said.

She tossed her hair lightly and gave him a benevolent smile.

'It's cool, Lukey,' she said sweetly. 'I know you wouldn't compromise us. Besides, after Jayney and I've had a coffee, I think we could all do a bit of surreptitious snooping.'

We went upstairs to the kitchen and while the coffee machine – an expensive espresso number donated by Abby – did its thing, she outlined her approach to 'surreptitious snooping,' as she had so alliteratively put it.

'We'll just look at what's trending locally: see if PIVOT or POW are there. We could also search for innocuous terms like subway, or maybe even graffiti. But don't for god's sake search

POW. I think if we searched PIVOT it would probably be okay, but that's a last resort.'

I agreed, although I thought she was being a tad over-cautious – hopefully there were hundreds of people or more searching for POW after seeing our work on the subway line. We grabbed our coffees and tablets and joined the boys. Bevan had given up hurling large pieces of cast iron about, and was settled down in the beanbag watching some crap on television. Abby and I dropped into our armchairs, and she explained the strategy. We all set about exploring the various social media channels – Instagram, Twitter, Facebook, Snapchat and so on, for evidence of our crime. I logged into my Twitter account, @High_Ho_Silver, and checked the feed for results on the words 'subway' and 'PIVOT', while the others took on other apps. The results electrified us. A lot of people had posted photos on Instagram, Tumblr and Facebook showing our work, and we were cursed and blessed in equal measures across every platform.

The ones who supported us generally reacted as we had wished, asking out loud why on earth our country, or this PIVOT crowd, should have any say over what happens in Venezuela, and decrying the crusade for another war. We had started a conversation about the justice of calling for war based on a country's plans for its own resources, and we had laid bare the cynical brutality of US foreign policy.

On the other side, there was an unhealthy dose of hatred and vitriol. Of course, there was no official reaction from PIVOT – they were too clever to give us any oxygen – but their supporters vented dismay, disgust and anger. Many assumed that we were Venezuelans, and voiced their opinions on this in the worst possible terms, calling us taco niggers, petroleros, Hugo lovers, car thieves, and many more quite inventively pejorative words and phrases, plus the usual, unimaginative ones such as spics, greasers, wops and wetbacks, and of course the mandatory cunts, cocksuckers, motherfuckers, assholes and dipshits. We spent a couple of alarmed, intimidated but ultimately encouraging hours browsing the internet, laughing almost to the point of tears as we took turns sharing the most ludicrous, outrageous, hilarious or downright stupid slurs with each other, and practically glowing when we read out the positive messages.

Many on both sides of the argument asked, 'Who the fuck is POW?' – a question we were eager to answer in full, but not before we had put some security screens in place. There would be time to address that later – for now, we were just relishing our mysterious notoriety and the elevation that comes with knowing you've made a difference, however small.

By the time we were finished, we were fired up to do more, and right away. Bevan, who had missed out, was eager to become a fully-fledged POWer, and desperately keen to commit some heinous act that would give him the kind of rush and afterglow that we'd had.

In all of this, there was only one thing missing: Nevin. I looked up from the tablet that had been occupying my attention for so long that my neck ached, and asked, 'Hey, where's Nev?'

Lucas looked up absently – I think he was looking at some celebrity titty-watch by then – and said that as far as he was aware, Nevin had gone out early in the morning. He thought he'd heard him messing about in the kitchen at some ungodly hour, and then definitely heard his heavy footsteps stumping downstairs not long after.

We started talking about what we might do next – whether another hit on PIVOT posters on the subway would be enough or if we should do something else – and forgot about Nevin. It was a charged discussion, and from a reasonable start in which we uncovered a number of good ideas that we would later implement, we were soon striving to outdo each other in the preposterousness of what we proposed. These ranged from protesting outside PIVOT and military recruitment offices, to hiring a skywriter to write 'POW' over Manhattan,to hijacking Rush Limbaugh's microphone, and escalated all the way to kidnapping the president of PIVOT, Arkady Zenstl, using drones to deliver paint bombs to the façade of the UN headquarters, and even crucifying the secretary of state in Times Square. Clearly, we were losing focus, so Abby called a halt to further speculation about what we might do next, promising that she would formulate a plan.

We were just settling down again when Nevin came through the front door, a shit-eating grin on his face and a bundle of shopping in his hands. It was easy to see that he had, at least in his own mind, achieved something marvellous.

'Good; you're all here,' he said as he walked into the room and set down his shopping bags. Out of them he produced four items: two cell phones and two little packages containing some sort of electronic gadget.

'Okay,' he said with a self-important flourish and an ill-disguised glance at Abby to elicit her approval. She gave him a barely perceptible nod, but it was enough to make him smile gamely as he plunged into the speech he'd obviously prepared on the way home.

'We need to create a social media presence, but one that doesn't leave a trail for anyone who disagrees with what we're doing. That means keeping strict discipline around our social media usage at all times, and never once deviating from it. I propose to give everyone access to our POW Twitter, Facebook and Instagram accounts, but only under the conditions I am about to describe.

'First, I have picked up two "burner" cell phones,' he said, pointing out the two cheap phones from his bag. 'Phones we can use to set up bogus email and social media accounts that aren't traceable to our own accounts, and which we will never use again. Later today, after we've set up the accounts, I'll visit my grandmother in the home in Trenton; there's a vegetative old man in the next room, and I'll sneak in there and put the phones in a bottom drawer somewhere in his cubicle. That way, if anyone does a geolocation search on the phones, they'll turn up a beautiful red herring.

'Next,' he said, picking up one of the little packages and starting to tear it open, 'is the most important item in our arsenal. This is called a Speakeasy.' He held up what looked like an ordinary thumb drive. 'They were developed a few years ago, but for some reason they didn't take off. They are pure gold. You attach one of these to your desktop or laptop computer, and you do your emailing, POW-related social media work and – as the designer first intended – your banking through them. What they do is, every time you switch them on, they create a virtual machine that is completely separate from your hardware and your software. The virtual machine is generated in a data warehouse somewhere around the world – chosen at random from a roster of locations so it's impossible to predict – and it pops up a virtual keypad so you can do your business without touching your own hard drive or even your keyboard. Even if there is keylogging malware or any other monitoring software embedded in your hardware, you're safe.

'As soon as you finish your secret business, you log out of the Speakeasy, and the virtual machine it created evaporates. It's like it never existed. I got two – I'll keep one on my laptop, and Abby, you may want to keep the other one on yours. I would also suggest that we all set up anonymous email accounts via Tor or similar. As I said before, use the burner phone numbers to secure the email addresses.'

He shot a shrewd, submissive look at Abby, and she grinned madly. This was the kind of initiative she loved and rewarded handsomely.

'Brilliant, Nev,' she said. 'That's exactly what we need to get our message out there, but protect ourselves at the same time.'

Beaming like a cat that had just swallowed an entire aviary full of canaries, he added, 'I've also set up a virtual private network on my laptop, and I'll do the same on everyone else's. That means we don't leave an IP trail, but it's not foolproof, so for added security, any official POW business must be conducted via Speakeasy. Bev and Lucas, you two can use my laptop or take my Speakeasy any time you want to conduct POW business online. I would also suggest that we use it any time we are going to do sensitive searches on things like the locations of PIVOT offices, or the names of politicians who back its agenda. But it's essential that we use these clever little fuckers every single time we do anything even remotely related to POW. One slip and they'll have us.'

'Wise words,' said Abby. 'We have to be absolutely rigorous on this. Right now, we're nobodies, but when we start hitting PIVOT hard, they'll come looking for us. And we don't want to be found.' Regarding each of us in turn with those gorgeous blue eyes and an imperious yet somehow imploring gaze, she added, 'Our actual freedom and the success of POW depends on it.'

We all nodded, and I'm sure the others were as encouraged and as excited as I was. With this sort of alluringly furtive cloak and dagger thinking and technology at our service, our mission really did have a chance of succeeding.

Working very much as a team, we set about creating the accounts we would need to spread the POW message. Once we had a presence, we set about answering some of the questions and criticisms that our first act had generated. Our first tweet under the handle @POW_Power was, 'We are POW. We are Patriots Opposed to War. Expect to hear more from us you warmongering assholes.'

This was followed up with, 'We are not Venezuelans, we are Americans who remember what democracy, justice and freedom are really all about,' and then, 'PIVOT, you're just the first POW target. We won't stop until there is no more war.'

This last gained a lot of traction and was favourited and retweeted over a dozen times. We were on our way. In the meantime, we started work on a Facebook page. We realised that we would need images to populate it, so we started talking about what we might use. There was a certain amount of reasonable paranoia floating around the room, which coloured our thinking. Lucas suggested that we have a selfie as our main image, with our faces covered, but Nevin was against it.

'What if the FBI, or the CIA, the NSA or whoever the fuck it is that hates us the most and is the most keen to shut us down, examines the image and gets the location data, or worse, the user information off it? Or if they just undo the Photoshop work? It can be done.'

'Let's get a shot of one of the posters we fucked up off Twitter or Instagram and use that,' I suggested, and this drew general agreement.

'We can download and then upload it to our account via Speakeasy so it will never have any of our data on it,' said Nevin.

It was a learning process for all of us, and we were fully engaged, finding new things to like about our group and each other as we went on. We were building something: starting a genuine conversation about the filthy foulness of war and the benefits of peace, which we vowed to spread to as many people as possible before we were through. When and how we might be 'through' was not a topic we were prepared to entertain. We were at the beginning, and it was, for all of us, the greatest thing we had ever been involved in.

The only dark spot in the day came late in the afternoon when Bevan came across an Instagram post by some PIVOT operative or other – a picture of a clean PIVOT poster in the subway, with the caption, 'The last of the PIVOT posters defaced by a cowardly, anonymous group has been replaced. Look out POW, you're next on our clean-up list!'

'Fuck you, motherfuckers,' screamed Abby, her face distorted in pain and anger. 'We'll fuck you up, you fucking war-loving killers!' It took us all aback a bit, to see her so livid: even though we all shared her dismay, she had taken it really, deeply personally, and it was a little frightening to watch.

To calm her down, I suggested we go to the bodega for a couple of six-packs. It was that time of the day, after all. As we walked down the cold, leaf-blown street, she shook with rage and resentment. It was as though she was a mother and her baby had been attacked, and she was not going to rest until the attacker had paid in blood and pain for his audacity. I tried to focus on what we had achieved, given that it was less than twenty-four hours since POW had swung into action, and eventually she calmed down. By the time we got to the bodega and saw Jihad lounging around outside, his hands thrust deep in his coat pockets and his gaze somewhere far off, Abby was almost entirely back to her own self: confident, cheeky and disarmingly lovely. I went inside for the booze while she flirted with Jihad, which was becoming their ritual.

There was a good Black Friday crowd in the bodega, and by the time I came out with the drinks, Abby had clearly filled Jihad in on the whole scenario. This wasn't, incidentally, a breach of the confidentiality that Abby had hammered into Lucas, Nevin and Bevan so rigidly: Jihad was considered an honorary member of POW. Besides, we valued his opinion and hoped that he would play a starring role in future acts in our little drama. He was nodding and looking somewhat impressed but not overwhelmed, and as I approached, Abby was telling him that PIVOT supporters had already undone all of our good work. He appeared to stop and think for a moment, and then said, 'Abby, PIVOT is a symptom, and you should be attacking the disease itself: war. You need to get the message across that all war is bad, not just this particular one.'

Abby took this in, but we shared a look that said we were both sceptical.

'Even if you stop this war, another one will rise up in its place,' said Jihad, with that sagelike slowness he used when making profound pronouncements. 'You must deal with the very notion of war itself.'

'But surely that's not specific enough,' said Abby. 'How can we get our message across if it's such a wishy-washy, catch-all nebulosity as "war is bad, children"? No one would disagree with us – even the most hardened neocon claims to abhor war, but then declares that it's necessary to stop bad people from doing bad things. Let's not forget, in the past we've bombed people in countries across the world in order to hypothetically protect them.'

'True,' said Jihad. 'And making people see the futility of that, and helping them to understand that violence only begets violence, is a big task. But you have to start somewhere. May I suggest that for your next act, you aim for a bigger bang.'

'How do you mean?' asked Abby, interested.

'Be audacious. Think big, and above all, be offensive. Your little PIVOT stunt was fine, but it was limited in scope and ambition, and it was all over almost as soon as it began. Aim higher.'

'Will you help?' asked Abby. 'With the planning and the execution?'

Jihad smiled indulgently, as if he was used to people relying on his superior intellect and strategic skills.

'I wish I could, Abby,' he said. 'I really do. But my occupation is already high-risk enough, and my name and skin colour make me an immediate suspect in everything from international atrocities to the loss of a set of car keys on

Graham Avenue. I'm afraid I'll have to bow out.'

Sadly, but with a nod that showed that she understood, Abby looked at me and said, 'I was afraid of this.'

'Me too,' I said. Jihad could have been a great asset to our group, but I'd always had my doubts about his ability to commit. His was always, I suspected, going to be a philosophical rather than an active contribution.

Just then, a customer sidled up and Jihad hastily excused himself to conduct his illicit business. Abby and I walked away, disheartened to an extent but not shocked. I think in both of our minds we became determined to prove to him that we could succeed without him, and I, at least, held onto a distant hope that once we started to gain fame and followers, he would be begging to rejoin.

9. A bigger bang

We walked home in silence, thoughtful. We'd had a long day of POW thinking, reading and talking, but neither of us was quite ready to stop. My mind was alive with thoughts about what Jihad had said and how we could achieve the 'bigger bang' he spoke of, and I'm guessing that Abby was the same. Just as we got to the front door, she grabbed my arms and said, 'Jayney, our friend gave me a little sample of something nice, but not enough to share with the boys.'

This was not an unusual occurrence; Jihad often gave us little presents like that, especially if he had a new strain or something quite wicked in stock.

'Shall we give the boys their beer and disappear?' I said. She nodded vigorously.

Our boys were already distracted by some gory shit on television, so we handed out the beers and left them to their bombs, blood and guts. It was one of those nineties movies with an intensely high body count, but where the broadcasters, sensitive to what passes for morality, had bleeped out whenever one of the characters said 'shit'. The gore was uncensored, but the swearing was excised, and they had also pixelated the scenes where the native prostitute girls – and in those movies almost every female native in the country we're destroying to save is a prostitute – exposed their breasts.

None of the boys so much as grunted as we handed them their cold cans, inhabiting not our world but yet another foreign jungle battleground. Abby was appalled, both at their reaction and their distraction. I had to stop her from going back and delivering another lecture on the link between screen violence and the real thing.

We sat in my room and Abby rolled a thick, beautifully tapered reefer, like a tiny cornucopia of mellow Zen, and we rugged up so we could take it outside into the yard. As we perched on the back step, a crushed box under our butts in an underachieving effort to shield them from the chill of the concrete underneath, we stared at the sky and the bare cherry tree, and watched the blue smoke from our joint curl and fold over itself as it snaked its way up over the roof and out of sight.

'Do you think there's such a thing as a good war?' I asked as the warm buzz of detachment spread through my limbs and set my mind whirring again.

Abby was momentarily startled. I guess she was off on some other tangent and not really ready for my question, so I prepared to repeat it, but when I turned to look at her and say it again, I could tell that she was fully awake to what I was saying. It was like she'd been thinking the same thing.

'Why do you ask?' she said.

'Well, I was just thinking about today being Veterans Day,' I said. 'Given that its date is Armistice Day from World War I, it obviously began as a tribute to the men that fought in that war. But the ceremonies also emphasise World War II, and, you know, a lot of people believe they were good wars. I don't know if they're right or not.'

I handed the blunt to Abby and she took a deep toke that opened her eyes up wide and pushed her chest out half a foot. She held it and then blew out a torrent of grey smoke mingled with silver condensed breath, which looked magical as the next -door neighbour's back porch light made it halo and glisten. I was entranced.

'That's what we're up against, Jayney,' she said. 'There are no good wars, but there have in the past been necessary wars, and World War II is a great example of that. It was something we didn't choose to fight – although I could argue that we chose to create the conditions that forced us into it – and in which all those clichés about courage, honour, sacrifice and blah blah blah actually meant something. But the trouble with that "good war" as you call it, is that it has made every war after it seem good and necessary too. Even when they've clearly been aggressive and invasive, our leaders have characterised our offensive actions as being defensive. Notice how we're always fighting for our freedoms, even when the people we're attacking are so far away and so under-resourced that even the idea of somehow curtailing our freedoms would never have occurred to them? You can put that down to the story that came with World War II.

'Our propagandists learned from that war, that if you claim to be under attack, and everything you stand for – which is naturally good and right and just – is at risk because of the horrid, godless, barbarian hordes waiting to swoop in and crush your liberty, people will allow you to commit all sorts of atrocities. The funny thing is, they learned that from fucking Hermann Göring, of all people. What does that tell you? The guy was a fucking Nazi!

'Anyway, the idea of being attacked, and especially anything connected with the word freedom, works like magic now – all a politician has to do is say "freedom" once, and we the people will be falling all over ourselves to green-light any and all crimes they see fit to commit to advance their agendas. And that's despite the fact that what they want, which is war, has nothing to do with freedom and everything to do with power.'

She had been holding the reefer all this time, so I nudged her and she handed it over, and I took a solid pull. It was getting near the end and the smoke was hot and harsh. I loved it. Abby's eyes burned with passion and her cheeks glowed red in the cold night air. With the neighbour's porch light behind her, I could see the fine, downy blonde hairs on her face in silhouette. I passed her the joint and she turned to look at me and smile.

'So, no, sweetie,' she said. 'There are no good wars.' She took another good long toke, and continued. 'Sure, there may have been one or two once, but I doubt it. And in any case, even the necessary wars are the reason we now have so many unnecessary wars – our wars of choice. We use them and the people that fought and died in them to glorify the business of soldiering. The act of killing people has become something that we've come to treat with an almost religious reverence. The mantra is always, "support our troops", not because the people behind that slogan feel the soldiers really deserve our support – as you can see by the way they treat veterans – but because it feeds the idea that war is good. How can war not be good, if our brave, selfless, heroic young men and women give their lives in service to our country by travelling to other places and killing the people there?'

I stared at her and felt as light as a feather. Or a snowflake.

'So why did you ask, darling?' she said. Her face was turned to me, and it was deep in shadow but her eyes glittered, and the way her lips moved when she said "darling" made me quiver. I tried to ignore it.

'Because I've been thinking about Jihad's bigger bang,' I said, 'and I think I have the answer. We need to stop people from venerating soldiers before we can turn them against war.'

Abby nodded and closed her eyes, as if she was trying to see my thoughts by looking into her own. 'Mmmmmm.'

'I have two words for you, my darling,' I said sweetly. 'Battery Park.'

Abby's eyes sprung open and she was once again forcefully present, almost shimmering with energy and inspiration. She wrapped her arms around me in a bear hug, and laughed.

'Oh, you are so right, Silver!' she said. She only ever called me Silver in moments of extreme elation, so I knew I had scored a direct hit.

'Battery Park,' she repeated. 'The biggest bang of all!'

Battery Park is holy ground to Americans in general and New Yorkers in particular. It's home to all manner of memorials and monuments, including the Sphere, a remnant of the fabled 9/11 attacks that gave our glorious country even more licence to wage war around the globe. But our target, as Abby well understood, was to be the East Coast Memorial – a series of huge granite panels inscribed with the names of over four thousand US servicemen who went missing in the Atlantic Ocean during one of the "good wars", World War II. The eight massive blocks would provide a vast canvas for our paint cans. We would create a sensation.

'Leave it with me, my genius friend,' said Abby, still hugging me. 'We're going to nail this.'

We went inside, pretty stoned now and holding suddenly empty beer cans, and collapsed into our armchairs. Abby sent a willing Bevan upstairs for fresh drinks, and we turned into good American zombies until, at last, hunger pangs forced me out of my stupor. I ordered pizza and relapsed into my semi-comatose state, my second beer half-drunk on my chair's arm. Nobody else stirred.

But Abby didn't look as catatonic as the rest of us; she had that thousand yard stare, and I knew she was creating our next big hit, and that it would make our reputation. I sipped my tepid, flat brew and went back into tv stupor until the pizza delivery knocked on the door.

We spent the next week working hard on our social media presence, madly tweeting and Facebooking and so on, and checking our profile. After the flurry of activity on the day after Thanksgiving, our mentions had begun to slide, and reaction to our online activity was waning. Clearly, people needed something to spike their interest.

The following Thursday, Abby and I took off on another thrift shop and hardware store expedition. This time we bought mostly black – black pants, black skivvies, black jackets, black balaclavas (ski season was coming up, and Abby spun a marvellous tale about Aspen in her best Boston accent) – but we also bought a few brightly coloured sweaters in extra-large sizes to cover our burglar outfits while we were on the subway and walking through heavily surveilled areas. At a couple of hardware stores, we bought cans of black spray.

Before anybody could knock the top off an evening brew that night, Abby gathered the team in the living room and explained the plan. We were going to hit Battery Park, for the reasons outlined above. It had only been a week since our first assault, and although some of the excitement had worn off, Abby and I were expecting a rush of positive reaction to the plan from the boys. We'd been talking about the Battery Park assault between us days, and were both jumping out of our skin with anticipation. The boys looked excited to hear it, but were uncomfortably low key when we had fully explained the plan. Almost dumbstruck, I'd say. Abby and I looked at each other and frowned.

At last, Nevin shifted his gaze to a blank piece of wall off to the side of where Abby's face was, and hesitantly addressed it.

'Um, I thought we were targeting PIVOT,' he said. Lucas nodded with unnecessary vigour, and Bevan looked troubled.

'Well, our ultimate purpose is to stop all war, isn't it? So that's what we're doing now. This operation is about reminding people that wars can't go ahead without soldiers as cannon fodder. It attacks the disease, not the symptom,' Abby said, echoing Jihad. 'We won't forget about PIVOT, but this is an opportunity too good to miss. We really need to get POW noticed, and this will do it. You can thank Jayney for the idea,' she added. As if attaching my name to it would do anything to inspire our reluctant warriors.

Fidgeting, looking at his lap and grimacing as he spoke, Bevan said, 'Look, I work with some ex-troops. Most of them are really nice guys. I don't want to dishonour them.'

'Yeah, what the fuck, Abby?' said Lucas. 'Why bring the troops into this? It's the politicians and the corporate assholes who send kids off to war. Why don't we stick to targeting them?'

Trying not to look exasperated, and speaking as slowly as if she was addressing a kindergarten class, Abby said, 'Those kids keep signing up, Lucas.'

He almost winced at the venom she put into his name, even though I thought she was actually holding back.

'And anyone who's signed up over the last twenty years or more had to know that the politicians who dictate what they do were going to send them off to invade other countries. That makes it at least partly their fault. Yes, they're poor, they're stupid, they're completely without hope, and they're convinced – by the media, by the state and by the bumper stickers saying, "support our troops" – that if they go to war and kill a few brown people, they can get shot up themselves, or run over by one of their own jeeps or tanks or whatever they do, and come home and everything will be just fucking rosy. But they know that the last thing they're going to be doing is actually defending America, so they have to bear their share of the blame. Okay, some of the names on those slabs are actual selfless heroes, but let's just call them collateral damage, hm?'

The boys weren't looking convinced, although there was some truth in what Abby was saying about the culpability of people who sign up to an army they know is all about waging aggressive war as defined by the UN. She changed tack.

'Bevan,' she barked. Bevan snapped to attention. 'Those friends of yours. All nice guys, eh? Big drinkers, some of them?'

'A few,' he said.

'A few heavy drug takers among them? Maybe a couple of steroid freaks?'

'Yeah.'

'And when things get a bit rowdy, when customers get a bit out of hand, these fellows are a picture of restraint, are they? Or do they turn nasty and crack some heads?'

Bev squirmed. 'Okay, a few of them are a bit fucked up and they kind of lose their cool. But it's not their fault.'

'I know!' said Abby. 'It's the fault of the wars they've been in. And what are we trying to do?'

'Stop the wars,' I said. My expression was bright, my voice peppy, and my eyes unconvincing. 'Bev, you have to understand,' I continued. 'Nobody wants to dishonour the troops. But we need to make people pay attention to what we're saying, and this is a way of doing it. Besides, did any of your friends have friends who died in the Second World War?'

He shook his head.

'Lucas?' I knew Abby needed my backing on this, and I was determined to provide it.

'That's not the point,' said Lucas. 'We just don't want to be disrespectful.'

'Oh. So you'd rather that thousands – millions – more young people are tricked into signing up, and go off and kill millions more people in fucked up invented overseas wars, because you don't want to be disrespectful; is that it?' said Abby. She was losing it a little bit, and it was kind of alarming. Lucas, strangely oblivious to the fact that he was poking the bear, persisted.

'But they haven't done anything wrong.'

'What?' Abby cried. 'Who? The soldiers that go overseas and strangle children and burn villages and rape whole countries? Are you fucking serious, or are you just a fucking moron? Ever heard of My Lai, Lucas? Or Abu Ghraib, or Fallujah? Sirte? Cambodia? Laos, Bosnia, Korea, El Salvador? Yes, the politicians and the CEOs send them over there, but once they're there, those kids turn into fucking animals. They lose all respect for human life and decency, they stop feeling and keep killing, and when they come home they beat their wives and they abuse their kids and they end up on the streets, broken, fucked up and begging. That's when all that "respect the troops" bullshit breaks down – people don't look at them as the fine, upstanding heroes they supported anymore. Oh no, the troops they support are all those fine young men and women in crisp uniforms. The hopeless, smelly, shambling, crippled shadows who live on the streets and get drunk and stoned and disgust them aren't the kind of troops they respect. Not after they've been damaged.'

She took a couple of deep breaths and calmed down. 'Of course, I'm generalising,' she said. 'That's not the case with every soldier. Some serve admirably, uphold their honour beautifully, and come home to flowers and white picket fences. But you know that's the minority. The rest are discarded like last year's game consoles, and nobody gives a shit about them, least of all you. You'd cross the street to avoid one of those broken vets. So don't give me your pious crap about not wanting to disrespect anyone.'

Lucas was taken aback, but amazingly, he wasn't yet done. 'But Battery Park?' he said. 'World War II victims?'

'You asshole,' Abby said. 'I knew you'd be the first to turn to crap. You haven't got a fucking clue what we're trying to do here.'

All that time, she'd been sitting in her armchair, but now she stood up. She was flushed and her eyes were flashing. She was wearing a red tartan skirt that came down almost to her knees, and under that, thick black tights. She also wore a tight black turtleneck sweater, tucked into her skirt, so it looked as though she might have been wearing just a skin suit with the skirt over the top. Her command of the room was palpable. She looked around at each of us, and spoke evenly, almost without any emotion or modulation to begin with, but then becoming more – there's no other way to describe it – fanatical as she went on.

'Look,' she said. 'Last week we had a lot of fun. We got a buzz out of bombing those posters. It was an amazing moment. But we also did something important. And that's what we were there for. The important thing. Not for kicks. As we go on, the risks will get higher, and the exhilaration will increase. We'll get genuine thrills. But that's not why we're doing it. Remember that. Because at times it'll also get hard. Things will go wrong and people may even get hurt. It's unavoidable, and the pain will be real. And what we don't need is some chickenshit whining motherfuckers bawling about disrespect.'

She fell into deadpan delivery again. 'So, now is the time. Declare yourselves – are you in, or are you out? Starting with Battery Park tomorrow night. Nevin?'

Staring into her eyes, immersed in her heated glow, Nevin nodded solemnly.

'Bevan?'

He nodded, and even smiled approvingly. It's like he knew that she was manipulating us all, but he couldn't help but go along with it. She had a lot of power right then.

'Jayney?' she asked.

'You know it, Abby,' I said.

At last, she turned and faced Lucas full on. He was on the beanbag and she was literally standing over him. He looked sullen, even sulky, but he couldn't resist her.

'I'm in,' he said.

She burst into a huge grin and gave him her sweetest look. The change in her demeanour, and the way it instantly altered the atmosphere in the room, was remarkable. It was as though someone had opened the curtain and let the light in.

'I knew I could count on you,' she said. Then she laughed and pulled a piece of foil out of a hidden pocket in her skirt and threw it at Bevan. 'Let's get stoned.' As he started unravelling foil to get at the pot, she added, cheekily, 'They don't all strangle children,' and we all laughed like demented jackals.

10. Assault on Battery

Sunday night, or early on Monday morning, we put our plan into action. The mood on the subway was sombre. I had a knot in my stomach, and the rest of the crew looked as though they did too. It was after 2 a.m. and the subway was fairly quiet. Those that were aboard were almost all drunk, stoned, wired or some combination of the above, and those that weren't looked scared and out of place. Like us. Under our overcoats, we were all wearing the large, colourful sweaters Abby and I had bought, and in retrospect they kind of marked us out from the crowd. Maybe they were a bit too ostentatious. In any case, we were stuck with them.

Abby and I sat with Bevan, and Lucas and Nevin were in a different carriage so we didn't look like a group. I put my head on Bevan's shoulder and closed my eyes. I didn't have to try to look tired: I was. My nerves were exhausting me.

The 1 train we were on took us to the South Ferry station, and we walked up to State Street to cross into Battery Park. No one said a word, and we all walked with our heads down. We each carried a small backpack with one can of spray paint and the regulation two pairs of disposable gloves so we didn't have to get back on the train with paint all over our hands. The plan was to split up, exhaust our paint, our creativity or a maximum of three minutes, whichever came first, and get the hell out of there. We each had different escape routes, and mine was the longest – I had to walk all the way up to Little West Street, follow the path to the overpass above Rector Street, and cross over to the Rector Street subway station at Greenwich Street.

THE WORLD WITHOUT MIRRORS

The memorial was, thankfully, poorly lit, but there was enough ambient light for us to see what we were doing. The night was cold but clear, and conditions for vandalism were perfect. I managed to get three messages in large, thick, black lettering onto the huge grey panels carrying the names of those long dead mariners, writing, *Support for troops = support for wars, Dying in wars of invasion is not heroic* and *Murder is not bravery.* The others wrote similar messages – *Not all soldiers are heroes, Americans, we are not exceptional, we are killers, War kills humanity, Hey Mr President, send your own kids to war,* and *Remember Nuremberg.* This last one was one of Nevin's, but I was pretty sure people would look at it and say, 'What the fuck does that mean?' Nobody remembers anything about the Nuremberg Principles or the Supreme International Crime any more. If they did, we wouldn't have the hyperaggressive foreign policy we do. Then again, if it got people looking for the answer online, I guess it was worth it.

The adrenaline surge that I'd had when we hit the PIVOT posters came back, and while I was busy spraying my messages, I felt potent, virtuous and good. I had this idea that people would see what we had done and suddenly wake up. 'Fuck!' they'd say. 'You're so right.'

My three minutes passed in a blur of paint and righteousness, and then I was striding as fast as my legs would carry me across the park, my gloves and spray can safely stashed back in my backpack along with my bulky, ostentatious sweater. I could dimly see the bulky figure of Bevan half-running up towards Pearl Street. My mind was buzzing with fear, but I felt stronger and more principled than I ever had before.

My escape route turned out to be the scariest part of the whole adventure. I had to cover the length of the park, and then walk up a very deserted Little West Street. Worse, I had to pass a playground up near the overpass, and I was terrified. Who knew what degenerate, lowlife criminals were hanging out there?

I got to the subway station okay, and as I waited for the train my racing heart rate began to slow down. The sense of accomplishment was awesome. I felt important and visionary, and I wondered if the other people at the station could see a special glow about me. There were only three people, though, and two were making out in shitfaced slobbery, while the third, a middle-aged man in a crumpled suit, dozed. The adrenaline kept surging through me, but I felt a strange, welcome control. The stakes had been higher this time around, and the aura that surrounded its success was much brighter.

I was the last home, and I found my partners in crime in a boisterous, celebratory mode. I joined in the noisy self-congratulations, and got amongst the beers and bongs. We all agreed that, while the first hit was the most electrifying, the buzz from the Battery Park stunt was in many ways more satisfying. Bevan, who had popped his cherry on Battery Park, was near delirious. Hours after, he was still sweating, rubbing his forehead and saying, 'wow', and 'fuck' a lot, and along with the rest of us amping for the next event. We partied until after dawn, and as the world woke up and went to work, we all went and crashed.

11. Crashing

Waking up the day after the Battery Park job, we discovered that we had made national news —as the most despised people in America.

Everyone, on all sides of politics, religion, activism and commentary, and even the most apathetic of drones who didn't care about anything at all, had turned on us. The commentariat and the common people all joined together to describe us as disgusting, sacrilegious, unfeeling, monstrous, treasonous, traitorous, blasphemous, obscene, beneath contempt, undeserving of life and liberty, and a good many other less complimentary terms. Death threats, promises of improbable physical punishments ranging from dismemberment and torture to gruesomely detailed sexual acts, and hatred expressed in a rich spectrum of colourful phrases, poured into our social media accounts. Even supposedly antiwar groups and individuals weighed in with denunciations, declarations of horror and disbelief, disavowal of any knowledge of or association with POW, and assertions of solidarity with our troops. Right-wing commentators called for us to be hunted down like the animals we reportedly were, and shot on sight.

It was all more than a little bit over the top. If we'd decapitated a statue of George Washington; shat, spat and peed on the flag; or mutilated a disabled veteran in the middle of Times Square, the reaction could not have been more virulent or elicited more promises of impending vengeance. We had hit a positively religious nerve in the American psyche, and for a while it seemed like the entire population was lined up to put their hands on their hearts and swear that this was the most evil thing they had ever encountered. Our violation of the bond between our nation and its military had left a gaping, raw and bloodied wound, which would be picked over, prodded, reopened, examined and analysed until the next unspeakable act arrived to dominate the news cycle, or outrage fatigue set in and the media simply forgot about it. Thankfully, one or the other would happen with remarkable swiftness.

But on that first afternoon, as we emerged wearied and hungover to check out the effect of our stunt, the reaction was shattering. Almost instantly, I went into a state of panicked paranoia. I pulled the curtains, locked the doors, checked the window locks and switched off all my devices. Lucas was almost paralysed with fear, but somehow found the strength to wail about how we were all 'dead'. Bevan was walking around looking shocked, unable to form a coherent sentence but shaking his head and wringing his hands a lot. Nevin sat with his face in his hands, groaning softly.

'I knew it, I knew it, I knew it,' he kept repeating.

Alone among us, Abby was far from being afraid or abashed: she was in a fury. A tower of malice and loathing, she stalked about the house, raging at the stupidity, worthless gullibility and sheep-like mentality of the people of America.

'Those fuckers!' she screamed. 'You can't reason with 'em. They're so deeply mired in the propaganda, so brainwashed and brain fucking dead that they can't see what's right in front of their faces. My god! I had no idea that the masters of war had been so brutally effective in creating this nation of killer-lovers. We really are up against it, Jayney,' she said, turning to me. 'This proves that we've come along not a moment too soon. We need to get to work on these fucking sheeple immediately, harder than ever.'

Startled, appalled looks crossed each of the boys' faces, and if the situation had not been so serious I would have laughed. They looked like guilty kindergarten kids whose ringleader was pushing them into another misadventure while they were still in trouble for the last one. I took Abby out of the room and spoke to her quietly.

'You're right of course, sweetie,' I said. 'But I don't think now is just the time to be making plans for any future events. These boys are frightened – and so am I, a little. Let's let this thing settle down a bit and go back to where we started – stopping the attack on Venezuela. Hmmm? If we concentrate on one war at a time, we might have a breakthrough, and if we can stop it, we will have genuinely achieved something. But if we go down the Battery Park road again, we'll never get through to these blockheads, and they really will hunt us down. Attacking something so dear to them only served to heighten their attachment to it and the lie that it represents.'

To her credit, Abby listened to this and thought about it for a good couple of minutes. 'You're right, Silver,' she said. 'Fuck Jihad and his bigger bang. Let's take smaller steps.' She grinned a bitter, scornful grin that spoke of retribution. 'I'm gonna cut Jihad's balls off and feed them to him in a hoagie,' she said.

We rejoined the boys and Abby addressed them quietly but fervently.

'I'm sorry,' she began. It made them all look up. Her blue eyes were like saucers and her lips drew into a tiny pout that made her look vulnerable and remorseful all at the same time. Her hair was still messy from sleep, so it was adorably tangled and frazzled, and she wore just a t-shirt and a pair of leggings, so even at that moment she was magically beautiful. I could see the forgiveness in the boys' eyes before she even got the next word out.

'I should have listened to you all. You were right. I'll never do that again, I swear. Everything we do now, we all agree on or it doesn't get done,' she said. 'But please, please, please, don't give up now. It's too important. This shows us just how much the American people – our people – have to learn about war. And we'll find a better way to teach them.' We all sat and looked at her dumbly, in love but still in the grip of fear and paranoia.

'I'll make this right,' Abby said. 'We'll take a break, this thing will blow over, and we'll get back to being protestors, not desecrators. Okay?'

A silence hung over the room. The air was repressive, but a little less so than a moment before. 'We need coffee,' said Abby with a bright smile. 'Jayney and I will get dressed and go get some, and maybe a few croissants, and we'll forget about this for a little while, hmmm? Bevvy darling, maybe you and Nevvy could go out the back and burn the clothing we wore last night? And let's make a foolproof plan for getting rid of those paint cans, sooner rather than later. Remember, we covered our tracks very well last night, and we can get rid of the evidence long before anyone suspects a thing, if they ever do. We'll get through this, my boys.' They didn't look overly convinced, but at least they had something to do, and they knew there were croissants coming. Abby and I went back to my room to get dressed.

Later, along with our coffees and greasy breakfast, we tried to digest the incredible volume of hate pouring out of every corner of the internet and the wider media onto us. Yes, there were one or two people that supported us and said so, but that was no help. They were mostly anarchists and nihilists who advocated tearing the whole thing down and lining just about everybody up against the wall so they could start again, and we didn't really want to be associated with them.

After a while, we became numbed to the death threats, the pledges of violence and the endless waves of profanity, invective, vituperation and vitriol. You can only be offended the first thousand or so times, and after that you've already got the idea. To say that we were downhearted, though, would be an understatement. The weight of all that hatred was oppressive, and the boys and I remained gloomy, scared and, to be candid, ready to quit. Only Abby seemed to take strength from the outrage we had generated.

'We scored a goal here kids, make no mistake,' she said. 'Power doesn't react like this unless it's been hurt. This is kind of what we wanted, only maybe not so much so quickly.' She wasn't trying to be sweet or manipulative, or to cajole the boys into going along because they all loved her; she was being absolutely earnest about it. And while that in itself was undeniably attractive, we were all too far down in the dumps to be swayed by her argument.

'We're the most hated people in the country,' said Lucas, echoing my thoughts. 'We overstepped the mark, and now we have a giant target painted on our backs.'

Given Abby's prior fury, I thought she'd bite Lucas's head off, but she was calm and reasonable.

'I know it looks bad,' she said, giving Lucas a soulful look. 'And I accept full responsibility. But we'll get through this. In some ways, it really is what we needed to do, even though it doesn't look like that now. But I swear, one day we'll look back and say that this was a turning point. And the one thing we can't do is give up and let the innocent people of Venezuela suffer because we shit our pants over a few empty threats.'

'It's more than a few empty threats Abby,' said Nevin. 'There are thousands of these things. Even if only one in a thousand is genuine, that's still a lot of people out for our blood.'

'Don't forget, we're protected,' said Abby. 'If the cops and the FBI can't find us – and I'd say by now they are looking for us even if they weren't after the PIVOT hit – then a few moronic rednecks certainly won't. As long as we follow the protocols, keep a low profile for a while and let the madness pass, we'll be fine. I promise you.' Those blue eyes! Jesus, they were persuasive.

As this conversation had been going on we had all, as is the way of our generation, been glued to our various devices, scrolling through the messages of odium and abhorrence that our act had spawned. Abby, of course, had control of the official accounts, and we were all looking at hashtags such as *#FuckPOW, #KillPOW, #ECMatrocity, #SupportourTroops, #VetsagainstPOW, #POWyourdead* (there is no correct spelling or grammar on the internet) and so on.

Abby gave a little squeal of delight and surprise. 'This might be our shot at redemption,' she said. 'I've been getting a lot of PMs from journalists and news organisations asking for a statement, which I'm ignoring. But this one is from a producer at Tanner French Tonight. They say they want to give us a chance to tell our side.'

I liked Tanner French. Although, like most of her fellow actors, she had made her share of movies glamourising violence, her roles had also aimed at empowering women, for the most part, and she seemed thoughtful and intelligent. Her late-night TV show was highly regarded because she was witty, insightful and not afraid to question authority, without being contrary just for the sake of it. She had even on occasion been accused of being left wing, which as we know is about the worst insult one American can fling at another. It's one small step from being a full-blown commie, for Christ's sake.

Still, appearing on her show seemed like a dangerous move. Even with someone as seemingly sympathetic as Tanner, it was the producers' job to lure interviewees into a trap by telling them that they had a right to air their views, and when they agreed, those poor schmucks usually found themselves being pilloried, or worse.

The feeling in the Devoe Street lounge was suspicious. The idea that we would be fairly treated, or would make any headway against the tide of loathing that had engulfed us, was difficult to accept. It was much more likely that we would be exposing ourselves, perhaps seriously compromising our anonymity, purely for the sake of putting a face on the currently nameless target for revulsion our act had created.

'Don't do it, Abby,' was the prevailing sentiment. But Abby was, as always, persuasive. And crafty. Somehow, she had already thought it all out.

'We can't let this beat us,' she said. 'We have to take control of the situation. To stay silent or to disappear is to tacitly admit we were wrong.'

'We were,' said Lucas. He was worried, as we all were, that this could lead to arrests, maybe even prison.

'Then let us admit it,' said Abby. 'Look at every politician or public figure who's ever been caught screwing their best friend's wife, sneaking off with bags full of money, or snorting coke off a hooker's tits. Do they slink away and disappear? Of course not. They cry and say they're sorry. They claim to be flawed and say that makes them human, and they promise to try harder next time, which means they'll just try harder not to get caught. And because the only thing the media loves better than cutting people down is granting them redemption – which proves that it holds the keys to public adoration or aversion – it facilitates it all. The newspapers, television stations, magazines and online media all work together to coax the public into believing that the act of owning up is a wonderful statement of character and fortitude, and in the process, the crime itself is virtually forgotten, or at least whitewashed. Now I'm not saying we'll emerge from this as heroes, but we will get to have our say. A lot of people will admire our courage in admitting our mistake, and they may give us a second chance. They say there's no such thing as bad publicity – but if we don't do this, the bad publicity we've just had will kill POW on the spot. If we do go ahead, we might salvage the situation. Besides, if the alternative is to end up being a bunch of those good people who let evil happen by doing nothing, we don't have a choice: we have to do it.'

The boys still looked dubious. Nevin, who'd been nodding in agreement with Abby's assessment of media culpability in the destruction and resurrection of reputations, spoke up.

'That's all very well, Abby, but we're in a dangerous place right now. If the FBI gets even a hint of our identities, they and the cops will come down on us heavy. I'm talking jail time for all of us. Serious jail time.'

Lucas looked aghast, and Bevan screwed up his face. I think Bev figured he could at least fight his way out of trouble in prison, but Lucas knew he would be somebody's bitch in no time at all.

Abby's expression was sympathetic, but her eyes were resolute. It was really just a matter of time before we all capitulated. In my heart, I already had. I knew that if anyone was going to drag us out of this, it would be Abby; the strength of her convictions would carry us all along like dust in the tail of a comet.

'We already have the tools to ensure we don't expose ourselves,' she said with patience that, surprisingly, did not sound patronising. 'I'll only agree to the interview under very strict conditions – online via our little friend Speakeasy, and without any of us appearing on camera. Here's the plan...'

Spelling out her scheme in detail, Abby drew us in and one by one convinced the boys that this was the best thing we could do for POW. It all seemed legit, but it was a line ball really. There was so much potential for disaster. But, as usual, by the time Abby had finished laying out her plan, along with a little pep talk about the importance of our work and a reminder of what an amazing feeling it was to do something that involved both risk and reward, the whole team was onboard. She smiled a gentle, soft smile to herself and started punching out a message to Tanner's producers, detailing the conditions. Surprisingly, they agreed.

That night, we gathered around the television, sober and straight – not only because we wanted to be, but because none of us had had the courage to leave the house all afternoon, even to pick up booze. There was a lot of other fluff, with inane guests and lame musical acts, before Tanner introduced the interview that had been prerecorded late in the afternoon.

Looking down the barrel of the camera lens and adopting a very serious face, Tanner said, 'As we all know, there was a shocking, terrible event last night in Battery Park here in New York. A group calling themselves POW – Patriots Opposed to War – defaced the East Coast Memorial in the park with messages insulting, defamatory and distressing to veterans. This previously unknown group came to local attention last week when they daubed antiwar messages across a series of advertising posters placed in the New York subway system by PIVOT, the Project for an Independent Venezuelan Oil Trade, whose goal is the privatisation of the oil industry there. Although that act of vandalism caused a minor sensation locally, the reaction to POW's latest stunt has been tremendous and rightly so. The East Coast Memorial pays tribute to the US servicemen who died during the battle of the Atlantic, off our very own shores. It is to many Americans a sacred and beautiful place in which we remember those who gave their lives for our freedom, and the notion that it has been violated has upset and enraged citizens across the spectrum. It is important to know who would perpetrate such a vile act, and why, especially as POW has until now been a virtually unknown underground organisation. We have been in contact with the group, and under condition of anonymity, their leader, Eirene – a pseudonym – has agreed to talk to us.'

The camera cut away from Tanner to a shot of a Skype screen. There on the screen, against a background made up of a dark blue blanket, stood a miniature Hulk figurine, which belonged to Bevan. It had, of course, been Abby's idea to use that as a substitute for any of our faces on screen, and the show's producers had reluctantly agreed. The screen then split into two, showing on one side our little green monster, and on the other, a bemused Tanner French.

'Eirene. I'm told that your name is taken from the Greek goddess of peace; is that right?'

'For sure, Tanner,' replied a voice that was sort of like Abby's but not. She'd raised the pitch a half an octave, and adopted a beautifully naive sounding Canadian accent. We all burst out laughing the second we heard it – it was pure Abby gold. There was no way anyone would ever recognise her voice from that, so we all relaxed a little, too.

'We're all about peace,' Abby continued, making the *ou* in about sound more like an *oa*, as in boat, and prompting fresh hysterics from us. She blushed and laughed along with us. Tanner French, not in on the joke, remained gravely poised.

'Defiling the memorial in Battery Park last night has been described by the Secretary of State, whose grandfather's name is said to be on the memorial, as an appalling act of treachery. Veterans associations, city officials and ordinary Americans are shocked and horrified by what you've done. Do you have any excuse at all for such a shameful act?' she said with unexpected emotion.

'No, Tanner, we don't,' said Abby in that suddenly no-longer-funny Canadian voice. 'Our intention was never to offend or defame any veterans, or the memories of those who have died defending peace and freedom,' she said. Her voice was full of what sounded like genuine contrition.

'We made an error of judgement. We wanted to get our message across, and we chose the wrong way to go about it, and we apologise to all Americans unreservedly.' I thought this was laying it on a bit too thick, but Tanner French appeared to be lapping it up. Meanwhile, the side of the screen that had been showing the Hulk figurine was taken up with images of our handiwork at Battery Park, and some grainy web shots of the PIVOT posters we'd touched up.

'But the fact is, you not only chose to denigrate one of the great symbols of heroism and sacrifice in this country, you wrote some terrible, brutal things about our troops. You wrote, "Not all soldiers are heroes…" How can you expect anyone to take your message seriously after that?'

'Well Tanner, we're an antiwar group,' Abby replied in a sober, sorrowful tone. 'We know how destructive and damaging war can be, and we know that, unfortunate as it may seem, even our troops do sometimes commit horrendous acts that no one could possibly call heroic. But, I'm afraid I have to agree with you that we didn't put that well. We didn't mean to denigrate soldiers. For sure, we aren't blaming the soldiers themselves for the fact that sometimes they lose sight of what's right and wrong, in places and circumstances where their world has been turned upside down. One of the reasons that we are an antiwar group is because we see the shocking toll it takes on those who are forced to fight in our politicians' wars. These young men and women, often they have little choice but to sign up because they come from poor backgrounds. They want to leave their homes, where there's no work and no future, and they go along looking for adventure and success. But they have to be made into efficient killing machines, so they have the humanity drilled and beaten out of them. Then they go into these awful, brutal environments, and they become inured to the horror, and the result is that yes, some of them commit war crimes – that's an unavoidable truth. So, let me ask you a question, Tanner: don't you think that we would be better off avoiding that scenario altogether?'

French had been listening to this intently, and even nodding in places, as could be seen on the split screen. The producers had thoughtfully cut away to shots of battle scenes and injured soldiers on 'our' side of the screen, rather than just left the immobile shot of the Hulk there looking incongruous, and it even seemed as though they may have been helping our argument along.

Ploughing on without waiting for an answer, and without ever once dropping her absurd accent, Abby continued.

'Let's face it, Tanner, we abandon these men and women when they come home as, really, shells of people. What's worse: us saying that these soldiers are not all heroes, or the fact that none of them is actually treated like a hero? Our Veterans Affairs is in a deplorable state, and getting worse. Vets are often substance abusers, domestic violence perpetrators, suicidal, homicidal or prone to psychotic episodes. That's what we want to stop. That and the killing these poor, formerly innocent, defective human beings commit at the behest of our nation's leaders. The politicians and the warmakers don't care about what happens to our troops once they're out of the killing zone, but we do.'

'I can accept that,' replied Tanner, who had been trying to get a word in. 'Except that you chose to put your message across on what many Americans would regard as almost a sacred site.'

'Oh, Tanner,' said Abby – or should I say, Eirene – tearfully. 'We caused such a kerfuffle, and Jesus Murphy I'd give anything to make it different. I speak on behalf of all the members of Patriots Opposed to War – and there are quite a few of us, actually, across the nation – when I say once again that we apologise for desecrating the Battery Park memorial, and we won't be doing anything like that again, for sure.'

'Well, I'll be honest,' said Tanner French, bless her, 'your heart seems to be in the right place, but you really do need to think about your tactics. We're out of time now, so I'll let you go in a moment.' She brightened her smile, and assumed a more quizzical look. 'But before I do, I have to ask, why the Incredible Hulk?'

'Ha ha, I was hoping you'd ask that,' replied Eirene/Abby, cheering up. 'It's because we let our emotions run away with us, and we did something stupid and destructive. But the beast is contained now, I promise you.'

'Eirene, Greek goddess of peace, I thank you for your honesty and your genuine remorse. Hopefully, next time we hear of Patriots Opposed to War it will not be in such negative circumstances.'

'I guarantee it, Tanner. Thank you for your time,' said Abby. And the television cut to an ad. Beaming, Abby turned to us all. Shrugging her shoulders and holding her hands out palm-up, she was just far enough this side of self-satisfied to elicit literal cheers of approval from the boys, and applause from me.

There was still, after that, quite a good deal of merciless opprobrium and more threats of violent death on the various social media channels, but there were also many people commenting that we'd brought an important issue into the light. To some, our claim to be supporting the troops we'd vilified seemed acceptable, so we came out of it better than we'd hoped we would.

Later, in my room, Abby said to me, 'Tomorrow we'll go and have a word with our little friend. He owes us.' I nodded agreement, because I knew she wouldn't be too hard on Jihad. After all, his bigger bang had put us in the spotlight on a nationally broadcast television show watched by millions.

'You're such a hoser,' I said to her in my best Canadian accent, and we dissolved into tension-relieving laughter, hugging each other. The day had ended so much better than it had begun.

12. Losing Jihad

We had clawed a tiny bit of ground back with Abby's Canadian
-Hulkish performance on the Tanner French television show,
and the initial furore then died down fairly quickly. Two days
after our stunt, an obliging politician managed to get caught
in a public toilet with a famous sportsman's dick in his mouth,
and we were pushed out of the news cycle as the media relent-
lessly pursued that little slice of newstainment.

But there was still a lot of anti-POW feeling out there in
the cyberscape, and we all deemed it prudent to keep a low
profile for at least a couple of weeks. We didn't even leave the
house for several days, helped in this by an extended spell of
freezing sleet sweeping the borough, stripping the few remaining leaves off the trees and keeping all movement to an absolute
minimum. Gradually, all those terrible anti-POW hashtags fell
into disuse, and the somnambulant citizens of pathologically
patriotic America fell back into their usual pedestrian slumber.
We agreed we would do our best to rouse them only with
actions that pricked their consciences rather than incited their
ire. Rule number one: only ever hit those who are regarded as
fair targets. Rule number two: actual combatants are not, oddly,
considered fair targets.

By the time the weekend arrived, the grey sky was beginning to show hints of blue, and late on Saturday afternoon,
the sun finally showed his weak, white face. Having smoked
our last piece of herbal goodness that morning, Abby and I
decided it was time to pay both the bodega and our friendly

neighbourhood weed salesman a visit. There was a devilish smile on Abby's face when she suggested we walk down to pick up supplies. I knew she had been crafting a few well-chosen words of wisdom for Mr 'Bigger Bang', although these were mostly in good humour by that stage. We had been under no obligation to follow Jihad's advice, and it had been my idea to hit Battery Park, so we couldn't really blame him for our choices. Still, I knew Abby would relish raking him over the coals, and I knew he would take it in cool good grace.

Rugging up against the biting cold, we ventured out the front door for the first time in almost a week, trying not to appear furtive. We had all, at one stage or another during the preceding days, spent time peeping stealthily out the windows at the front of the house, and had spotted no suspicious persons or vehicles that might have been placed there for the purpose of gathering evidence against us. We felt that we were in the clear. Nevin even went as far as suggesting that the authorities couldn't be too cranky at us.

'We've done them a big favour,' he said. 'Out of nowhere, we've generated a powerful upwelling of emotion around the idea of soldierly heroism and the need to pour adulation on our troops – just at that post-Veterans Day point when a bit of exaltation exhaustion might have been setting in. In fact, if I didn't know it was us, I'd say it was a perfect false flag operation designed to induce exactly the response it did.'

We all laughed, but Abby was semi-serious when she said, 'Yes, we need to stop doing their work for them.'

Devoe Street was lively. Like us, most of our neighbours had spent as little time as possible outside through the cold snap, and people were cleaning up their front yards, clearing leaves and other debris off their cars, and checking for signs of damage or trouble. Abby and I walked arm in arm, chatting with our usual abandon, rosy-cheeked and watery-eyed at the cold, as innocent as the day is long. Nobody gave us a second look, and with every step we got more comfortable.

As we turned into Graham Avenue, with its wide, almost tree-less pavement and grubby shopfronts, a chill shivered through me, and my growing confidence was replaced by a sudden fear. I could tell Abby felt it too, and she gripped my arm just a little more tightly. Approaching the liquor store, we saw that Jihad was lounging in his usual spot by the entrance to a narrow alleyway, his hands in his pockets and a scarf wrapped around his head. There was only a slit out of which his eyes peeped, and they were darting backwards and forwards, watching every car and checking out the passersby intently. His head swung in our direction and as he saw us coming towards him, he theatrically tried to duck into the alley, 'realised' that he'd been seen, and stood facing us, his head hung low. As we approached, he pulled his hands out of his pockets, opened up his scarf mask so we could see his face, and put his palms up towards us.

'Hey,' he said. 'I said go for a bigger bang, not the nuclear option. Or, as we used to say in Pakistan, if you're going to pull the pin, you have to actually throw the grenade.'

Chuckling indulgently, Abby gave him that look that said she didn't hold him responsible, or if she did, she'd forgiven him. She threw a sideways glance at me and said, 'Oh, I think we all know who's really to blame, don't we Jayney?'

There was laughter in her voice, but a touch of ice in her eyes. I got the message.

'But,' she shoved Jihad in the chest with both hands, 'I blame you for inciting this poor girl. You know she hangs on your every word. And she just wanted to impress you.'

'Hey!' I said. 'That's not true.'

Jihad was staring at me, but in a warm and proud way, and Abby was back to being genuinely jolly, so I went along with it.

'Well maybe just a little bit,' I said. 'And what's this bull-shit about Pakistan?' I added. 'The closest you've ever been to Pakistan is Coney Island Avenue.'

'I've got brown skin, haven't I?' he said. 'I could have been to Pakistan.'

'I hear they have very good hash there,' said Abby.

'The best,' he nodded. 'Rich and creamy brown, like me. Just as intoxicating, but not quite as addictive.'

'You're an idiot,' I said. I did love him very much at that moment. 'So, have you got a handful of that wonderful Jihadi hashish for us, or what?'

'Alas, no, but I do have some of the finest hydroponically grown buds imported all the way from the exotic reaches of Queensbridge. Will that do, my ladies?'

'We'll take a quarter, thank you sir,' said Abby. 'We'll just go into ye bodega and use the card to purchase some booze and get some cash. Please wait one moment.'

We went into the shop, bought beer and got folding money for the transaction, and came back out to find Jihad looking very pleased with himself. It was probably his last bag, which meant he could go somewhere and warm up. I wanted to ask him to come home with us, but I didn't want him asking too many questions about Battery Park, and I didn't want the boys to think I was letting our neighbourhood drug dealer in on the secrets we'd hassled them to keep. They had no idea his comments had been the catalyst for the Battery Park hit. He palmed the weed to Abby, she palmed him the money, and he kissed me on the cheek and said, 'You're a big thinker, Jayney; don't let this little hiccup stop you from being that,' and we walked away.

We hadn't gone fifty yards when a cop car came screaming up the avenue and skidded to a halt right in front of the liquor store. In milliseconds, an officer had jumped out of the car, his gun already drawn, and pointed it straight at Jihad.

'Freeze, motherfucker,' he shrieked, so loud it was perfectly clear to us. Jihad complied instantly, literally freezing in place.

'ID,' yelled the cop. 'Now!'

Slowly, carefully, his eyes glued to the barrel of the gun pointed at him just a few yards away, Jihad started to move his right hand towards his coat to get his wallet out. And that was all the cop needed. He unloaded five shots into our friend, advancing a couple of steps as he pulled the trigger with a hideous rhythm, to make sure he wasn't going to miss with any of them. The noise was incredible. The shots were so loud and explosive it was as though they were going off in my head, and then there was this distant crumpling sound, which was Jihad folding onto the ground, collapsing into a little heap of blood and wool and cotton. His life was gone in an instant, blown away like an autumn leaf.

'You saw him,' yelled the cop to his partner, who had by now gotten out of the driver's seat and was standing, weapon drawn, next to his partner. 'He was going for a weapon.'

'He was going for his wallet, you fucking murderer,' I screamed, starting to run to the little pile that had formerly been my funny, intelligent friend. 'Because you fucking told him to!'

Abby bounded after me, and before I had gone three steps she had caught my arm.

'Stop, Jayne,' she said. I stopped.

The two cops were looking at us questioningly. A crowd was starting to gather – people appeared from houses, shops, stopped cars and seemingly nowhere with astonishing swiftness – and, luckily, they obscured us from the clear view of the cops.

'We didn't see anything,' Abby said brusquely, giving me a shove in the opposite direction. 'Let's go.'

There were forty-five yards and a growing gaggle of gawkers between me and the cops by that stage, and Abby was tugging urgently on my arm. Suddenly I understood her meaning, and turning on my heel, sobbing and shaking, we dissolved into the gathering gloom of the evening.

It was the most calculated, ruthless, ferocious act I had ever seen in my life, and my friend, my dear, sweet, witty, warm and completely harmless friend, my one-time lover, was its target. Abby guided me home in shock, and led me straight to my bed, where I lapsed into howling bawls of terror, horror and anger. It was beyond belief – beyond contemplation – but it was real. We had watched it happen. The blood drained from her face, her eyes tear-stained and her voice shaking, as she tucked me into bed, Abby told me she would go and tell the boys.

I'm not sure what happened next; I think I kind of blacked out for the rest of the night. When I woke up hours before the sunrise the next morning, Abby was sleeping quietly beside me, curled up like a little girl. Opening my eyes, I knew just one thing: war had come to us.

Not content with sending young people off to war to dispose of them, the authorities in my country were actively killing their own people, my generation, for 'crimes' as fanciful as pulling out a wallet. Jihad was the first person I had ever seen dealt with in this summary way, but I knew that he wasn't by any means the only one. His was merely the latest name added to a long list of victims of our police state.

I began to have my doubts about the possibility of peaceful revolution, but I couldn't conceive of a world in which I would fight violence with violence. Then again, I couldn't escape the reality that I was already part of a war – one I had neither started nor wanted any part in, but which it seemed I would not be able to avoid. And wars get bloody.

13. Regrouping

Coming on top of the blowback from Battery Park, Jihad's murder terrified us. If they would do that to a simple dope dealer, what the fuck would the authorities do to us? We had besmirched the memory of those who were deemed to have died heroically; they would cut us down without mercy.

It was becoming increasingly obvious to us that some law enforcement officials in America had decided that they would, wherever possible, dispense with the cumbersome processes of 'justice' and bureaucratic documentation, and simply execute anyone they thought might be guilty of anything, even if that was just being brown. It was more important than ever that we keep our heads down and continue to apply our own security protocols with meticulous diligence.

Incidentally (oh, Jesus, Jihad, did I just make you an incidental footnote? I am so sorry, my friend), we later heard from Lester in the bodega that Jihad had been complaining of harassment by the FBI. It seems that, having discovered a nominally Muslim man with a name like his, the Feral Bastion of Ineptitude had decided he would make a terrific informant. They had visited Jihad on the street a couple of times, and wouldn't believe that he couldn't tell them what was going on at his mosque because he didn't attend. That didn't compute with the G-men, who figured he was holding out because there was something big being plotted at the Williamsburg branch of al-Qaeda and they wanted part of it. If Jihad wouldn't provide the fictional intel they wanted, they would get him out of the way and find someone who would. So they had notified the local cops that a drug dealing potential terrorist was loose on their patch, and the flatfoots had done the rest. No need for anything as tedious as an arrest and trial.

As winter froze time and the weeks dragged on, the festive season spread its usual false cheer and empty talk of peace and goodwill to all, and we kept close to home. We didn't even talk about any possible missions, let alone carry them out. For the first few nights after Jihad was shot, Abby didn't even show up at our place – she was at home with her parents, regrouping. I missed her terribly, and our boys appeared lost without her leadership. If there had ever been any question who was in charge, it was now well and truly answered.

But I'll say it again – I don't blame Abby for decisions I made and the things I did, and I hope Nevin, Bevan and Lucas would say the same. Although we were all shaken by the Battery Park backlash, and both shattered and shit-frightened by Jihad's brutal execution, when we eventually went back to work as a group, we were all self-aware actors, not automatons driven by Abby's will.

Anyway, I digress. Back to that gloomy, grey, shockingly cold Christmas. In a matter of days, Jihad had been replaced. I guess the folks behind the business regarded him as dispensable. We were soon back buying dope off the new guy, whose name was Diego, but we never struck up the same kind of friendship; it was mostly just business, partly because he was a mean, menacing man who didn't talk so much as growl. We needed our pot, though. We stayed in through the long, icy days and smoked and drank and didn't say much, watching those execrable movies and TV shows that featured shootings, bombs and screaming in equal measure.

There was some minor attention paid to the lesser activities of POW, just to keep it ticking over. We kept up a stream of carefully vetted social media posts, pushing out lacklustre blogs refuting PIVOT's bullshit and condemning US armed forces for what seemed a lot like intentional blunders, such as when they 'accidentally' bombed a hospital in yet another war-ravaged Middle Eastern hellhole that our troops were rescuing from independence and peace. In that particular incident, our heroes had kept the accidental barrage up for well over an hour, long after receiving calls identifying the site as a hospital and pleading for a respite from the bombs. Just another day in the Pentagon.

In retrospect, we'd become just another lazy cluster of 'slacktivists', expecting a few indignant sentences tossed haphazardly into the wasteland of the internet to make a difference, but not really knowing or caring if they did. And we took a break even from that to try and eke a little joy out of Christmas.

My parents have always been fully-fledged Christmas crazies, so I spent a bit of time in the physical warmth and familial chill of my parents' place over the holidays, attempting to reconnect with them. It was fun, but it was also hard work at times, and I realised how little I missed my family. I had a new one of my own, I guess.

Abby reluctantly went home a few times during the holidays but, typically of her parents, they wanted to turn a time of relaxation and joy into a 'learning experience', so every night over the twelve nights of Christmas they explored some usually gruesome alternative to the Christian myth. These ranged from Gryla, the Icelandic giantess who devours bad children, to La Befana, the Italian Christmas witch, and Kwanzaa, the African American harvest celebration held at Christmastime, which goes all the way back to its creation by an activist in 1966.

One night, she came back to our place after grinding out her family duties to ply us with cheese and biscuits and tell the story of Judith, which is a Jewish Hanukkah legend. This courageous wench infiltrated the camp of an enemy general, fed him cheese, which made him thirsty, and quenched his thirst with copious quantities of wine. When the general was completely walloping drunk, she cut off his head – a neat progression from faceless to headless! Such are the uplifting stories religion tells us at times of celebration.

On New Year's Eve, Abby and I joined the throng in Times Square, and felt a little of the joy and hope a new year always brings. We agreed that the coming year couldn't be any harder than the one we were leaving behind, we acknowledged that we had made some mistakes and vowed to do better, and made one resolution together: to fight war in all its forms.

Early the next morning, partying back at home in the 'Burg with our boys, all drunk and stoned and happy – Abby having dispensed new year hugs and kisses to them all to make them cheerful and compliant – we discussed what the coming year would bring for POW.

'I know it's been a tough time for all of us,' she said. 'We've made some missteps, Jayne and I have seen senseless tragedy right on the street in front of us, and we've all lost a friend. But if anything, that should strengthen our resolve. It's time for us to get back to action. Am I right?'

Cautious agreement from the foot soldiers, who were probably a bit too sodden and slack-jawed to be having that conversation right at that moment.

'One of the things we need to do in the coming year is refine our focus,' she continued. How the fuck she was so bright-eyed and articulate at such a time is still beyond me. We'd both drunk and smoked the same amounts, and I was feeling seriously over-refreshed at the time, but she was a daisy on a spring morning.

'Stupidly, we've been thinking about war as something that happens "over there",' she said. 'And that's only natural, because our foreign policy is all about invading other countries and making them into client states. But we overlooked the fact that there are some serious wars going on right here at home. We had a taste of it when Jihad was killed.'

Quizzical looks from the gallery, struggling to follow the narrative, although the general tendency was acceptance of Abby's thesis. Maybe they'd understand it later. She clarified it anyway.

'I'm talking about our domestic wars, both declared and undeclared,' Abby said. 'The war on drugs, which has been going on since long before we were born and has never done anything but criminalise, incarcerate and liquidate a huge number of young people whose only sin is to enjoy a toke or party with Molly occasionally. Allied to this is the undeclared war on blacks and other non-whites, and the war on poor people which is waged by stealing their pensions and cutting the entitlements that they've worked and paid taxes for all their lives. Then there's the war on dissent, the war on privacy, the war on transparency, the war on equality that deprives women of control of their own bodies and denies gays the right to enjoy the same privileges we take for granted. The war on information and the war on education – because a dumbass population is an easily managed one. We're at war on many, many fronts, and sometimes I even wonder if the granddaddy of them all, the war on terror, which has never done anything but produce more terrorists, is simply there to distract us from all the others. Think about it – by making us focus on the war over there, we don't even see the wars over here!'

This latest thought had obviously only just struck Abby, and she probably should have thought it all through before she blurted it out, because it confused the boys, and even me to an extent. There were so many wars, it was hard to see how we could possibly fight in all of them, let alone win one.

Recognising that she might have drifted into murky territory, she recovered. 'Anyway, the point is, POW is going back into action, and soon. But we're going to be smarter, sneakier and less open to misinterpretation.'

A rousing cheer from the cabbaged crew. They sensed that it was the end of the speech, and they were willing to agree to just about anything if it meant they could return to their new year depredations. Abby sat down, and someone, I think it was Lucas, got out the stash and started rolling a joint.

Towards the end of that long, nightmarish winter, the trauma that kept revisiting me began to abate, thank Christ. For a while there, I was in full flashback mode. I kept seeing Jihad being ripped to bloody pieces by police bullets, feeling my own heart explode at the sight, and being ashamed that I hadn't gone to help him because I had been so desperate to save my own skin. That was the worst part: the guilt and conflict. Sure, I could intellectualise that he was dead before he even hit the ground, that there was nothing I could do and that I would have given myself up for nothing. But until you've been in that situation, where after it's all said and done you know you'd have come out of it feeling like shit no matter what you did, it's hard to describe the weight of despair it can bring down on you.

I'm pretty sure Abby was almost, if not quite as badly, as affected as I was. She masked it better, of course, and in her it manifested as a kind of brutal resolve to beat the bastards, but I knew she had been stricken, probably in ways I could never understand.

Yet, the Jihad business did bring us closer together, if that's possible. We'd been through something horrific together, something totally outside of our experience and expectations, and we'd come through it together. I could never forget how Abby saved me from myself that day, and I think she found a new respect for me in seeing that I had been willing, if just for a moment before I thought about it, to sacrifice myself for our friend.

The boys, none of whom had been close to Jihad and who may even, in retrospect, have resented him or seen him as competition they didn't need, were less affected by his death than we were. To them it was a tough, sad and inconvenient event, but their concern was more with the loss Abby and I were feeling than any sense of loss they might feel themselves. I don't know. Maybe I'm just projecting all this. Maybe they were crushed by his passing, sickened by the brutality and finality of it, and terrified by its unexpected capriciousness. Who knows? They were boys, and those fuckers are impossible to read sometimes.

Anyway, as my psychological shudders subsided and Abby seemed to grow stronger and more determined, the holiday season and the memories of the previous year receded into the past. We all started getting more motivated, and feeling more able to get back to work.

Our preferred method was, again, graffiti. Applied only to deserving targets, of course, and never against anyone who could be construed as a hero, a put-upon minority group, or some kind of symbol of freedom. It was, at least while it was still cold and difficult to get around, pretty hit and miss. We blagged a few PIVOT posters in the subway, but only in small numbers, never again such an ambitious multi-target hit as that first intoxicating mission.

We also defaced a couple of recruiting stations, and even though this was bordering on an assault on 'our troops', it didn't draw anywhere near as much backlash. Apparently, as long as their targets were still just dumb kids looking for a way out of the ghetto, we could say what we like about the people whose job it is to smile, welcome those kids to the forces and destroy their lives. Those same dumb kids only become heroes who require our unquestioning support after they've signed up and put on a uniform. And they stay heroes only as long as they are whole, unaffected by battle and still wearing a uniform.

For the first time, we hit a couple of political targets – the offices of congressmen and senators who had made idiotic statements about needing to protect the freedom of Venezuelans by removing their right to decide who would profit from their own oil.

The weeks moved by, and slowly but surely, we began to make a little difference. I can say this with confidence because the number of followers we had on our various social media accounts grew steadily, and although we got a good number of trolls, we also had a lot of encouragement from people right across the country. We weren't going to start a revolution any time soon, but we were gaining some traction.

We also started talking, in our blogs and other online forums, about the other wars we had suddenly noticed were being prosecuted on our home grounds. We weren't really breaking any new ground here, of course; various groups had long been very vocal about the futility and cost of the war on drugs, Occupy had railed against the excesses of the moneyed classes, and the Black Lives Matter and associated movements had been pleading with authorities for years to stop randomly killing non-white people for infractions that may or may not have occurred, and which in any case didn't warrant an instant death sentence. But we provided another rallying point for people who were sick and tired of all those wars and all that killing, and we started to gain respect.

We also began to get quite a lot of private messages from people asking us about joining POW and offering to mount operations of their own. Given that we were New Yorkers who had operated only within the city limits – with the exception of one wonderful white-knuckle evening in which Abby, Lucas and I travelled to Washington DC to daub a few nasty words onto a politician's office – getting people to act for us in other states seemed like a terrific idea. We wanted to spread the net, as it were, but at the same time we were not too enthusiastic about letting anyone, especially some random from the internet, into our group. Not if it would mean giving away our identities and exposing us. It was almost certain that at least a few of those messages of support and even more of the requests to join were sent by spooks from any of the bevy of three- and four-letter agencies that litter the 'security' and 'intelligence' industries in this country, so we were wary.

Instead of allowing anyone to join our group, we suggested to them that they start their own cell and act in our name. With their (preferably anonymous, encrypted) email address we could send them soft copies of our logo, archives of our blog posts and other informative material picked up along the way, to get them started. We stressed, of course, that if they were to act as POW, they needed to adhere to our way of thinking – that is, non-violent civil disobedience rather than overt revolutionary acts.

Lucas actually sat down one day and penned a manifesto to send our new cells – a kind of ethical and spiritual guide. It was pompous and overwritten to the point of officiousness, but that was part of its charm. Some people would even have been drawn to its bogus legalese tone and language.

MANIFESTO

Whereas the resolution of any issue, disagreement, conflict or controversy by violence is abhorrent to the values, rights and honour of human beings;

Whereas the makers of war – the producers of the means of destruction; the politicians in their pay and sway; the media which they own, influence and direct; and the religious pretenders who offer their blessings upon the wanton annihilation of individuals, communities, societies and races – will never willingly relinquish or renounce their ability to manufacture, prosecute, promote, extol and exalt war;

Whereas the economy, political framework, spiritual structure and social management of our nation appears to be predicated on the continuance, expansion and dominance of war;

We, the Patriots Opposed to War do swear and avow to work and strive for the following:

1. *The peaceful and amicable resolution of all issues, conflicts, disagreements and controversies by means other than violence or coercion.*

2. *The education and enlightenment of all people as regards the true nature of the intentions, agendas, plans, strategies, tactics, devices, systems and schemes of the makers of war through any and all means available, excluding violence and coercion.*

3. *The dismantling, dismemberment and dissolution of the war apparatus by peaceful revolution and popular assent.*

4. *The construction of a society in which peace-makers rather than warmakers are revered, honoured, heeded and elevated to positions of influence and authority, although that authority shall henceforth exclude the power to initiate war or to create the conditions, means, mechanisms, organisations or structures that make war feasible, viable or inevitable.*

We, the Patriots Opposed to War, understand that attaining our aims is improbable in a world such as this, in which the makers of war are also the shapers of opinion and the wielders of authority, yet this makes those aims no less honourable, peaceable or ultimately achievable.

Lucas was, of course, inordinately proud of his work, and although we often teased him about its florid pretentiousness, it was as good a representation of our thoughts, ideas and approaches as any we could come up with. Even Abby was pleased, and that of course kept Lucas on cloud nine for days.

It was also a big hit online, and got lots of shares and reposts across a range of social media.

In light of its success, we started thinking about ways to make hard copies of the manifesto and other writings, drawings and cartoons we had produced or that were being sent to us regularly by now. This was solved in a low-level, hilarious way by Abby and I heading off to the first local flea market of the year in April.

The air was still fairly chilly, but the sun was doing its best to brighten proceedings, the streets were peppy with people and the early colours of spring, and we cheerfully strolled the markets, making our usual facetious observations and being our hysterically funny selves. At one stall of old, broken-down machinery we came across this weird little machine that looked a little bit like a bread maker or a mini pizza oven, with a curved metal top, but also a flat plate jutting out of it, on which a crudely printed recipe could be read.

Intrigued, we asked the seller about it. He told us it was called a Ditto Machine; it would print copies of anything we wanted, cheaply and quickly; and he wanted twenty-five bucks for it. Sold! After we'd paid him for it, he offered to sell us a little portable typewriter, which we would need to make it produce legible type, for fifteen dollars. Cheeky monkey. We paid him and laughed, and lugged our two items of ancient technology home.

The Ditto Machine was limited in its applications – it only printed in a weird purplish blue and the print was usually a bit blurry – but we had a lot of fun creating small pieces of artwork and making copies of our manifesto to hand out. We didn't want to be seen handing out these pieces of seditious literature ourselves, so we would take to the streets with a hundred or so copies of whatever we wanted to distribute, and pay homeless people a few bucks to do it. This was my idea. I'd become completely paranoid about preserving our anonymity by then, and I was, according to Abby, hilariously cloak and dagger in my approaches to the homeless people we picked to do our dirty work for us. We also mounted a few night raids on various locations to paste up our crude little Ditto posters, but since the machine couldn't print them on anything bigger than letter paper, the effect was muted at best.

One night as we were sitting around at Devoe Street, we talked about what we might do to make more of a splash. It was early in the week and we were all straight and sober, for a change, and talking about targets for our little posters, graffiti raids and so on. Bevan walked in on this conversation; he'd been working the door at some bar or other, but because it was a quiet night, they'd sent him home early.

I should put in here that, even though he was still the same cuddly bear to me and Abby, our Bev had become a lot more assertive in recent months. Maybe it was that he spent his nights dealing with obstreperous drunks and hanging out with steroid abusers and war vets, and his days working out in gyms with more of the same, but he seemed much tougher, and much less cushy and Zen.

Still, the way he reacted to our discussion was startling and even a bit frightening. And ultimately, it changed our whole future. At first, he'd just heaved his now solid, toned and remarkably well-shaped bulk onto the couch, and listened. I'd had an idea, which I was sharing with the group.

'I got to thinking, we need to make a splash like nobody's ever done before. Make it colourful, bright, just a little bit damaging so it costs them time and money to remove it, and gets our message across. I have this image in my mind of an actual splash, a splash of colour. We get water balloons and fill them with paint, and throw them at the windows and walls of the places we want to hit. The balloon will burst and the paint will create a huge, colourful explosion on the wall or window. Then, wearing gloves of course, as we always do, we step up and finger-paint POW in the biggest letters we can, right in the middle of the splotch. Simple, fast, effective, and a bitch to clean off.'

Abby laughed, and Lucas and Nevin nodded with passable enthusiasm. But Bevan sat stony-faced for a moment. Then he spoke: more words, more heatedly and more heartfelt than I had ever heard him speak.

'Can you hear yourselves?' he asked. The effort it cost him to speak out, almost against his will, made his voice shake and distorted his face, but he was unable to stop because this was so important to him and to our cause. The easy laughter stopped and the room turned cold. Abby's eyes popped wide and white rimmed, and her mouth remained open.

'Finger-painting? Homeless people as the distributors of our message? Posters and that idiotic fucking manifesto printed on tiny pieces of paper fed through a machine that was out of date fifty years ago? A Ditto Machine! Is that how we're going to stop wars? Are you fucking serious? They're laughing at us!' he said. 'We're a joke. A minor nuisance. A tiny bunch of paranoid stoners whose big idea is to appeal to the intellect of the people and the better nature of the warmakers. What's wrong with this picture, people? It's doomed. It's a waste of fucking time. The only thing it's achieved is to get the fucking FBI looking for us so they can make an even bigger laughing stock of us. What the fuck?' he asked in rhetorical despair.

'If we're ever going to have even the slightest effect – make even one person who matters think for a minute – we have to make them hurt. Make them pay. Make them ask if it's worth it to keep going in the face of such towering, committed and relentless opposition. Take the fucking fight to them!'

He looked around at his dazed, stunned and speechless audience. We were all just staring at him, astonished at the power of his words and the command in his voice. He was sweating like he'd just worked out, the blue veins in his neck were standing out and pulsing like crazy, and his breath was a rasp. His head swivelled around and his limbs followed loosely, and then he started moving.

'Fuck this,' he said. 'There's only one way to show you what I mean.' And with that he swiftly crossed the room, picked up the Ditto Machine, and marched out of the door, slamming it as he went, and out of the house, almost splintering the front door as he slammed that, with even more savage force. He carried that heavy iron machine like it was a little kid's toy, and I had this vision of Abby and me struggling to carry it home from the flea markets. It struck me just how strong he'd become while we weren't paying attention.

14. Make them pay

The crashing hollow boom of the front door seemed to echo for long minutes, and we all stared at the blank timber of the hall-way door as if expecting Bev to burst back through and shout 'joking!' But he was gone, and after a lengthy pause, Abby at last breathed out and said, 'What the fuck was that?'

Lucas giggled, and Nevin joined in. I was still in shock, and Abby's expression changed from one of deep concern to bemusement.

'Must've had a bad night at work,' said Lucas. Maybe he and Nevin had observed the animal change – that's the only way I can describe it – in Bevan more perceptively than Abby and I had. He'd always been just gentle Bev to us, and we'd been wrapped up in ourselves and each other through the bad months since we lost Jihad. Then again, because he'd been working lots of nights at various clubs and bars, we didn't see much of Bev. It could have been that this was the first time that he'd allowed his true feelings to erupt in front of us. Or, as Lucas had said, maybe he'd just had a bad night at work. Whatever it was, it transformed the way we viewed our brawny housemate and, as I've said, it was to effect an even bigger revolution in the way POW worked. Our dynamic had just changed again.

An hour later, we were still sitting there, kind of stunned but having recovered quite a lot, and Abby and I had talked about taking more notice of how Bevan was feeling and acting in the future. We heard the front door open, and I half expected to see Bev's big baby face sheepishly peer in as he opened the door into the lounge room. Instead, there was a bit of grunting and the sound of something heavy hitting the floor in the entrance. Then Bev opened the door and regarded us with triumph in his eyes. Once the door was opened, he turned around to pick up the heavy object we'd heard thumping onto the hallway floor, and brought it into the room. It was a huge, expensive looking and almost brand-new colour printer for pieces of paper up to poster size. He put it in the middle of the room and stood back to admire it.

'What the...? Where did you get that?' Abby asked. 'What happened?'

'You know that asshole Druitt?' Bevan said. Lincoln Druitt was a member of the state legislative assembly with an office in a small commercial centre in Green Point. He was a big supporter of PIVOT, and had been a cheerleader for all sorts of violent interventions. He was the worst kind of warmonger, the kind who always couches his calls for death and destruction in terms of humanitarianism and protection. We all hated him.

'He donated it,' said Bev with a shit-eating grin

'What do you mean?' I asked. Although I'd already guessed the answer.

'I tossed that stupid Ditto Machine through the window of his office, climbed in and helped myself to a machine that we can actually use,' said Bevan. 'It'll slow down his pro-war activities, even if just for a second or two, and it will give us a much-needed equipment upgrade,' he added.

'Jesus, Bev,' I whispered.

Lucas and Nevin looked thoughtful, and studied Abby's face to see how they should react. She peered inquisitively into Bevan's eyes, but she didn't seem overly troubled.

'You didn't leave the Ditto Machine in the office, did you?' she asked.

Smiling, Bev shook his head. 'It's in the East River.'

'Okay, tell me exactly what happened,' said Abby.

'Dude, we're a non-violent group,' interjected Lucas, hoping to gain the moral high ground and perhaps curry Abby's favour.

'Did anyone get hurt?' Bevan asked with a shrug.

'Shh,' said Abby. 'Go on, Bev.' She was watching him like a cobra watches a mongoose.

Dropping with studied nonchalance onto the couch as Nevin gave way with a grudging stare, Bevan looked coolly straight back into Abby's eyes, his pupils bluer and brighter than I'd ever seen them. If his whites hadn't been so clear, I would have suspected chemical assistance of some variety.

'I've been thinking a lot about how namby-pamby we've been,' he began. 'I mean, we're dealing with some hard nuts in the military, in politics and especially in business, who want to make more war, not less. And here we are, playing softball. I haven't said anything because I feel like I'm not really part of the inner group on this, just a helper, I guess. But I want to be more. And then, tonight, it all came home to me when one of my vet buddies at Hoskin's, the bar I was working at, showed me a screwed-up copy of the POW Manifesto that some hobo had given him. He thought it was the most pathetic, stupid and laughable thing he's ever seen. And he's antiwar! It just made me embarrassed and mad, and I thought, well it's time for us to piss or get off the pot. So when I got home and you were all talking about finger-painting, I just lost it. I went back to Hoskin's and borrowed my buddy Jet's van, and I went around to Druitt's office and I smashed my way in, and I smashed up his office, and I stole his fucking printer. So sue me.'

Trying to suppress a grin, Abby nodded.

'Well, we could certainly use a new printer,' she said. 'But I'm not sure that breaking and entering and theft are, umm, commensurate with our philosophy.'

'Why not?' I asked, before Bevan had time to formulate a reply. 'Our philosophy is pacifism, not inaction. I'm with Bev – if no one gets hurt but it slows down our opposition's work, what's the harm? Besides, it's costing us a lot of time and money to make the tiny little ripples we're making now. Why shouldn't we get a little assistance from those who can afford it, and who we want to hurt?'

'You said it yourself, Abby,' said Bevan. 'If we're going to succeed, we have to take bigger risks and seek bigger rewards. I'm just acting on your thoughts.'

'Damn! You *have* been listening, haven't you? And you're absolutely right,' said Abby. It was as though she'd had an epiphany, right there and then. Or was this an idea she had been waiting for us to discover ourselves? Had we just found the Easter egg she'd planted a long time ago?

'We're still pacifists, right?' she asked rhetorically. 'Well, we need to understand exactly what that means,' she said. 'Pacifism is about renouncing violence, right?'

'Yes,' we all said, nodding.

'Well, violence applies to people. You can't be violent to property, can you? You don't hurt a plate glass window by smashing it. You don't upset a printer or ruin its life by stealing it. You don't traumatise money by putting it into someone else's hands. But you can do those things and piss off the people who own those items, and upset their plans, without physically hurting them one little bit. We just need to redefine our terms. We can be destructive without being violent. We can take the fight to our adversaries without so much as harming a single hair on any of their heads. And if that means we steal a little bit from them to pay for our fight and retard theirs at the same time, is that such a bad thing?'

I had a feeling that we were already starting to split those hairs we wouldn't harm, but I couldn't find a way to refute the logic, and besides, what Abby was saying was just an extension of my own argument. It was true that the actions we'd taken to that point had cost us quite a lot of money and time, and we'd gotten nothing for it. It was also true that in spite of growing support from others, our actions to date had regrettably had no noticeable effect on PIVOT or its backers, and it was in fact likely that they viewed us as some sort of half-assed joke. So what if we did up the ante a bit and make ourselves more of a nuisance? We still wouldn't hurt anyone, so we'd be true to ourselves and to our mission.

Lucas and Nevin were nodding to each other, and Bevan's eyes were shining.

'You're right, Bev,' said Abby again. 'We've been too nice. Pacifism isn't passivity, is it? And if we destroy a little property along the way, who's to say we're not doing the right thing if it hampers their destructive agenda? These motherfuckers would tread on us whenever they got the chance – why don't we tread on them for a change?'

'Make 'em pay!' said Nevin, his face alive.

'Damn right,' agreed Lucas.

'I don't know how much I've spent on costumes, cans of paint, subway rides and all that other shit, doing POW's work,' said Abby. 'It's time we took something back.'

'Make 'em pay,' repeated Nevin, and we all nodded and grunted our agreement, stopping just short of leaping up and belting out a cheer.

'So, tell us the rest of your story,' I said to Bevan, to calm things down a bit.

'Once I had the printer in the van, I went back in and got the Ditto Machine, took it to the East River and threw it in,' continued Bev. 'It's amazing: the whole break-in only took me about two minutes, if that – and I did a hell of a lot of damage in that time. That fucker didn't even have an alarm,' he said. 'I guess he's too arrogant to think that anyone would ever break into his office. Douchebag.'

He ran his hands through his hair, pushing its thin, strawberry blond wisps back over his pink scalp, and looked around the room. He shrugged.

'Then I came home. And now I have to go drop the van off at Hoskin's. My buddy is waiting.' He stood up, looking quite proud of himself, and a lot more manly than I'd ever imagined him to be.

'I'll come with,' said Abby, jumping up quickly. She had a strange, bright-eyed look about her, and she was almost girly in the way she said it. Lucas and Nevin watched with undisguised envy. That night, Abby didn't sleep in my room – she stayed with Bevan in his room, and I could hear clearly that there wasn't a whole lot of sleeping going on.

I don't think Abby consciously threw a bang (or two or three) Bevan's way as a reward for pushing us into a new facet of our crusade, and to an extent reactivating or re-energising it. I think she found Bevan's newfound audacious vitality alluring, and she couldn't resist exploring it sexually. It wasn't a calculated move; it was more of a physical, hormonal or even an evolutionary response. Her subconscious had tagged him as a potential mate, as it were, and she couldn't help the instinctive urge that it raised in her. She did no more than surrender to it.

I felt more than a little the same; suddenly he was sexier, cooler, and more powerful than he'd ever been before. It wasn't as if I'd never really noticed him as a sexual being before – I've already mentioned that I had – but as I said earlier, there had been an animal change in him, and it was tempting on a visceral level. I didn't feel it to quite the same extent that Abby did, and I never acted on it – but then again, I didn't share a couple of victory drinks with him at Hoskin's.

Abby told me about her conversation with Bev in the van and at the bar that night, and because it was important, I'll distill it here. It started with Abby questioning Bevan as to why he'd changed his tune so much about what POW did. After all, she reminded him, he'd been reluctant to hit Battery Park on the basis that he didn't want to offend his veteran friends, and as it turned out, she'd said to him as they drove the damp streets to the bar, that he was right.

'No, I was wrong, actually,' Bev had said. 'In fact, we all were wrong to count that operation as a mistake. That was our biggest success, and we should have used it as a jumping-off point to a much more forceful and hard-hitting campaign. That publicity – that was powerful and widespread, and we let our notoriety slip away. We fell from being heavy-duty risk takers to being snotty little apologists for our best work. It was the worst thing we could have done.'

'But what about offending the vets and the troops?'

'Turns out I was wrong about that, too,' said Bev. 'When my friend turned up with that copy of the manifesto tonight, it started a conversation about POW. Of course, I kept quiet about my involvement, but I did say something like, "aren't they those assholes that desecrated Battery Park?" And my friend said, "yeah, that's them. But they disappeared after that, and it's too bad. Because I think they made a really good point, and I reckon they got through to a few young people. I wish someone somewhere had told me that kind of truth before I signed up. I was a stupid teenager and I believed all that bullshit about service and sacrifice, but those guys nailed it: there really aren't too many heroes in the forces, it turns out." That blew me away. But I had to know, so I said, "what about supporting the troops?" And he said it's just a meaningless slogan that people who never have to go to war use to dupe young people into thinking that they'll be respected and looked after when they come back all fucked up, but that nothing could be further from the truth. He also said that the veterans' groups and others that came out against us did so because they're all run by the establishment.'

There was much more, Abby told me, about the need to be more antagonistic to the pro-war types. We needed to take the fight to them, was the takeaway. But we've already been through that, so I won't bother going through it again. Suffice to say that by the time Druitt got to his office in the morning and found it trashed, we had well and truly turned a corner.

So we set about planning an operation that would 'make them pay'.

15. Next level

If being a poorly skilled graffiti artist was a thrill, becoming a burglar and vandal was definitely next level. Breaking and entering is no misdemeanour, it's a proper crime, and the consequences of being caught are much more serious than if you get busted with a spray can in your hand. So your heart rate is elevated long before it starts, and the adrenaline courses through your system in great waves. Only, they're not waves: they're like the successive surges of a tsunami, piling more and more on what's already there so that you feel sick and inundated and suffocated. But you keep going because you have to, because suddenly you're there and doing it before you know it, and the only way out of it is to finish. It's frightening and inspiring, knowing that no one can stop you, unless they do stop you and then it will be the last time you're ever free, so you feel freer than you ever have before.

Afterwards, the release is intense. Your limbs are jelly and your mind is bursting and your heart is bursting too, and your eyes are like scimitars, knifing through the darkness trying to discern any threat and searching in vain for the audience you wish you had but know you can't have. It's a rush that beat any drug or any feeling I'd ever had before, and would only be exceeded later when things got even crazier.

I won't bother to catalogue all our crimes in this phase; we have a prosecution team for that. But the first major felony, like so many other firsts in your life, is a signal moment: a memory seared by fear and the density of the rage that rises in you when you're engaged in destruction, an inescapable turning point in your story. So I'll tell you about that.

Of course, the target had to be PIVOT. Although we'd consciously expanded our sphere of interest to include the other wars, battles, skirmishes, invasions and incursions that are regrettably still being started or carried on by this formerly great country of ours, averting the invasion of Venezuela on the spurious grounds advanced by PIVOT was still at the top of our list. Theirs was a plan to instigate a whole new batch of war crimes – to pile up a fresh new mountain of corpses – and it was getting closer to happening every day.

The media was compliantly pushing all sorts of wild accusations about the Venezuelan government, repeating allegations that will be treated as laughably transparent bullshit by historians but were made with apparent sincerity by those whose job it was to act shocked and plot an invasive response. The idea that 'we' could protect people by dropping bombs on them had not lost any currency, in spite of the disastrous outcomes of similar misadventures in Libya, Iraq, Syria, Somalia, Cuba and so many others it was impossible to remember them all.

The trouble with attacking PIVOT was, and still is, that it's impossible. Their offices are in a secure skyscraper on Fifth Avenue, where the schemers conspire war and death in lavish comfort thanks to the generous donations of American tax-payers, oil companies and other corporate backers. So we had to think of another way.

Earlier, we'd hit on the idea of targeting companies that worked with and for PIVOT as suppliers and confederates, as well as politicians and other vocal supporters of the group. We figured that if suppliers, in particular, felt the wrath of POW, they might have second thoughts about continuing their dealings with PIVOT. Of course, it had to be genuine wrath, not just the feather slap of an online diatribe or a couple of inflammatory posters pasted on the subway wall and removed a couple of hours later by MTA buzzards or glue failure. If we could at least enlighten those suppliers as to the calibre of the scum they were dealing with, we might disrupt the relationship. During our ongoing campaign, we went after PIVOT's printing companies, completely fucked up several vehicles belonging to their limo provider, and even trashed their local lunch bar after Nevin saw some PIVOT operatives munching on a couple of Reubens there. But for that first job, we settled on a relatively easy target: a PR company with offices in a small commercial centre in State Street, Hackensack.

Even though this firm dealt with a number of mayhem-oriented clients like PIVOT – they were serial promoters of war and injustice – they obviously never conceived that they could end up as collateral damage in the retribution their clients so richly deserved. Their security was absurdly lax, and their computer system was top notch, as we found when Bev, Abby and I conducted a sly reconnaissance mission a couple of days after Bevan's successful Druitt bash.

The first thing we needed was a vehicle. Bevan's friend Jet, whose van he had borrowed on the night of the Druitt break-in, was actually looking to sell the van, cheap. There were a couple of irresistible sales points about this vehicle. First, it was deliciously nondescript. There are thousands of these older grey-white, poorly maintained and virtually unidentifiable vans running around New York. Second, and more importantly, Jet was happy to provide an accessory he claimed never to have used himself: a set of bogus licence plates. These artificially aged plates were practically unreadable, and coated with a reflective surface that made photographing them difficult. The inclusion of these plates, and the ridiculously low price Jet was willing to accept for the van, sealed the deal.

Technically, the van belonged to Bevan, and he used it most often, but he always parked it a block or more away, and never in the same street two days in a row. If we needed to drop anything off in Devoe Street – shopping, stolen goods and so on, he would temporarily park it in front of our place or as close as possible, but as soon as that was done, he would drive a block or three away. As the paranoiac says, you can never be too careful.

Abby and I did a costume shop, bought a new pack of disposable food handling gloves, stocked up on spray paint and got some POW decals made. There was a delightful little business in Greenwich Village called Anonyprint, which we made much use of as time went by. Buying from these guys was simple: you placed the artwork and the details of the order anonymously online, and this process generated an order number. Also anonymously, via mail or a hole in the wall outside their premises, you then dropped them a money order for the required payment, quoting the order number of course. When the job was done, they messaged your cell phone (we had expanded our stock of 'burner' phones so that we all had one) or emailed you (sham address, natch) with a locker number and a code that would unlock it, and you went and picked up your order. Once it was picked up, the artwork and all evidence of your order, except for the bare accounting details, was destroyed. It was quick and easy and cheap, and it was comforting to know that we weren't the only subversives around who needed such a clandestine service.

The irony of using Anonyprint was that we never got to make proper use of the beautiful new printer Bev had pinched from the Druitt office. It ended up rotting away in our basement, because it was so much easier getting Anonyprint to do it, and the people selling colour print cartridges are much worse robbers than we ever were. Oh well, *c'est la guerre.*

The night of the job, it had been one of those horrid wet March days when the drizzle is relentless and it seems as though the air is sweating, except in the regular intervals where it rains properly and great gobs of water fall like baseballs from the sky, and the gutters gush and overflow. In other words, it was perfect. No one in their right mind would be out on a night like that.

The entry party was to be Abby, Bevan and me. Lucas was to keep watch out on the street, and Nevin, who was the only one apart from Bevan to have a driver's licence, was to keep the van running a short distance up the road. The plan was to get in there, choose a couple of portable and easily hocked items to liberate; break or disable any electronic items we didn't want to take, smash the phone system; put a few POW decals around the place in prominent positions and generally cause maximum inconvenience. We had an agreement that we would spend no more than four minutes in there – I had lost the argument for three – carry whatever we could and get the fuck out of there.

I must say, for our first coordinated operation, it worked beautifully. Like clockwork – perhaps more organic and chaotic, but just as precise in its result. Within seconds of Bevan breaking the door open with preposterous ease, Abby and I had located a couple of near brand-new laptops and placed them near the door, and Bevan had found and was noisily disassembling the main computer server. The racket from this swift and uncompromising demolition was startling, and made the whole deed seem much more risky and therefore exciting, but out on the street, Lucas claimed to have heard nothing, and nobody in the neighbourhood seemed to have taken any notice. By the time we'd been in there just two minutes, we'd pasted stickers on just about every surface, destroyed their communications system, trashed the random souvenirs placed around the walls (I took particular delight in defacing a photograph of the founder with the odious Hillary Clinton), and visited destruction and disorder on a scale I wouldn't have thought possible in such a short time.

At the three-minute mark, Nevin drove up to the front of the building and stopped, and we started our exit process. Meanwhile, Lucas broke out a can of spray paint and daubed a nice message from us on the front wall: PIVOT support = Warmakers. FUCK YOU! POW.

We walked out of there with several laptops, three tablets, a laminating machine – which I thought was overdoing it but didn't have time to quibble about – and, best of all, a cashbox with almost a thousand dollars in clean, crisp bills in it. An unexpected and very welcome score.

By the time the four-minute deadline was up, we were driving sedately down the street, Nevin and Lucas in the front while in the back Abby, Bevan and I wriggled out of the costumes – wigs included – that we'd worn in case of internal surveillance cameras. We were passing Columbus Park and heading for the George Washington Bridge before I even breathed.

The rush was unbelievable. I felt as though I'd just saved the world, or flown around it like Superman. I was invincible, inexorable and, frankly, at least a little bit insane. At that moment, I also became incorrigible. Irredeemably addicted to crime. I learned that punishing people, bringing violation and stress and horror to their lives for daring to support something I knew to be wrong, could bring me unalloyed ecstasy, unshackle my most primal emotions, and elevate me to heights of vitality I'd never known.

I was not alone, of course. We were all feeling it, and giving vent to the spirit that overtook us with squeals of elation, whoops of victory and the laughter that so often comes with the release of unbearable tension.

We had done it. We'd fucked up their work and trampled on their dirty little lives, and sent them an unmistakable message: POW will not be denied! We were no longer just a cut-rate clutch of slacktivists sitting at home, getting stoned and composing feeble dissertations to hurl at their edifice of evil. We were a force to be reckoned with. Once a trifling annoyance, POW had become an adversary that demanded attention and commanded respect.

Not only that, we had walked away with the spoils! Glorious cash, top-quality computers – new toys to play with, and some left over to turn into more cash. This first operation alone would fund several more, and maybe even begin to pay us back for the long months of paying for everything ourselves, sinking our own funds into POW's thankless and, let's be honest, until then ineffective, work.

As you, dear reader, are surely aware, none of us came from poor or parsimonious families. Our parents were already generously supporting all of us (okay, just Abby, Lucas and me: Nev and Bev supported themselves), and if any of us had asked for more, we would have received it. But this was different. Stealing money felt like earning it. It's easy, with the clarity of hindsight, to see how utterly ridiculous that statement is. But at the time, I genuinely believed that this theft was in fact my first truly earned pay packet, and I revelled in the feeling that aroused in me. I felt like I had grown up or entered a new world. And I had.

When we got home, we celebrated like stars. We settled down long enough to announce via social media what we had done and why we had done it, attributing to ourselves the noble motive of disrupting the work of PIVOT through its despicably venal suppliers, and neglecting to mention the theft we had indulged in. But once that was done, we descended into decadent festivities. We made pigs of ourselves on beer and tequila and ganja, many a back was slapped and every head was affectionately tousled and playfully slapped. It was a long, riotous and laugh-filled party, and every time we received a plaudit from one of our adoring readers, we chugged our drinks and slapped each other's backs again.

16. 'For protection'

Things started to gather pace from that point. We were really fighting, on several fronts. In addition to urgently trying to stop the invasion of Venezuela, we took up the cudgel for the victims of all those other wars, spreading articles and information on police brutality, whistle-blower persecution, the annihilation of privacy, the mass incarceration of black and brown (but not white) drug users and so on and on and on. There was so much abominable shit going on in our world, everywhere we looked we found viable targets for our scorn and our notorious activities.

We hit all kinds of businesses and organisations that may or may not have had links to the perpetrators of our many wars, smashing up their premises and appropriating their tools of communication and oppression. Stolen goods like laptop computers, tablets, cameras, jewellery and even art, we 'flipped' by handing off to our man on the street, Diego. He may not have been as close a friend as Jihad, but he was an excellent fence – he would hand the goods on to someone else, and that person would hand them to a wholesaler, who would then send them off to his retailer. By the time these things got to the person who sold them to some slyly complicit member of the public (*come on, a legit laptop for that price? fuck off*), there were several degrees of separation, and neither the buyer nor the seller had any idea who we were or where the goods came from. We didn't make much from our theft this way, but it was safer and hassle free.

The best thing to 'find' was always money. Folding stuff. Filthy lucre, 95 percent of which is still physically tainted with cocaine powder residue in this great country of ours. We always searched for the cashbox on our raids, because there is nothing like coming across a wad of greenbacks, which were readily convertible to the things we needed, like paint, costumes, booze and weed. It's odd that so many businesses seem to find it necessary to hold large sums of cash, for doubtless legitimate (*cough*) purposes. It wasn't unusual to collect several thousand dollars from a small business that had no apparent need for so much currency.

As our activities expanded, we also borrowed a trick from so many other small time political terror organisations by claiming responsibility for all kinds of actions we didn't really have any clue about. If a factory was robbed – whether it was in New Jersey, Philadelphia, or Alaska – we not only proclaimed our involvement, we found a connection between them and the military-industrial complex, the police state or the surveillance behemoth, and we let them know that they had earned the wrath of POW for that connection.

Our 'associates' around the country were encouraged to do the same. 'Take the fight to the next level', and 'make them pay' became our catch cries, and we busted them out as often and as loudly as we could. Of course, many observers noticed and remarked upon our newfound aggression. There was much discussion around the values of pacifism and the benefits of passive resistance. But we were having none of it.

Abby penned a blog post, under her usual pseudonym of Eirene, entitled, 'A Case for Disruption'. In it, she outlined what she called a subtle twist in our philosophy. This became our new manifesto, and we stopped printing or disseminating the old one.

Here's what Abby said on her blog:

Patriots Opposed to War (POW) is a peace organisation. Our aim is to secure a just and lasting peace for all Americans, and for every nation of people on the earth. We are all humans together, my friends, and we need to break down the tribal barriers that divide us and pit us against each other. When we can see each other as fellow inhabitants of this great big globe of beauty, then wars will stop and happiness can be allowed to spread.

When we Patriots started POW, we believed that the truth of our mission would carry it forward. We believed, and still do, that reason, common sense and our shared humanity should be more than enough to stop war and encourage people to work together for our mutual benefit, no matter where we were born or where we live.

The trouble is, my friends, that the forces of power, money, domination and war are much stronger in this current world than the forces of logic and humanity. The men – because they are usually men, although we are sad to see so many women becoming warmakers – behind the wars being fought on our American soil and across our world have a vested interest in the prosecution of those wars. No amount of logic or reason, or even pure love, is going to dissuade them from their course, because they believe that killing and death, and control over other living things, is their right and their purpose.

So how do we, the Patriots Opposed to War – who dispute these assumed rights to start and to never finish wars – get these boneheaded warmongers to change their minds? We know that speaking reasonably, calling upon their empathy and appealing to their higher natures is just not going to work. When we do that, when we advance our argument rationally and quietly, they ignore us. They think we are weak and inconsequential, and they know they can just carry on with their brutal ways because we won't do anything concrete to stop them. They believe that we are all talk, and so far, we haven't given them too many reasons to believe otherwise.

Well, that all changes now, my friends. Because we, the Patriots Opposed to War, have learned that if we are going to be taken seriously, we have to act emphatically. We have a duty, as humans and as pacifists, to disrupt and impede their plans. That means taking the fight to them, and making them pay for our fight – the same way that these warmongers take the fight to innocent owners of assets that they covet in faraway places, co-opt those assets, and then use the profits to extend and recoup manifold their investment in bloodshed.

How does this subtle twist in our philosophy affect our status as pacifists? Not at all, because our ultimate goal is to put an end to all wars, to ensure that all human beings are not just seen as but are treated as equals. That will never change. We still abhor killing, and we do not kill to achieve our aim. But if we can use the inanimate objects and so-called property that the one percent seem to care for so much, to grab their attention and to prove that we mean business, then we will. Disrupt them. Break their toys and upset their minions, slow their businesses down and make them fear us for what we can do to their profits.

It's our patriotic duty, our obligation as members of a species that belongs together, to stop the people that would divide us so they can conquer us. Don't take it anymore. Be ruthless, be strong, be committed and be loud about it. Make them pay, and we can win!

Yours in peace and love, Eirene.

This, along with the fact that POW had, almost overnight, changed from being an occasional nuisance to an unstoppable crime wave, made quite a few people sit up and take notice. We were, of course, condemned by the regular press, which takes its orders from the warmongers in charge. But beyond that stinking pile of craven bootlickers, our new approach was well received. Other protest groups started promoting us, bloggers used us an example of genuine activists who maintained high principles but achieved results anyway, and people all over the country demanded and received more decals, more information, and more encouragement to go out and be disruptive themselves. We were busy, and we were loving it.

Beyond all the difficult back-office stuff – the writing and posting, emailing, responding, talking and strategising, which can be draining and tedious – there was the real work of POW: breaking and entering, stealing, smashing, defacing, wrecking, ruining and generally running amok. That was the part we loved: getting into some nice, clean, well-ordered office and turning it into the kind of shattered disaster zone that would break the hearts and spirits of the people who turned up to carry on their evil work the next day.

The risk attached to these actions was much higher than simple graffiti and low-level vandalism, so the mental payoff, the adrenaline surge and the feeling of raw achievement was incredible. It was fast and challenging, fearful and liberating. We felt as though every time we did it we got more out of it – certainly, as we became better thieves, this was true on a strictly material level – and we wanted to go and do it again, only bigger and bolder and nastier.

Through all this, Abby became even more assiduous about 'hygiene' – the practice of keeping our fingerprints and other DNA-carrying evidence off everything we touched. We had to be meticulous. Abby made us wear hair nets under the beanies and hats we wore to cover our faces from prying cameras, we wore two sets of disposable gloves under our outer gloves, we wore clean thrift shop outfits every time and we disposed of them piecemeal in a hundred different locations and ways, and we stuck rigidly to the plan at every job. No deviations, no extensions or creative diversions; just in and out exactly as dictated by the scheme and schedule Abby had devised, which we practiced with rigour and diligence.

It worked beautifully, because we never once left behind anything that was sufficient for investigators to trace back to us.

It was hard to gauge just what level of attention the police were paying to our crime scenes. Even if it seemed quite a lot to the office managers, to the local cops, us breaking into an office and walking off with a couple of computers and a tin of money was still pretty small cheese: a petty crime of the kind perpetrated by junkies and juveniles every day in thousands of places. The addition of political messaging may have given the cops more of an incentive to catch us – our war was in part against them, too – but whether they went full CSI on us and we were just too hygienic, or whether the investigation was just the usual cursory nod to procedure that characterises most law enforcement in this country, it was hard to tell. Thinking about it now, I also ask myself if it was a question of competence. For all their urban assault vehicles, massive arsenals of semi-automatic weaponry and flash grenades, acres of thick black body armour and bilious volumes of righteous bluster, a lot of cops were (still are, I guess) semi-literate, barely numerate idiots whose intellect extended only as far as arguments started and ended by squeezing a trigger. Their own limited capacity for deduction and inference may have augmented our intentional failure to leave behind blatant evidence. All I know is, we never got caught. Remarkably, we never came under any scrutiny at all, as far as I know. Our techniques for evading detection, our scrupulous online habits and our crime scene caution let us keep on carrying out our felonies, and keep escalating their scope and payout, without ever being molested.

Nothing that good lasts forever, though, right?

There came an incident that was terrifying in itself, and far reaching in its consequences. It was another step in this world without mirrors, in which we slowly metamorphosed into what we were to become without noticing.

It began with an announcement in the venerable newspaper of record that PIVOT had added a new board member, one Alvarez Elitto. This fellow was an architect of some renown, an 'artist' with a remarkable ability to design ugly piles of twisted steel and glass that had no readily apparent function, aesthetic appeal or public amenity. However, his real genius was in marketing – that is, his ability to wield bombast and floridity to make his monstrosities seem magical. He described his designs in terms such as 'diaphanous', 'ethereal', 'facete', 'elemental', 'lustral', 'heteroclitic' and 'transilient', usually stringing several such overblown terms together to create absurd agglomerations. Because they were impressed by the opaque grandiloquence of Elitto's descriptions, his peers instantly proclaimed his work as genius. Anything endowed with such pompously pretentious prolixity must be pure perfection, right?

Coming from a family who were all stalwarts of the Venezuelan oligarchy, Elitto was a first-class dissembler and kleptocrat. He added his voice to that of the PIVOT board in the hope of maintaining the pretence that the organisation had the Venezuelan people's best interests at heart, playing on his heritage to achieve the deceit.

Incidentally, PIVOT had been very active through the early part of the year, accusing the Venezuelan government of doing precisely what PIVOT itself was plotting – to control Venezuela's oil reserves for its own reprehensible purposes. There had been a number of 'peaceful protests' in which large numbers of demonstrators had turned out on the streets. The rumour was that the great majority of these people had been paid to be there, and among their number were squadrons of serious agitators who were mysteriously well trained and organised, dangerously armed with guns and petrol bombs, and given to savagely provoking the local police. If these provocations didn't work – and sadly, they often did – the agitators would simply start shooting or lobbing bombs themselves, and claim that the police started it.

Recently, the newspapers, websites and broadcasters that routinely spread government fabrications without doing their audiences the courtesy of a fact check had been full of reports that there was a 'humanitarian disaster' in the making in Venezuela. The fiction was that the government was starving the people so that they would, in desperation, agree to radical new laws that would allow the government fat cats to walk off with the oil bounty and leave the population to, um, starve. Presumably a little more effectively the second time around.

It didn't make even the slightest sense, but that was of no concern to the pundits and politicians who maniacally repeated the words 'humanitarian disaster' like demented parrots at every opportunity, or to the millions of dross-fed viewers who reflexively winced every time someone said those magic words and demanded that 'something' be done.

Into this heated arena came the oligarchs' representative, Elitto, the token Venezuelan (expatriate, of course) acting as though he gave a dried rat's turd about what happened to his countrymen. As he explained from the comfort of his Manhattan eyrie, Elitto had joined the board because, 'As a native of Venezuela, one offers a vision for her future that creates a conscious interface between economic and social dynamism in order to elevate her to the plane of harmonious empower-ment and collective gratification, on which she belongs.'

'Oh, we are so destroying that bastard's office,' said Abby when she saw him spouting that meaningless tripe on one of the right-wing television channels we regularly watched for the purpose of outraging ourselves. His objective, plainly, was to ensure that his family, generations of which had happily plundered the wealth of their country, was at the front of the line to get their grubby hands on the spoils of war that would proceed from its final destruction. He was despicable.

Nevin found out he had a loft studio office in SoHo that had been so minimalistically refurbed that most people who came to the door assumed that the renovation hadn't even begun yet and went away. It was ideal – we could most likely sneak our way into the building unseen, do our dirty work and slip away undetected. The big debate was whether we could do any damage to a place where everything was distressed, the brickwork was partially exposed where render had been ripped away with what looked like a fork, and the furnishing was so sparse as to be almost imaginary.

We were becoming old hands at smashing and grabbing by that time – although it was a fresh challenge and a brand-new buzz every time – so we were all keen. This does not imply that we skimped on the preparation. We cased the joint, as Lucas loved to put it, and we made a meticulous plan based on who would be where and at what time – who was to carry out the cashbox search, lift the laptops, vandalise the furniture and so on. And we put it to a strict timetable. Then we rehearsed it, and everyone enunciated their role clearly so that we all knew what we had to do and what everyone else would be doing at the same time.

On the appointed night, Bevan was suddenly called in to work at Hoskin's Bar, and that threw our plan into disarray. Usually, Lucas was on street watch, Nevin drove the van, and Abby and I burglarised with Bevan, using his strength to its maximum advantage. Without him, we were one man down, and our best one at that.

Rather than call it off, which in retrospect we should have done, we decided that we would, for once, dispense with the street watch. After all, Nevin would be sitting in the van just up the road, and he could toot the horn to alert us if there was anything untoward happening at the front of the building.

The entry went well. Although Lucas wasn't as strong as Bevan, he managed to break us in quite neatly, and with the clock running, we set about our individual tasks. I was assigned to ferret out the cashbox and any other random valuables, so I started going through drawers, levering open any locked ones with a screwdriver I carried for the purpose. Abby checked computers and communications devices, either disabling them or selecting them for resale, and Lucas was to quietly effect some physical mayhem – breaking and vandalising things, and spraying the usual POW tags on walls. Or in this case – to our immense satisfaction – across incomprehensible but obviously expensive artworks.

Out on the street, Nevin did what he always does at these events, which, as we found out, involved sitting in the van and playing with his fucking telephone. Abby had banned phones on these outings, as they could conceivably be used to track our movements by isolating and tracking the signal, and because they are a monumental distraction anyway. But Nevin reasoned that as it was a burner, it wouldn't matter. The fool. He was playing blackjack or any one of a million time-killing, life-wasting games, so he didn't see the security vehicle cruise straight by him and park out front of Elitto's building.

As the guard got out of the vehicle to check the doors, we had already started down the stairs carrying arms full of loot, feeling very smug. At that point, Nevin's buzzer went off, so he started the van, only noticing the security company car in the spot where he wanted to stop when he looked up. He says that he wisely elected not to beep the horn to signal us, as that would have also alerted the guard to his presence, and possibly ours. I submit that in reality, Nevin froze, and sat there like a stunned mullet waiting for something to happen.

Luckily, he then found the presence of mind to drive to the entrance to Elitto's building and double park next to the security company vehicle.

Right then, we came face to face with the guard at the front door, and the only good thing about that was that we were on high alert because walking out onto the street with our plunder was the riskiest and most watchful moment of the whole operation. In effect, we were expecting the guard, but he was not expecting us. I was in front, and I almost kissed the guy as he opened the door when I was half a pace away. My heart skipped three beats, and I'm sure my pupils widened to saucers, but at the same time, I almost burst into laughter at the priceless look on his face. I was startled, but he was beyond astonished; I can't be certain he didn't shit his pants.

For a few milliseconds, I had him at a disadvantage, and I used that time shrewdly. I shoved my load of laptops in his face, upsetting his balance and pushing him off his feet, and as he and the electronics clattered to the ground, pushed past him. Abby and Lucas whizzed by him while he was still recovering, and in a flash we were outside, where Nevin was waiting with the van doors open. We piled in and slammed the door just as the guard, shouting and carrying on like a madman, stood up and started to run towards us. Nevin pushed the accelerator to the floor and the heavy old van took off at its disturbingly slow fastest, which was luckily still quick enough to elude the flustered security guard.

Horrified, I watched out the back window as he reached into his holster and pulled out a revolver.

'Shit!' I yelled, as he squeezed off a couple of shots; I ducked away from the window, in spite of the fact that he was waving the gun around like an out of control fire hose and couldn't possibly have hit the van, let alone me.

'He's firing at us,' I bellowed unnecessarily as the van at last gathered pace and Nevin threw it around a corner without even touching the brakes. We three thieves were flung about inside the van, but we were away, and that was what mattered.

Almost instantly, the post-peril euphoria kicked in, and as Nevin drove, his teeth chattering and his knuckles white on the steering wheel, the incursion party collapsed into giggles, gasps and gales. We'd had an excruciatingly close shave, losing a couple of laptops in the process, but we'd survived. The relief was orgasmic.

This was the most dangerous, potentially lethal thing that any of us had ever done, and surviving it was like standing on Everest. I was shaking like a freshly set jelly, my heart was thumping with near-audible palpitations, and my breath was coming out of me in short rasps, but I don't know if I had ever been in such a state of heightened awareness. My fellow intruders were the same, and we shared not just a bond but a complete union of consciousness that night. We were one. At least until Abby came down long enough to verbally beat the shit out of Nevin for his inattention and stupidity.

When we got back to Devoe Street, having changed the license plates of the van in some dark corner of Bushwick and parked it several blocks away, the fact of our escape rather than the cause of it was still fresh in our minds. Our brains were all drenched in serotonin and our bodies awash with endorphins. So we took that as an excuse to party the night away like crazed conquerors, hitting the usual substances with abandon.

Late in the night, a tired-looking Bevan came through the door, not entirely thrilled to find us all in the terminal stages of inebriation and babbling about our adventure. He made us quieten down and tell him from the start how the thing had gone down, who did what and how it all came out roses in the end. It was while Lucas was recounting the sorry sequence of events at the tail-end of what had been an otherwise ordinary operation that Abby's eyes started to narrow as she regarded Nevin. I could tell she was not satisfied with his excuse that he had been distracted by something else and that was why he had neither seen the security guard arrive nor felt it necessary to give the requisite signal when he did twig to the situation. I guess she had it all figured out there and then, but not wanting to interrupt Lucas, who was feeling unusually heroic, she'd decided to wait to grill our driver.

Lucas, as I say, was the most buzzed of all of us. It had been his first actual break-in, as opposed to his normal role of street rat, and not only had he handled it well, he'd been at the back of the line in the getaway, so he was closest to the action. Or so he obviously felt. He told the tale with flailing arms and a flurry of verbal flourishes, and as he did, we all laughed and clapped. It was his first time as the centre of attention for a prolonged period, and he lapped it up.

The only one not impressed was Bevan. He had a look of deep concern on his face when the security guard's weapon was mentioned, and this evolved into alarm when he found that actual shots had been fired. Being sober, and hearing it as a story about how his friends were shot at, he didn't find it as amusing as we did. Then again, he couldn't have known just how far we were from being hit by the wildly flying bullets. He sat quietly, carried on looking perturbed for a while, and then excused himself and went to bed.

It was odd, but not completely out of character; he'd declined to be the sober loner in our fucked-up midst before, and of course he'd missed what had been an exciting operation, so he was probably a little miffed at that, too. We let him go off to his room and carried on celebrating. Somewhere in there, Abby casually mentioned to Nevin that he could have called or texted us when the guard turned up, and in his addled state, he nodded energetically.

'Shit, Abs, why didn't I think of that?' he said.

Instantly, Abby's face darkened, and Nevin's clouded. He knew he'd been trapped. He could only have messaged us if he had a phone – but if he'd done so, he would have messaged phones that were sitting quietly at home.

Abby didn't pursue it right then, most likely because it was very late and we were all pretty poleaxed by that time, but we all knew Nevin would be taken to task sooner or later. Poor bastard: I can just see him now, his rubbery lips suddenly dry, his cheeks sucking air and his eyes, as close to being crossed as it's possible to be, trying to focus as he realised that he'd been busted and wondered how he might get out of it.

Not long after that we all called it a night. Lucas, feeling very much the man of the moment, cast a meaningful look at Abby as he headed up the stairs to his room. His thoughts may as well have been projected on the wall: he felt that as a primary actor in the drama that we'd played out, he had earned the same Abby reward that Bevan had once taken off. But Abby was not in that sort of mood, especially after her suspicions about Nevin's actions had been aroused, so she pointedly ignored him. I kind of felt sorry for him, and to be honest, the whole episode had given my physique such a shake-up that I was feeling very horny, so I considered, for the briefest of moments, compensating him myself. Common sense, and the knowledge that Abby would be disapproving if not downright disappointed, kept me from following him up there.

The next day, Abby tore large strips off Nevin and made him swear on his life that he would never again put his fellow Patriots at such unnecessary risk. He of all people, she said, should have known that if the authorities checked mobile phone geolocation records at the time and place of the event, they could likely use that information to determine the number and present location of the phone, and start tracking it in real time – even if it was a burner. She made him destroy the phone right there and then.

He was so thoroughly chastened that he went off to work early that afternoon, and stayed there long after the evening news he worked on was finished. Abby, affecting to be crabby but, in reality, pleased that she had an opportunity to turn success (of a sort) into a lesson, watched him go with a sense of accomplishment.

Late in the afternoon, as we two were lolling in front of the television while Lucas was up in his room, presumably masturbating or playing some shoot-'em-up game on his computer, or masturbating while he played, and Nevin was still hiding out at work, Bevan came home.

He walked into the room slightly hunched over, his hands weirdly cradling a bulge under his sweater, stealing his steps furtively and trying to keep a crafty look off his face. Abby and I watched as he dropped onto the couch and plunged his hands into the folds of clothing across his belly. Eventually, out came the thing he had been hiding: a semiautomatic pistol with a ten-round clip in its bulky handle.

'What the fuck, Bev?' said Abby, knowing the answer.

He passed her the black, bulky piece, handling it as though it was a delicate flower rather than a heavy instrument of death.

'I've been thinking about this for a while,' he said with grim reflection. 'But after last night, I'm sure. You need this, Abby. We need it. For protection.'

17. Casing the joint.

I looked at the shiny metal object covering Abby's pale palms as she stared at it, her eyes wide and unblinking. I asked myself, if I had been holding that gun when the security guard had started shooting at us – at me – would I have fired back? In the shock of the moment, at a time when everything seemed to be happening in a blizzard of slippery speed, I doubted that I would have had the presence of mind to have raised the gun, pointed it, switched off the safety and squeezed the trigger.

I tried to imagine a scenario in which I might have loosed a few shots. The first one would have shattered the rear window of the van, splattering me with glass and possibly injuring me. The sound, in that enclosed space, would have deafened me, and the muzzle flash may have blinded me. It would have been a terrifying, sensually overloading experience. Part of me was wondering, though, if the guard might have reconsidered confronting us if one or more of us had been visibly armed.

'Where did you get this, Bev?' Abby was still transfixed by the weapon.

Bevan shucked a grin and shrugged his square shoulders.

'I meet some people.'

'Can you get more?'

This was unexpected. More?

'What are you talking about, Abbs?' I was as casual as I could be.

'Yup,' Bev replied.

'You're not serious, are you? Abby?' I tried to shake her near-hypnotised gaze off the gun, waving at her as I spoke.

'Why not?' She was turning the gun over in her hands now, touching its barrel indecently with her long white fingers, running them slowly along its solid length and wrapping her hand slowly around the grip, tightening it and then holding the weapon up in the firing position, sighting along the top, drawing a bead on an imaginary foe.

'Really?' I said.

She turned unhurriedly and looked up at me, as though she was sitting on the porch of some frontier shack in a golden sunset, and her lover had just called from away in the field. She could have been emerging from a long and satisfying sleep.

'We're pacifists, Abby,' I said. 'These things are completely against what we preach.'

'No, we preach that these things shouldn't be used to kill people in any of the declared and undeclared wars going on here and abroad,' she said. 'I am not for a second suggesting that we use them to kill or hurt people. But I think there is a case for having a couple of guns handy. For protection, as Bev says.'

There was a strange, dark glint in her eye, seemingly reflected off the oiled metal.

'For protection? Please.'

'Think about the Cold War, Jayney,' she said. She was beginning to come further out of her trance and become the familiar, didactic Abby. 'All those nuclear bombs. What were they for? To blow people up? No, to stop us, and to stop the Russians, from blowing people up. We're talking about a quality deterrent, sweetie. That's what a couple of little pistols could do for us: make us less vulnerable to fucking madmen like that security guard last night.'

I could see the logic, in a twisted way, but it was difficult to adjust to the idea that wielding guns would make us less vulnerable, because it would make any situation undeniably more dangerous.

'If one of us had been carrying that thing tonight, it could easily have escalated the whole shit-show and created a far nastier outcome.'

'Ah, but if all three of us had been carrying "these things", as you call them, then the security guard would have had no option but to stand down,' she said with a tiny little serrated edge of triumph. 'No shot would ever have been fired, because he would have known he was outgunned from the start. As it was, he didn't hesitate to start firing shots at us, and we were unarmed! In fact, he shot at us *because* we were unarmed. What does that tell you about the battle we're in?'

'It's just the tip of a greasy slope, Abby,' I said. 'Guns have a nasty way of going off when you least expect or want them to. It's almost inevitable.'

'You're thinking of Chekhov, aren't you?' she asked with a twinkle. 'Me too. And maybe even that's not such a bad thing. If at some stage one of us fires off a couple of rounds to scare off an overzealous security type, it will only enhance our reputation for fierceness. It's not as if anyone will get hurt. I mean, the chances that any of us could hit the side of a barn with one of these things are negligible. Beyond negligible. Minuscule.'

'I don't know, Abbs…'

She cut me off. 'Just think of it as a preventive tool. If we come across someone who wants to hurt us, they'll back off if they're outgunned. It's common sense. And if it's you, me and Bevan – that is, the rational ones – handling the weaponry, then we'll be fine.'

I wasn't convinced of anything, but further dispute would be pointless. Abby had made her mind up, and that was that. Bevan promised to look into getting some more guns.

Our 'reputation for fierceness,' meanwhile, had been given a significant boost by the Elitto raid. Alvarez Elitto himself had helped by whining loudly and inanely to the press. He claimed, foolishly, that we were a bunch of foreigners seeking to subvert the will of the Venezuelan people by trying to intimidate him, and implied that he somehow represented the grass roots of Venezuelan society. This was too much even for some conservative commentators, who reminded him that he was an expatriate, while left wing pundits pointed out that he came from a family that had been systematically siphoning wealth off from the state through generations of 'public service' that had inexplicably enriched every office holder, until they had abandoned the country altogether. There followed a spiteful debate between the left and right wings of the various social media platforms, in which POW came off looking a lot like the voice of sanity.

Our new strategy of taking what we called 'direct action' (it sounds much better than larceny, demolition and sabotage), made us look like fearless warriors for peace, which is exactly how we wished to see ourselves.

The trail of wreckage that we had already wrought was considerable, and even the mighty began to take note. The president of PIVOT, Arkady Zenstl, wrote an op-ed in the *Times*, bemoaning the new trend towards destructive protest.

He didn't mention POW, but it was clear that he was talking about us when he wrote, 'People who have no interest in the outcomes of policy beyond its disruption are now seeking to bolster pathetically weak counterarguments to that policy by visiting cowardly destruction and outright theft on its instruments. It's a recipe for anarchy, and a new variant strain of terrorism that must be comprehensively stamped out. We must silence these busybody vandals who wear a cloak of righteousness to mask their childish vandalism as activism.'

We loved that. In a moment of unintended transparency, Zenstl had admitted that he and his ilk had an 'interest' in the outcome of a policy, and berated us for not having one! By doing so, he was confirming the worst that anyone could think of his organisation – that it was about achieving the aims of the rich (their 'interests') – and helping people to see that our motivation was pure: we had come from what was right rather than what we simply wanted. What a dick. We paraded this statement of his, and our response that our only interest was peace, all over the internet for days. We dined out on it, and it was delicious.

His call to 'silence' us, however, was neither funny nor easily dismissed. We had a powerful and now quite angry enemy lined up against us, and we were certain he would be using his undoubted influence in legal and law enforcement circles to press for our detection and suppression. I started to think that the acquisition of guns for protection was perhaps not such a bad thing.

Bevan duly delivered two more pistols – 9mm automatics, guaranteed to be untraceable and complete with plenty of ammunition – just a few days later. The purchase of these, which was only dropped to Lucas and Nevin after the fact, depleted our cash reserves, so it was decided that we needed to take on another project. The boys agitated for guns of their own, which we should have expected, but Abby was steadfast in her refusal.

'Nevin, you're driving the van. You couldn't possibly do that and handle a weapon safely or effectively. It doesn't make any sense. And you, Lucas — Really? You're out there keeping watch and jumping at shadows. What are you going to do if someone comes up and asks you the time? Probably blow their fucking head off. Believe me, we're much safer if only Jayney and Bev and I carry these things. It's not like we want to, but we have to.'

There was plenty of grumbling and sulking, but the boys knew they wouldn't talk Abby around. Oddly, my meagre pacifist objections were the only ones ever raised. The boys accepted the need for guns without a second thought.

So we needed to plan our next big heist, and there was a meeting as to just what that might be. Nevin, who'd been trying to find ways of redeeming himself since the Elitto raid, had been doing a lot of research into Arkady Zenstl, the president of PIVOT. This fellow was a Russian immigrant, a man who'd found it expedient to bail out of his home country when Putin cracked down on the oligarchs who were bleeding the country dry. He'd managed to get billions of rubles out of Russia over a long period, having been helped into America by corporate types who admired and had profited from his ruthless 'business acumen' – meaning his unprincipled exploitation of people and resources. These corporate types had helped Zenstl skirt the economic sanctions against Russia with ease, which was always the way with favoured kleptocrats.

Arky's interest in Venezuela was always purely commercial, and it's doubtful that he ever met a Venezuelan outside of its one percent. However, in what we considered a transparent attempt to shore up his credentials, he owned a restaurant on the Upper East Side called The Venezuelan. This upmarket joint was at the time very hip, and was always crowded with try-hards desperate to wax lyrical over dishes concocted of beans and plantains and pulled pork. Interestingly, our friend Arkady probably used this place to launder money, because it only took cash. That's right, food fans. If you want to dine at The Venezuelan, better bring a wad of greenbacks. A large wad. That made it very much an oddity in these days of the cashless society, but one the financial and legal regulatory authorities somehow failed to remark upon.

Perhaps unlike the food it served, The Venezuelan itself was too delectable an opportunity to pass up. We knew we would have to relieve Arky of at least one night's takings, which would undoubtedly amount to a pretty sum.

It so happened that my birthday was coming up, so I called my dad and arranged for a family dinner at The Venezuelan.

Daddy was bemused at my choice of restaurant – it was the kind of adventurous gustatory experience that he and Mother loved but which neither of us kids had ever expressed interest in – but he was chuffed. Maybe he thought I was growing up or something. The important thing is, he was happy to agree. As Abby's birthday was a couple of days before mine, and since she had been present at just about every family event I could ever remember, she was naturally invited.

On the day, Daddy sent a town car to pick us up, and we met the family at The Venezuelan. We were a picture of filial happiness, even if the pleasantries – especially between me and my brother – were kind of distantly relayed. He was a little reactionary for my liking – a right winger by choice rather than upbringing, and a snotty, entitled one at that: the worst kind.

Mother and Daddy were, as always, jovial and generous, and apparently more interested in the restaurant and the food than their own family or each other. I wondered what kind of booze-soaked social event we had dragged them away from, and felt vaguely sorry for them.

Abby and I forced ourselves to play the part of willing food adventurists, spouting the kind of laudatory superlatives so favoured by gourmands everywhere despite the fact that the food tasted a lot like cooked carpet and boiled string. The fact that we were able to wash it down with copious quantities of good Russian vodka – Arky was not a compete idiot, it seems – helped a lot. The dishes may have been all tomatoes and corn, but the vodka was all top-quality potato spirits. Just the kind of vegetable I prefer.

The décor was, predictably, appalling – overuse of bright red, yellow and blue, too many horses and too much decorated timber. Thick, hairy, hideous rugs, seemingly designed to induce a kind of geometric epilepsy, hung on the brick walls. The salient feature to us, though, was that there was one door in and out of the restaurant, and just one door between the dining room and the kitchen. Logically, the manager would exit from the front door with a large bag of cash each night, but if he (a big ugly Russian man, a brother or cousin of Arky, I would guess) left through the rear kitchen door, that would be more than acceptable because it opened onto an alley. We would, as a matter of course, follow up this initial visit with a more comprehensive reconnaissance mission.

At midnight, we thanked the portly Russian gentleman, who ogled Abby with ill-disguised lasciviousness, air-kissed the various members of my family and thanked them for their attendance, and stepped back into the waiting town car. It had been a fun and instructive night out.

The next night we went back with Bev at around midnight, parked a hundred yards away and sat quiet watch as the last of the customers straggled out, the lights dimmed and the staff left one by one. At about two thirty, the big Russian left, locking the street front door behind him. He carried a heavy looking backpack, and his round head swivelled about on his thick neck as he nervously surveyed the street. Assured that he was safe, he darted across to a car stopped close by on the other side of the street with its engine running, and jumped in. We'd seen this ostentatious vehicle – a large white Cadillac – arrive a couple of minutes before, and guessed that the Russki had called the driver to let him know he'd be locking up shortly. The vehicle roared away and we left a few moments later.

The following night, we parked a little closer and Abby stayed in the van. She had instructed Bev and me to be walking slowly down the street, acting like lovers, stopping frequently to clinch and make out, so we could get a close look inside the pickup car when it came. It seemed like a setup to me. I was sure Abby was trying to get Bevan and me together, perhaps to save her from the guilt of having slept with him, or maybe to divert his affections away from her. Either way, it wouldn't work. But we had to put on a show, and we did.

I must say again that Bevan's physique had become quite magnificent. Several times as we meandered up the street, he wrapped me in those muscular arms, pulled me into his steely chest and dug his face into my neck, whispering, 'Is the car coming? Or should I just nuzzle a while longer?' or a variation thereof. He smelled of musk and gun oil, and it was sexy and intoxicating.

The first time he pulled me into his arms like that, I laughed and pushed him away with an overplayed 'nooooo'. He took it in good grace, laughing with me and letting me go but holding my hand so I swung on his weight like a child. We walked on a couple of paces, then he grabbed me again. This time, I let him burrow his face into my neck a little longer, delighting in the feel of his short stubble against my skin and his hot breath on my collarbone, then pushed him away less forcefully and scolded him more softly. We tarried on the same spot for a few seconds, laughing and whispering gibberish to each other, and he grabbed me again just as the Russian's ride swung around the corner. We both tensed a little but carried on the pretence we were enjoying so much; I escaped his loose grasp and took a few short running steps away from him, stopping directly in front of where I thought the car would pull up and beckoning him with a harlot's grin.

He caught up to me and swept me up entirely, lifting me with ease, and as the car stopped right next to us, did a long turnabout. Both of us got a good look inside the car, through windows open to the warm May air. We could see that the bored looking, lantern jawed flunky was travelling alone, and was completely unconcerned about us. He didn't even give us a glance.

Bev put me down and we pranced down the path a dozen or so steps, hand in hand. Then he hauled me in with a quick pull once again, and surprised me with a kiss full on the mouth. Just a short, sweet and shallow kiss, but a memorable one.

'We did it, beautiful,' he said, holding his face close to mine and looking deeply into my eyes. At that moment, he could have had me. But he let me go, and led me on down the dark, empty street as the restaurant manager got in the car and it pulled away from the kerb. We kept on walking all the way around the block, holding hands, just in case any other eyes were watching.

'This is going to be a breeze,' Bevan said, swinging his arm so that mine swung too. He was swept up in the beauty and simplicity of the job, and seemed to have instantly forgotten what I would have called our 'moment'. He never mentioned it again, nor did he ever try anything like that on me again; I suspect it had been a show to make Abby jealous. I also suspect that it kind of worked. And I had further developed the idea growing in my own mind that he was kind of hot.

We made light chatter as we tarried and sashayed around the block, and got back into the van relaxed and jubilant. Abby was uncharacteristically cool.

'That took a while,' she said as Bevan started the van and we drove away.

'We took a circuit of the block for authenticity,' I said. I could play it cool, too.

'Just playing the game,' said Bevan.

It was quiet for a while, but before we even got to the Williamsburg Bridge, Abby had loosened up a bit – she never was good at holding a grudge – and we talked about the job.

'Okay,' she said, 'obviously the goon parks around the corner somewhere and waits for the boss to let him know he's ready. He's close enough so that it only takes a few minutes to get here, by which time the boss is out the door and ready to go.'

'So we have two options,' said Bevan. 'We can delay the vehicle so that the big man is stranded on the street and we hit him there, or we can commandeer the vehicle so that the boss gets in none the wiser, and rob him at our leisure.'

'I think we find out where the driver parks and waits, and a couple of us stop him there,' said Abby. 'That way, you and I can deal with Mr Russki alone and minimise the chances of something going wrong.'

'So, how do we delay the wheel man?' I asked. I had fallen into the habit of using gangster lingo, like the boys; it made me feel dangerous.

'That's for Nevin and Lucas, and maybe you too, Jayney,' Abby replied. 'Nevin gets a camera and microphone from work, and they – you – wait near where the wheel man is parked until his phone rings. As soon as that happens, you switch on the camera light and shove the thing in his face – hopefully he'll have the window open again – and act like you're from some sort of news channel. You ask a dumb question that stuns him for a minute – the light will help with that anyway – and keep him as long as you can. By the time he takes off, the job is done, and Bev and I swing by with a bag full of money and pick you up a minute or two later.'

It sounded like a reasonable plan, and nobody else seemed to have a better one, so we agreed.

The next night, we all went out as a group, in low-level disguise – expensive clothes, swish hair and piles of makeup, all the boys wearing suits, and strolled the streets looking for our wheel man. We looked like any other group of smart young uptown yuppies out throwing our money and attitudes around.

We had a fair idea where our target would be parked because of where he'd come around the corner the previous night, so we concentrated on that area, and found him within a few minutes. The idiot – he'd parked in a dim, dark part of the street that made him an easy target. I was encouraged by how easy this was going to be.

18. No witnesses

The night of the job, we were tense. This was to be our first armed robbery, and because it was straight out robbery it was not to be conducted under the auspices of POW; it wasn't our MO and it shouldn't be something we'd be suspected of, even if the Arky Zenstl connection was made. Our purpose wasn't to make a statement but to fill the coffers, so we'd already decided we wouldn't claim it, would disavow any knowledge of it and if asked, would condemn it.

We left to go uptown early, around midnight, Bevan and Abby in the front, with Lucas, Nevin and your correspondent crammed in the back of the van. Abby was wearing a black, curly wig and a size sixteen outfit. She'd wrapped her legs in long swathes of cloth, and taped a number of small cushions and other "fattening" items around her belly and chest, with more cloth around her arms. She was a convincing chubby, which is what we called her; if the mood hadn't been so serious, we would have laughed about it.

Bevan was dressed all in black, and Abby had temporarily dyed his hair black as well. He had shoulder pads under his oversized shirt so he looked even bigger and more menacing than usual. He wore a hat over his newly blackened hair, and kept it low over his eyes.

I wore a straight blonde wig, which almost convinced me I needed to bleach, because I thought I looked hot; a large, bright yellow jumper that I filled by padding my boobs to ridiculous levels, which again made me pause. Should I get my boobs done? I asked myself when I caught my arresting profile in the mirror before we left home. The boys, who couldn't stop staring even though they knew they were fakes, would most definitely have said yes. I also wore a very short red pleated skirt over dark green tights, so I looked like some kind of cheap slut, ideal for my cover as a would-be television reporter. Especially once I applied more lipstick and eyeshadow than I'd usually use in a month. I was, if nothing else, unrecognisable – so the job was done.

Nevin and Lucas, who were to be a bit more background, dressed all in black with berets and fake glasses to obscure their faces as much as possible without being too obvious. They looked like earnest art students, which was what they were meant to be.

Abby, Bevan and I were carrying our guns for the first time. While we hadn't had an opportunity to practice shooting them, Bevan had made us go through the procedure of loading, switching off the safety, aiming and pulling the trigger with us so many times I could just about do it in my sleep.

I said that I would just as soon carry the thing without any bullets in it, but I was outvoted.

'A gun without bullets is an empty threat, Jayney,' Abby said. 'If you know it's not loaded, you're likely to treat it as harmless, and your mark will know it instantly. If it has bullets in it, you'll be careful and your threats will have substance. That's all you need. You have to look like you mean to use it – and to do that you have to be prepared to do so.'

'But I don't want to shoot anyone, Abby,' I said.

'I don't want you to, either. And I don't want to myself. But if either of us have to, we have to be ready,' she said. She was deadly serious.

I wasn't convinced, but I could see I wasn't going to win, so I shut up and loaded the clip. I suddenly felt lethal.

We three "arts students" got out of the van and unloaded the camera gear around the corner from where we knew the wheel man would be parking, and Bev and Abby kept going the couple of streets up to the restaurant. Bev was to stay in the van, and Abby, adopting a thick Russian accent – I swear she loved the drama of these charades – was to accost the manager and effect the robbery alone. I was worried about her but Bevan assured me over and over again that he wouldn't let anything happen to her, and I believed him.

I also had my own nerves to deal with, along with two excited and difficult to control boys, so as they drove away I anxiously waved goodbye to Abby. She waved back gaily, hanging out of the van window as though she was off to a fair. I helped the boys carry the camera gear down the street to where the wheel man was parked.

Getting close enough to the wheel man to hear when his phone rang was a piece of cake. There was an all night diner and a 24-hour convenience store, as well as two nightclubs on the short street, so there was a bit of foot traffic on the sidewalk, and a little noise. He'd parked with his driver's side up against the sidewalk on the wrong side of the road, and we stopped just a few paces away, pretending to be setting up a shot near his car. He sat there with the windows down, ignoring us, concentrating on the mindless game he was playing on his phone. Honestly, those things make getting the best of anyone such a doddle. It's like their whole brain gets sucked into the screen, and their senses are so completely dulled they don't even know what's going on until you club them over the head.

I was starting to wish we had actually planned to club the wheel man over the head, though. Casting surreptitious glances through the window of his Cadillac as we pretended to adjust the camera and talked quietly among ourselves about pulling focus and other such crap, I could see that he was a big, healthy specimen whose suit was tight over smooth round shoulders and protruding pectorals. His chin alone looked strong enough to stop an aircraft carrier, and his hands were massive. It was a wonder he could get his monstrous fingers to punch the tiny buttons on his telephone screen.

I was keeping a close eye on the time, knowing that the manager had been locking the restaurant door almost on the dot of two thirty the last three nights in a row, so we could expect it to happen again that night. At two twenty-five we were ready. Nevin was holding the camera, I held a radio mic in one hand and did my best to conceal the gun I held in the other – my preferred hand of course – and Lucas had the big hand light, ready to thrust it almost in through the car window. I was holding the pistol under instructions from Abby and against my better judgement.

'If he looks like he's going to just start the car and drive off, or if he looks at you with the tiniest threat in his eyes, you wave that fucking thing in his face,' she'd said. 'That'll make him think twice, and in the pause that hesitation creates, you scram. Got it?' I'd nodded but I was less than convinced. The gun seemed to be overkill – I was sure the plan would work fine without it.

Acting as though there might be someone I needed to interview on the other side of the road, I slowly manoeuvred myself around to the passenger side of the vehicle, standing in the middle of the road like a pelican on a rock. We waited, absolutely astounded that the goon hadn't thought to look up from his phone even once to see what we were doing just outside his car windows, and less than thirty seconds after we had finished setting ourselves up, the phone in the wheel man's giant goony hand went 'ping' very loudly. He jumped at the sound, unprepared for the device he was caressing to start ordering him around.

Lucas, on the sidewalk right next to him, switched on the light, and it filled the car's interior with what appeared to be broad daylight streaming in through the driver's window. If the hood was surprised by the phone, he was stunned by the light. Without giving him time to recover, and partially blinded by the light myself, I opened the passenger side door and thrust my head and the microphone into the car's interior, saying, 'Sir, the NYPD has suggested that it will begin stop and search operations on people lurking suspiciously in cars; what's your response to that?'

He swung his head wildly from side to side, but in the same motion dropped the phone on his lap, and his right hand dived into his coat pocket, emerging wrapped around the butt of a nine. Lucas ducked and the light went out, but I had seen enough. At the sight of the gun, I lost my mind. I thought of that asshole cop spilling Jihad's blood and guts all over the street, and I knew that this stranger meant to do the same to me. Fuck him. He wouldn't get the opportunity.

My mind on auto, my thumb flipped the safety on my own piece, and I raised it and squeezed the trigger three times in succession. The sound wasn't as abrasive as I'd thought it would be, more of a pop than a bang, really, but the muzzle flash was frighteningly like lightning, bursting out with intensity and blazing speed behind the bullets; one, two, three, as they left the gun. Two of them connected with the back end of his head, which exploded like a watermelon, all pink and fluffy, and the third snicked the end off his nose, which looked like it would hurt a bit. Except he was well and truly dead by then, and what was left of his head fell forward onto his chest, the gun still only just out of his jacket. In the sudden darkness that fell when the television light had gone out, the whole scenario had played out as if in a stroboscopic light show.

Then there was silence, and even in the dim street light I could see that there was blood and lumpy brain bits all over the interior of the vehicle, and presumably all over the sidewalk outside the open window. He wouldn't be making the pickup.

Lucas was first up off the ground, rising up out of the muck on the other side of the vehicle.

'Jesus, Jayne,' he breathed.

'Run,' I said, and took off up the street as fast as my legs would carry me. Behind me, I could hear Lucas and Nevin clattering along, dragging the camera, the tripod legs and the light, and doing their best to catch up. We hadn't gone more than fifty yards when the van swung around the corner in front of us and came barrelling down the street. Bevan stopped in front of us and we jumped in chaotically, all trying to get in first, with camera gear and lights and microphone all jumbled up together. This was something we should have rehearsed.

In a manic moment or three, we were all in. Bevan jammed his foot down and the crime scene receded behind us.

If I thought that the adrenaline spurt from previous jobs was pronounced, none of them had been a patch on this. It was hyper elation, a sense of invincibility and godlike pre-eminence, a trip like I had never thought I'd experience, and which I assumed I never would again.

Strangely, the horror and guilt that I'd always thought would accompany the taking of a human life didn't appear even peripherally. It was all good, that feeling. I'd met that man on an even battlefield, and I'd won. He would have killed me without a second thought; why should I give a fuck about him? Some second-rate gangster earning his dodgy dollars by ferrying around a fat man whose job was to run a money-laundering restaurant for an inscrutable oligarchical bastard. He deserved it. These and so many more justifications ran through my mind like quicksilver as I tried to hang onto that feeling of jubilation and achievement.

Incidentally, this is the first time I've ever admitted to killing that rag. We were never even looked at for it, so I guess I just dropped myself in it, again. Oh, well.

No one in the van spoke for a long time, and eventually I started to calm down. Lucas and Nevin were still breathing heavily from fear and exertion. They'd seen the wheel man's gun, and heard the rest from their positions on the ground, so their reaction was more of panic than awe. I almost laughed to see their faces in the dim flashes of light from the street lamps we passed as Bevan drove. In the front seat, both Bev and Abby remained silent.

I looked at Abby and could see spots of blood all over her face in the yellowish streetlight glow.

'You've got blood on you, Abbs,' I said.

'So have you, Jayne,' she said. Her voice was quiet, matter of fact. Almost dead.

I put my hand to my face, and to my surprise found that it came away with smears of what I guessed really was blood.

'What happened?' she asked.

'He went for his gun,' I said.

'So you shot him?'

'Yes.'

'Dead?'

'Yes.'

'Good. No witnesses.' She was curiously devoid of emotion, flat but with an undertone of triumph.

'You got the money?'

'Yes.' She held up the bulging backpack between her and Bevan on the front seat.

'And the Russian guy?'

'No witnesses,' she repeated.

'Fuck!' exploded Lucas, who was in the back with me. 'Fuck!' It wasn't an angry or a fearful fuck, but one of exultation, of excitement finally unleashed after a period of unbearable tension. 'That was fucking insane!' he yelled.

'How much did you get?' Nevin chimed in, the relief and release evident in his voice, too.

'Fucking thousands,' said Abby. 'Thirty, forty, I don't know. But a fucking pile!'

'Woo hoo!' Lucas sang. 'Holy fuck on a fucksicle, that was amazing. Jayney, you were like Alice from *Resident Evil*, like Ripley against the aliens, just all fucking business. Pow, pow, pow. Super, super, super intense. And we walk away with the cash. Bam!'

Only Bevan was still silent as the general hubbub in the van rose to a crescendo of glee.

'Abby, you executed that guy,' he said when there was, at last, a break in the frenzy.

'He deserved it.' There was ice in her voice. 'He was a low-level scumbag who helped launder money for a high-level shyster whose aim is to kill thousands if not millions of Venezuelans and steal their oil. Why should I let someone like that live? I – we – at least slowed their plans tonight. Put a dent in their smug little plot. We should be congratulated.'

'As long as you know what you're doing,' Bevan said. He wasn't pissed off, and he wasn't berating her; he was just telling it like it was.

'You got us these guns in the first place.' Abby wasn't accusing, just reminding.

'I did.' He nodded and smiled. 'I just didn't understand how you'd interpret the word protection.'

The celebrations that night were tinged with even more than the usual tang of hysteria. There was a manic quality brought about by a sense of justified paranoia, which was understandable: the authorities don't fuck around when you kill someone. That's a right and a pleasure they reserve for themselves. And when you have the mortgage on who lives and who dies, you tend to get a bit territorially pissed when someone else comes along and kills without permission, even if the victims are a couple of thugs.

As it turned out, the fear that fevered us that night was unfounded. The news carried the story that these two had been slain in the time-honoured gangster fashion by a highly professional team that was most likely a long way away already. This professional hit on his employees raised questions about the nature of the business and associations of Mr Arkady Zenstl, who was forced to answer for his commercial interests and those of his comrades. Even he could see, after the application of the media blowtorch, that he was attempting to defend the indefensible, and he quietly slipped from the public eye, resigning from various positions including the presidency of PIVOT. Chalk up another, perhaps unintended, win for POW, even if he did get to slink away to a zillion dollar rat hole located somewhere in the Caribbean.

The return from the robbery was stupendous. Given that The Venezuelan charged like a wounded tapir, it was likely that most customers ended up paying somewhere around $120 a head for their food and drinks. With four sittings a night, they could probably get through up to three hundred customers or more. That's about $36,000 – and we had walked away with over $50,000.

And Abby and me? There was no getting away from it: we had become killers, but we rejected the idea that we were murderers. For a start, we shared the conviction that we had performed a community service in ridding the world of those two. The more we discussed it – and we discussed it at length over two very large joints the next night – the more we convinced each other and ourselves that we should be applauded for our selfless act.

'The way I see it,' said Abby, 'I am still a committed pacifist, as you are, right?'

'Right.' I handed the reefer over.

'And we're antiwar. We believe strongly in the protection of innocent victims from the evil designs of warmongers, who kill people simply because under the ground they live on there's a volume of black, tarry stuff that burns well, or because their colour is wrong, or their choice of herbal relaxant is proscribed. That's never changed, and never will. Our objection is to war in all its forms, and our objective is to put a halt to those wars, correct?'

'Correct. Pass me that thing.'

'So we find ourselves in a position in which we are compelled, by force of circumstance in the pursuit of our objective, to carry out an act that is abhorrent to us as pacifists, namely to rid the world of a couple of brute criminals. This is not something we would ordinarily choose to do. As pacifists, we allow that even the lowest and most antisocial felon has a right to exist. And yet, in the name of our objective, we eliminate these two. Bang bang. We compromise our powerful personal principles, and take a path that is repugnant to each of us, in order to attain the higher goal – the eradication of the killing of innocents. You and I, Jayney, have made an extra-ordinary sacrifice. We made ourselves the last thing we wanted to be, because we can see that it's the only way to achieve our objective. I'd say that makes us heroes, Silver.'

'Fuck, you're right,' I said. 'I don't want to be a killer. But if that's what the task demands of me, then what else can I be?'

'Exactly. I know your heart is pure, Jayney, and you know mine is, too. Society would judge us poorly, even for offing those two dregs, but we know why we did it, and we know that if we have to, we could do it again. Right?'

'Right,' I agreed. Maybe the dope had clouded my mind a bit, and maybe in hindsight, the logic isn't all that clear, but the conversation helped to dispel the niggling doubts about what we'd done, which were bubbling away below the surface. On some level, I had begun to feel bad about my dead thug. What if he had a wife, kids, a dog and a housing loan? I guess there was a level of guilt there, but that would diminish over time.

And I couldn't forget the pulsating, almost sexual thrill that killing him had given me – something I am sure Abby also felt but we never spoke about – and more than feeling bad about his death, I felt good about killing him. That was why I agreed so readily to the idea of doing it again, if I 'had to'. More than anything else, I wanted to feel that raw, mystical authority over the life of another again, and to exercise my prerogative without mercy. I sublimated that longing as much as I could, because a part of me believed it was wrong to feel that way – I smoked a truckload of dope and drank an ocean of tequila to deny it. But the longing wouldn't go away.

19. Boom

Still, neither of us wanted to drop what we were doing and become full-time killers. That would have been tawdry. We chose to continue to profess to be the pacifists we were, and never did confess that secret desire to go out and kill people for the hell of it, even to each other.

So we went back to what we'd been doing with growing success, which was breaking into the offices of companies that worked with or showed even a smidgeon of support for PIVOT, trashing them, taking every valuable item on the premises, and leaving graphic POW signatures.

In these operations, it seemed that an underlying lust for more risk – more 'action' – as I put it to myself, started to manifest. By unspoken agreement, we started overstaying the schedule, strolling out slow and arrogant, and virtually begging to be challenged, but nothing ever happened. It was frustrating, in a way, because as fun as those burglary jobs were, they no longer delivered the blast of furious emotion that they used to, and we were hungry for a new rush. But with every new gamble with our safety and freedom we came up winners, which was in a way a loss – of restraint and care.

Meanwhile, PIVOT had been talking up recent unrest in Venezuela, and we got bogged down in a lot of boring but necessary online work to combat that. The President of Venezuela had announced that she was planning to buy as much gold as she could, with a view to building up enough of a stockpile to kick-start a gold-backed South American currency. Wall Street had been artificially keeping the price of gold down to protect the US petrodollar, so Madame President was getting a bargain, and she knew it.

This course of action was very dangerous indeed – the last person to even mention trying something like that had been Libya's Gaddafi, prompting NATO and the US to murder him and destroy the country back in 2011.

Madame President's plan clearly annoyed the shit out of the Military Industrial Complex oligarchs in charge of US foreign policy; they thought it very cheeky. So they spent a lot of time and effort spreading the story that the President was stealing all that gold for herself, and starving the poor peasants yet again. She did a lot of starving, did the President.

We put in a lot of effort into refuting that story in social media, writing blogs and so on, and while it was interesting to an extent, and absolutely vital because we were up against the corporate media, it lacked that carnal kick that we had become addicted to. As the rhetoric heated up, we got more bogged down, and even when we did get to burglarise and destroy, it seemed to bring less of an emotional payoff.

Just when it seemed that we might have to bust out and do something stupid, like stage another armed robbery for the fun of it, an opportunity popped up to do something different. Something on a grander scale. Something dangerous and therefore fun.

Nevin came home from work one day with some news. He'd been editing an interview that one of the reporters at his work had conducted with a bright, earnest-faced young thing representing Americans for Venezuelan Democracy, the unfortunate initialism for which was A4VD. This was a newish NGO, an offshoot of PIVOT staffed by eager youth who were indoctrinated and paid by their ultimate masters, the CIA, through the now ubiquitous National Endowment for Democracy. One of the founders of the NED, a charming and recklessly candid individual named Alan Weinstein, had once admitted that 'A lot of what we do was done 25 years ago covertly by the CIA.'

The sweet young thing in the video, all breezy smiles and transparent innocence, had been interviewed at a warehouse in Teterboro, New Jersey, next to the airport there. She explained that they were putting together cargo for a 'humanitarian mission' to Caracas, which would be used to help the poor democratic protestors being brutally treated by the filthy socialist government, while in the background similarly bright-eyed staffers packed t-shirts and flags into a box. The fact that those 'poor democratic protestors' were being paid to be there by the same people that trained them in civil disruption seemed to have escaped her.

Anyway, the important thing for us was that we had a new target.

'Okay, they probably have boxes of t-shirts, flags, flares, first aid kits, food packs, bottles for Molotov cocktails with wicks, batons, slingshots, Nuland brand cookies and all the other stuff necessary to mount a "peaceful" protest,' said Abby at the meeting she called to discuss a strike on the warehouse.

'So we go in there and ruin as much of it as we can, set off fire sprinklers and extinguishers, tear things open and smash as much as we can. Just our usual mayhem, probably without too much opportunity to liberate redeemable items. Unless anybody wants an A4VD t-shirt?' She cast a mischievous eye around the room and smirked. 'Didn't think so. Okay, tonight we'll do a drive-by just to check on the security arrangements, and tomorrow is go day.'

We all nodded, and the meeting broke for refreshments. Just our kind of meeting, really – short, to the point and culminating in booze. Although we didn't take too much liquid relaxation on-board because we wanted to be sharp for the reconnaissance mission to Teterboro, we managed to get a little buzz on. At about ten, Bev, Abby and I squeezed into the front seat of the van together and drove over to Jersey. We were using the GPS coordinates Nevin had downloaded from the hard drive on the camera used in the interview, and without them we would never have picked the A4VD warehouse. It was unmarked, unremarkable and identical to the row of such facilities all around it, in a commercial and industrial precinct that was deserted at that time of night.

The West Commercial Avenue property was in complete darkness and there was no sign of any security presence. We went past and parked a half a block further down, then walked back towards the warehouse, acting as if we were looking for something we'd dropped on the road. Not that there was anyone to watch us. At the actual site, Bevan ran over and got a closer look, and found a tiny plate that marked it as an A4VD facility. Bingo. Just to be sure, he knocked heavily on the door – he had an excuse at the ready about having broken down – but there came no answer.

On our way home, the discussion centred on the lack of security at the site.

'There can't be much worth anything in there if they have no security,' said Bev. He wasn't arguing against the raid, just wondering what we would get out of it.

'Who would want all that propaganda and protest stuff?' I said.

'Doesn't matter if it's cheap, valuable or priceless. We take what we want and we burn it down,' Abby said. There was a smouldering fire in her voice and I had no doubt she meant it.

'Burn it down?'

'The job here is not to find stuff that makes money; it's to stop that shit from getting to Caracas,' she said. 'Set them back and make them realise we're playing for keeps.'

'Whew,' Bev whistled. 'You sure got hard, Abbs.'

'My friend got shot in front of me, my best friend got shot

at and had a gun pulled on her, and these fuckers are planning to subvert democracy and steal a whole population's birthright. You're damn fucking right I'm hard,' Abby said.

'Well, I guess we better take some incendiary material along tomorrow night,' I said as cheerfully as I could. I didn't like seeing Abby so dark, although I could understand her motivation, and suddenly I had an itching to see that whole place in flames. Maybe that would give me the high I needed.

Bevan grinned a little to himself and said nothing.

There was no more partying that night. When we got home it was late, and Lucas and Nevin had passed out in front of another repeat of *24*, the television show that did more to normalise and promote torture than any other before or since. We switched off the TV and went off to bed. Sleep was difficult, not because I wasn't tired but because Abby was a bit restless and squirming all over the bed in her efforts to find slumber. I almost kicked her out and made her sleep on her sofa bed, but that would have been mean.

We slept in and didn't go to college the next day. This was unusual, as we'd been fairly conscientious about college through all of our nefarious activities, and clung on to it for the sense of normality and routine that it brought to our lives. The tension grew throughout the day as we prepared to try yet another new avenue of criminality.

The array of burglary and vandalism-related tools that we'd assembled as a result of the jobs we'd carried out in preceding months was quite impressive. Almost every time we'd raided a workshop, office, storage depot, printing house, art framer or simple merchant, we'd walked away with at least one item that we didn't intend to hock, but to keep for future use ourselves. These included several crowbars, a couple of handheld blowtorches (from a jeweller), hammers, handy metal spikes, a set of bolt-cutters (why on earth a small law office, the practice of a PIVOT apologist, would need these was anyone's guess), a couple of cordless drills, and several other types of hand tools.

We had a relatively quiet 'family' dinner in which Abby went over the plan, the hygiene requirements and associated regulations such as 'no phones', which she reiterated to Nevin probably one more time than was absolutely necessary. Then Bevan walked off to get the van, which was parked about half a mile away. He would put on the phony plates and come around to pick us up in Devoe Street, where we would be waiting with bags carrying the necessary tools.

A little after eleven, we were on our way, pumped to be doing something so massively destructive and physically challenging. As we drove, each of us silently went over the parts we had to play. The order of events was that Lucas and Nevin, in their first major role together, would break into the place through the front door, just lever it open with a crowbar, find the distribution box and cut off the electricity to foil any cameras. There was always a possibility that there would be battery backup for some cameras, so disguises were to be maintained at all times, and any cameras seen were to be smashed. Incidentally, as a special, ironic tribute to A4VD's intention to distribute anti-government t-shirts, we would each wear a new t-shirt (to be burned after use) from a batch we'd had made by Anonyprint. They all had the same message front and back – 'Humanitarian my ass!'– in case any camera should record our work. This is what a surfeit of cash – the proceeds of the Venezuelan robbery – does to an operation like ours: makes it just a little bit bloated and self-parodying.

Anyway, once inside and with the electricity shut off, the boys were to open the roller door and Bev would drive right inside. With the door closed behind us, we would all switch on headlight torches and start working our way through the shipment intended for the Caracas protestors. After all crates had been opened, contents appropriated, disabled or destroyed, and havoc played, we would set a large pile of material alight in the middle of the warehouse floor and get the hell out of there.

The area around the warehouse was deserted, and although every now and then we could hear the buzz of the planes taking off or landing at nearby Teterboro Airport, the silence remained otherwise unbroken. The break-in proceeded without a hitch and the power went off as planned, only to be briefly switched on again because the roller door was electric. But this was a minor hiccup, and with the van inside and the door closed behind it, the power was taken down again, and we set to work. I was to take care of the office, a small area at the front of the building, my jobs being to locate and disable or destroy the surveillance system and the telephone system, find the cashbox and seize the contents, and confiscate any items that might be of use or saleable.

I set to work while Abby supervised the opening of crates and the tearing open of packaging. Given that we were inside the building with the door closed and the area was generally free of traffic at that time of night, we'd set a generous time limit of ten minutes' activity, with a further two minutes to clear out. My work in the office was completed within four minutes – I'd become exceedingly efficient at find and destroy missions – so I was back out on the floor in under five. Using the torchlight on my head, I could see that there were boxes strewn all over the place – their former contents containing plenty of flammable material, I noted with satisfaction – and a sense of chaotic disorder had taken over. It was all looking very agreeable. But my colleagues, the slackers, were clustered around a large timber box, maybe four feet high and eight feet per side. Their heads were bobbing up and down and the beams of their torches were playing on the inside of the box, as if they were conducting some sort of light beam sword fight in there, and they were all whispering excitedly.

I threw my loot in the back of the van and went over to join them so I could see what was inside the magic box.

'What do you think of this, Jayney?' said Abby. I followed the line of her torch beam, and inside the box, for a second, all I could see was more timber boxes. But when I read the labels on the boxes, I could see what had grabbed their attention: these were boxes of semiautomatic rifles, AR-15s to be exact, plus flash grenades, ammunition and boxes of potassium nitrate. Potassium nitrate – the primary ingredient in explosives? What the fuck kind of protest were they planning down there?

'Holy snapping duckshit,' I whispered. 'What do we do with this?'

'We take as much of it as we can carry, and we burn the rest,' said Abby. 'AR-15s and ammunition first boys. Go!'

The boys leaped into action, and in five minutes had the back of the van piled with ten AR-15s, as many large boxes of ammunition, and a couple of boxes of flash grenades. Given that we had no idea what to do with the potassium nitrate, we decided we should probably leave it behind. It should make a spectacular contribution to the ensuing conflagration, anyway, so we placed cartons of the stuff around to spread the damage.

While the boys were thus engaged, Abby and I made a huge pile of paper, cardboard, cloth and packing crate timber in the middle of the floor and poured an explosive volume of gasoline, which we'd brought with us, on the pile. There hadn't been any Molotov cocktail bottles or wicks, but we'd brought a bottle we could use, just in case. Abby tore the POW t-shirt she'd had on over her sweater up to make a wick, and we put the last of the gasoline into the bottle.

Ten minutes was gone, and it was time for us to be gone too. Lucas ran to the power box and switched it on to open the door, and Nevin and Bevan and I tore off our POW shirts and threw them on top of the pile before getting in the van. Lucas chucked his on the pile on the way past, threw himself into the crowded back of the van, and Bevan got us going. As Bevan backed out, Abby lit the Molotov cocktail and, running to the door, lobbed it at the pile. I had no idea she could throw that far or that straight, but she got it spot on, and in a millisecond a prodigious detonation of flame erupted from the pile, blinding us all. Abby was almost knocked over by the shockwave, but she managed to keep her feet, and the second Bevan stopped she was hauling herself into the front seat, her face reflecting the orange glow from the colossal inferno that was quickly engulfing the warehouse. It was a shame that we had to get out of there as quickly as we did; I am sure I was not the only one who would have loved to have feasted on the sight of the flames and basked in the deliciously devastating explosions that were sure to rock the site.

As we drove off down the street, the first of the boxes of potassium nitrate went off with a booming blast that shook the van and probably woke up everyone in a fifty-mile radius. It was glorious, and personally very uplifting. We were back on 17 heading for the Lincoln Tunnel, watching the fierce red orange in the sky east of us, when we saw a fleet of emergency vehicles heading the other way. The mood was victorious, the memory of that titanic explosion and fire something that lives in me still. It was so bright, so loud, so overwhelmingly destructive and so palpably *our* achievement that we were all radiant with pride and bursting with energy and excitement.

And the haul. The artillery we'd so serendipitously stumbled upon in our quest to thwart the protest! Our minds were collectively blown, our wildest dreams exceeded. We were stunned, saturated with joy and swollen with conceit, even while we professed disgust that the supplies for a 'peaceful protest' should consist of such lethal weaponry. We were convinced we could do anything we wanted to, including imbibe near-lethal quantities of tetrahydrocannabinols and alcohol in celebration, which we planned to do that night.

But after spending two hard, filthy hours making space in the basement, cleaning it out and carefully storing our precious arsenal, all wrapped in blankets against the dampness, we were too washed out to even think about it. We were grimy, drained by the experience of the night, and after handling all those weapons, comprehensively aware of the gravity of our situation.

Abby and I were the ones who spent most of the time in that foul-smelling pit, cleaning and preparing the space for the guns and other toys of destruction, so we had time to talk while the boys shuffled in and out with small loads – out with rubbish and expendable items, in with ordnance. They brought the guns in one at a time, wrapped in blankets, on the premise that little armloads might look less threatening to any nosy neighbours, but we needn't have worried; we were left unwatched and unmolested.

As we worked, I wondered out loud why there hadn't been more protection for that toxic cargo of guns, ammunition and explosives. Surely such a valuable and dangerous stash merited a detail of armed guards? As always, Abby had already divined the answer.

'Sweetie, it's easy,' she said. 'Protecting that warehouse would only arouse suspicion about its contents, and by extension the activities of the so-called Americans for Venezuelan Democracy. Who would post armed guards at a warehouse full of Nuland cookies and t-shirts? They counted on the sheer ordinariness of the site and the goods supposedly stored there to provide all the protection they needed. They even went on TV and talked about t-shirts and humanitarian stuff. Shit nobody wants.'

There was no question as to whether POW could claim the job. Liberating a magnificent trove of weapons that could, in a pinch, make Devoe Street an impregnable stronghold, was the gravest of crimes. If we were to admit to POW involvement it would serve only to redouble the authorities' efforts to track us down, and they might even get so serious about it as to make some headway.

There was also the small matter of the devastating fire and series of sizeable explosions that had woken up half of Jersey, emptied out numerous fire stations and caused several million dollars' worth of damage as well as temporarily shutting down Teterboro Airport. Best to adopt a more understated approach: take to social media and innocently speculate as to how the benign contents of a humanitarian shipment could cause such a notable inferno.

The media had been on the scene almost as quickly as the emergency services – several television stations kept crews on alert at the airport in case there should be some sort of juicy disaster there – and they were all on hand to record the impressive results of the last of the explosives igniting. The audience-grabbing, entertaining nature of the vision meant that it was replayed endlessly for a couple of days on all local stations, and the story went viral across the internet. Human beings love nothing more than to watch things blowing up.

While the video footage was comprehensive, the reporting was not. No mention was made of the weapons that had been stored in the warehouse – to do so would have been to expose A4VD as a fomenter of violence – and consequently, neither was it mentioned that a portion of the arsenal had gone missing. The official story was that an electrical fault had started the fire, and the explosions had been caused by gas cylinders destined for homeless shelters in Caracas, and paint cans to be used in repairing damage caused by marauding government troops bent on destroying peoples' homes and property as well as their lives. It was all a load of unmitigated bullshit, but instructive of the way the government and the media worked together in such matters.

Deciding that even to 'innocently' inquire about the origins of the vast explosions that rocked the entire suburb could mark us as possible perpetrators, we kept reluctantly silent on the whole episode. We had achieved our purpose – to stymie the bloodshed they had intended to export along with ugly clothing and inedible food packs – so we enjoyed our victory without sharing it with the rest of the world. Shame, because we would have relished the notoriety.

Meanwhile, the war of words over Venezuela continued to heat up, and our Teterboro accomplishment had taught us, if we needed further confirmation, that our friends at PIVOT and their undoubted covert government supporters meant deadly business. We worked harder than ever to uncover and refute their plans, and of course we needed to plot our next escalation. Killing people and blowing things up had proven so stimulating that we needed to find a new outlet for our growing thirst for anarchy.

20. Bang bang

After all that work in the basement, I slept the sleep of the just and didn't wake until quite late the next morning. My dreams had all been fire and glory, and I awoke feeling rested, strong and just a little bit smug. We'd shown those fuckers!

I opened my eyes to find Abby sitting on the bed staring at me. But wait, was it Abby? The long blonde locks were gone, and in their place was ferociously short-cropped hair, coloured almost blue-black. The effect was stunning; her blue eyes stood out like clear Swiss-blue beacons, and her features had some-how suddenly taken on a startling chiselled, angular clarity. It was like she was a different person, and I blinked at her for several seconds.

'So, you're the evil twin,' I said at last. And she laughed, and the laugh and the brilliant white teeth and the way she tossed her head, as though all that hair was still there, was all the same Abby.

'You like it?' she said.

'I love it.' That girl could look gorgeous in a gunny sack with a face-full of mud and a head covered with thatch.

She threw herself at me and we hugged.

'I love you, Jayney,' she said.

'I love you, too, Abby,' I said. 'But why are we having this conversation now?'

'I've been thinking...' she tailed off.

I must have let out a little groan, because she instantly changed her mood and jumped up.

'Sorry, sweetie,' she said. 'I know you just woke up. I'll tell you what I've been thinking later – for now I'll get you a coffee.' And with that she bounded out of the room.

Because I'd slept so late, we were up against it to get to college in time, and once we were on the road and on the subway, she seemed disinclined to talk. Oh, we had our usual girly chat about inconsequential stuff, but there had always been an unspoken rule between us that we never discussed serious matters unless we had absolute privacy. So we prattled about the day's classes, passed judgement on the dress sense, tonsorial inadequacies and other physical peculiarities of the people sharing the train with us, and got creeped out by the number of males staring at Abby. Her fresh 'do had certainly given her face an amazing new frame, and it had not gone unnoticed.

It wasn't until that night, when we were in the lounge with all of our house boys, drinking beer slowly and without much enthusiasm, watching the news of our blazing adventure, that Abby finally gave voice to her thoughts. And she didn't just talk to me about it; she convened an unofficial house meeting by launching into an obviously planned speech.

'I think we can all agree that last night was an outstanding success,' she began, to much nodding and clunking of beer bottles. 'We killed a clandestine plan to launch a dirty attack on the government and the people of Venezuela by the scum at PIVOT and their deep state supporters. And not only that, we did it in such a spectacular, public way that it couldn't be ignored. Sure, they lied about what really happened, but we know, and we know what we got out of it. Which was probably the biggest orgasm any of us have had this week, am I right?'

We laughed.

'Anyway, the point is, we got a huge buzz out of it and we did some good. And you know why?' She didn't wait for an answer, because we all looked blank anyway. 'Because we played their game against them. We turned their own tools of annihilation against them. Hoist them with their own petard, quite literally. Boom!'

More laughter.

'Look,' she began again. 'The people who plan and send others off to these wars, one of the reasons they do it is because they are so removed from the consequences. There's no "boom" or "bang" in their cosy little worlds. All the shitty, bloody, destructive stuff happens miles – preferably hemispheres – away from their large, comfy offices and their ridiculously luxurious homes. They don't see blood and pain; they see neat little packages stored in grubby old suburbs, which get shipped off to other places where strangers get blown up and blood gets splashed around. It's all very neat and not in the least distressing. Last night, we gave them a taste of what it means to be less removed from the war zone. They saw their plans and their money going up in giant clouds of flame and smoke, a lot closer to their pampered lives than they're used to. It must have given them a bit of a fright.

'Well, I think we need to take the reality of what they do away from the realm of the purely theoretical, and into the midst of their snug suburban existences. Remove the insulation that makes it so easy for them to ignore the reality of war. If we take it to them, if we make them live the horror of war up close – even just a tiny snapshot rather than the whole disgusting, degrading, terrifying experience – it may open their eyes to the destruction they are bringing to untold, unknown victims.'

'What are you talking about, Abby?' said Lucas. I noticed that his eyes were shining, and although my mind was already rebelling at the idea of what I thought she was putting forward, my guts were tied up in a knot of anticipation and hope that she meant what she said.

'I'm talking about stepping it up,' she said. 'We've wrecked their offices and stolen their computers, and that doesn't even slow them down. Now we have to make it personal.'

'We have to hurt them,' said Bevan. I wondered if he and Abby had already discussed this. I guessed he was the one who'd clipped her hair while I slept that morning; it all made sense, and it was all very cosy.

'But we're pacifists,' said Nevin weakly. I was thinking the same, but I wasn't even going to bother bringing it up. I already knew Abby's answer to that, and while I only half agreed with her, there was a deep lust inside me to ignore philosophical objections and go with the sensual indulgence of inflicting pain and violence.

Abby trotted out the same reasoning we'd talked about earlier, about how choosing to compromise our principles in the name of something more important made us heroes rather than hypocrites. She made a reasonably convincing argument about being committed to stopping war rather than eschewing the use of force itself, particularly as force was the only thing the enemy understands. She reiterated the need, in this case, to use the enemy's own weapons against him. To make the enemy know what it's like to be the victim and to have naked fear, pitiless, searing pain and ugly, chaotic death descend on them and the ones they love at what feel like random moments. Compelling them to experience war, she said, was the only thing that would make them renounce it.

The boys didn't take much convincing. In fact, there appeared to be an impatient enthusiasm among all three of them to get their hands on the deadly toys downstairs and start playing Rambo.

'So let's hurt,' said Nevin. His voice had a savagery I hadn't seen in him at any time in the many months we'd all been together. Lucas – uptight, prissy, self-righteous and aloof Lucas, was almost frothing at the mouth.

'Easy up, killers,' said Abby. 'We need to be disciplined about this, or the only people who'll get hurt will be us. Have either of you ever handled a gun, let alone a semiautomatic?'

This slowed the boys down. Bevan sat back and put his put his hands behind his head a little too complacently. Abby shot him a look.

'I know you've at least fired off a few rounds, big boy,' she said, 'but we're not talking about a .22 calibre here. And we're not talking about knocking a bottle off a fence or missing a running rabbit. So listen. None of us knows anything about those things we've got in our basement, and we need to train in their use without anyone ever finding out. So how are we going to do that?'

'Google?' This was Nevin.

'YouTube?' I said.

'YouTube,' Abby echoed. 'And Google, accessed via Speakeasy,' she added, slinging a sly grin at Nevin. 'We watch, we learn, we practice and we practice some more. We download manuals and we find out how those things work, how they come apart and how they get put back together, how to keep them clean and how to stop them from breaking, jamming or blowing up. We become so familiar with them we're like that idiot in Jarhead, practically wedded to them. Understand?'

'This is my rifle. There are many like it, but this one is mine. My rifle is my best friend. I must master it as I master my life...' intoned all three of the boys together, barely containing their excitement.

'Okay, okay, I get it,' said Abby. She was spluttering a bit because she was trying to stifle a laugh. 'You understand.'

For the next couple of weeks, we all diligently studied and practiced. We fondled and played with our rifles, cleaned them and yes, dismantled and reassembled them until we could do it like experts. Never in under four minutes and certainly not with blindfolds on, though – we weren't fanatics, right?

The drills all took place down in our basement, which we made homelier by putting more light down there, adding furniture we could actually sit on, and generally tidying up.

It was a unifying time for us, because we shared a common goal, and we were all serious about achieving it. There was co-operation, respect for our commander and her lieutenant – Bevan, not me – and also for the instruments of destruction we held and loved.

Along with the physical training – those things are heavy and ungainly and it took a long time for us to become handy with them, able to swing them around and to do things like run up and downstairs with them confidently and capably, and then to have them ready to fire in less than a second – Abby maintained a steady diet of political indoctrination. Over and over again she stressed the inhuman callousness of the 'animals' we would be targeting: their indifference to the bloodshed, devastation and agony their actions caused, the cruel remoteness from reality with which they insulated themselves, and the cold calculation they unthinkingly applied to the lives of real, innocent human beings.

'These people, these targets, they're not innocent,' she would say. 'They're not even humans, really, when you think about it. What sort of a human being would target someone for bloody death or dismemberment simply for the money in their pocket or the oil under their feet? A monster. A bestial oxygen thief with no thought for anyone other than themselves. That's not us, and you know it isn't,' she said emphatically. 'We're engaging in this war reluctantly, out of need rather than desire, because they don't engage in it at all, they just cause it and they profit from it but they never experience it. They're inhuman but we – we're heroes. Champions of the innocent and scourge of the evil and the uncaring.'

She really did use words like that, and we ate them up. We studied the lives of the kinds of people we would be targeting, and we hated them more and more every day. They were indulgent, insensitive, arrogant, entitled, discourteous to their underlings and dismissive of their victims. All they cared about was plotting to get their own way, and mowing down anyone who stood in their path.

The new president of PIVOT, Ruben Vega, was a grossly overweight gluttonous pig of a man who perfectly embodied the disconnect between the ruling classes and the average person. His fingers were wreathed in gold rings, his huge suits were exquisitely tailored of the finest materials, and his shoes alone cost more than most Venezuelans make in a month. He hung out with other super-rich parasites whose wealth came from the hard work of his poor countrymen. His family had owned vast agricultural and manufacturing properties for generations, exporting pork (how very apt) and coffee to the United States, and making cheap, shitty shoes and dirty-to-make items like tyres. He lived in New York City during the spring and fall, commuted from the Hamptons through summer, and spent at least part of every winter in the mountains of Austria or Switzerland. The one place he never went was Venezuela; his purpose was to rape it, not to visit it. He had no idea of the hardship his exploitation caused.

Vega was married to a former model (aren't they all?) and was occasionally seen disinterestedly dragging around a couple of fat, clueless kids who had no doubt inherited his disdain for the source of their wealth.

Another target was Arthur Scarde, a massive contributor to PIVOT who owned a Wall Street vulture hedge fund. His specialty was identifying struggling South American companies and governments, buying their debt cheaply and then screwing them out of much more than the original debt was worth. He had more or less bankrupted a number of towns and cities in Venezuela, along with countless other victims across the continent. As a result of his devious manoeuvres and dodgy dealings, he owned (that is, had virtually stolen) a huge portfolio of assets across South America, including a large number of sweatshops. He was a loathsome, unabashed predator, a financial psychopath who destroyed people and lived for the sheer amusement of it, and who thought nothing of spending a million dollars to arm a death squad to bleed a village or state until it did his bidding. Mr Scarde was neither married nor apparently attached, but travelled with a retinue of very young, mostly hairless men with shiny skin and downcast looks, and there were rumours that he harboured a catalogue of revolting proclivities that made the dour demeanour of his travelling companions understandable, if not their willingness to remain with him.

Others complicit in the planned appropriation of the entire sovereign country of Venezuela through the actions, deceits and criminality of US NGOs, covert agencies and military actions included senators and congressmen, lawyers, financiers, and a ghastly host of representatives of the military-industrial complex who knew exactly which weapons would exact the most horrific toll on targeted populations. Plus of course journalists and other public figures who misinformed, disinformed and straight out lied to the somnambulant public. We knew who a lot of them were and where quite a lot of them worked and lived, and we came to regard them – well, most of them – as unworthy of remaining part of the human race. Some we eliminated from our kill list because we could see that they acted under duress or out of misplaced loyalty or ignorance, but many of them we convicted in our private court of opinion as being shameless purveyors of evil, illness, poverty and death.

Before we could shoot anyone, we had to go out and shoot at nothing, so we did that one midweek day at the height of summer. Bevan knew a wilderness place some way from the city, so we piled food, drinks, a couple of picnic blankets, a box of dope cookies, an AR-15 wrapped in a towel and some ammo into the van, and off we went. We did the normal picnic thing out there in the boondocks for a while, just to make sure we were truly alone and that no one would come upon us down our dirt trail.

Commandant Abby was strict: no intoxicants until after the live firing exercise. So after a good, healthy lunch and a tense, interminable quiet period listening out for coming cars, trucks, drones, choppers or troopers on horseback – a little paranoia can be a wonderful preservative at times – we busted out the firearm, or 'the piece' as Nevin and Lucas insisted on calling it.

We each took turns firing it just a few times, to get a handle on the recoil, the noise and the feel of an operational weapon. First a few single shots, then a couple of faster volleys, squeezing off six, seven or ten rounds in a single burst. It was intimidating, exhilarating and arousing to feel that prodigious weapon in your hands. To know that you were letting loose a little slug of hot lead that would close the gap between you and your target at around 975 metres per second.

A little later we set up a couple of empty bottles and cans on a rock and took a few shots, just to prove to ourselves that we were so inaccurate we would probably never even injure anyone, let alone kill them. It was fun and instructive, and we all got better at it, even though we didn't stay at it for long because Bevan thought we should conserve ammunition. Accuracy was improved by holding the rifle up and sighting along the barrel, but that was also a good way to get a bruised shoulder and maybe a black eye if your grip wasn't tight enough, so most of the time we held it down just above waist level. That made us feel like outlaws anyway, so that's the way we worked it.

Having made a hell of a racket and even destroyed a couple of bottles and cans, we made short work of the dope cookies and got back into the van. Bevan, bless him, stayed straight, and had to listen to our increasingly incoherent drivel on the long, surprisingly less uncomfortable drive back to Devoe Street. By the time we got there we were in high spirits, and had also consumed a couple of six-packs of beer, so we got the party started properly, and Bevan went off to work. Because he was the only remotely composed one among us, he put the gun away before he left. He really was a trooper.

It was time, then, to put the next phase of our plan into action: to purposely go out and assassinate someone. I say assassinate, because what we intended was not, and I believe this very strongly even now, murder. The men who were our targets were combatants in every sense of the word. That they planned and started their wars in the expectation that they would remain isolated from the battle itself was not our concern – far from it. Even more than the cannon fodder they sent to kill and die on their behalf, they were fair game, and we aimed to teach them that.

Now that we were equipped like an army, we found out what every army knows – it's difficult for even a small, heavily armed squad to do their work inconspicuously. If we were to attempt any operations with all five of us swaggering in wielding AR-15s like some junior Schwarzeneggers, our potential victims would likely see us coming from a mile away. It was in no way practical in the city, although it would be less impractical in the suburbs, where we hoped to do some of our finest work. But we had to hone our skills first.

So the first operation was a covert action, featuring the 'A' team – Abby, Bevan and your humble correspondent, using our handguns. And the target was our old friend Alvarez Elitto. He had earned the honour by being such a public crybaby over our generous remodelling of his office. His pouty, petulant pity party made him pathetic in our eyes, and he had made far too many pointed remarks about how we should be hunted down and shot to let him get away with it. We decided to illustrate to him the gruesome reality of hunting down and shooting someone.

Actually, we didn't even hunt him down. We simply went and knocked on the door of his plush Village apartment, and when he opened the door, Bevan popped him off. Bev got the gig because he was the only one of the three of us not to have made his bones – there's that crude gangster vocabulary again – and he acquitted himself beautifully. Before Elitto knew what was going on, he was wearing three bullet holes, his hallway was delightfully spattered with blood and parts of his anatomy, and we were making a swift getaway. It was so easy it was laughable – and as we exited the building and strolled casually down Ninth Street, laugh is what we did. How could we not? The stern, admonishing look on his face when he opened the door and saw us there, the indignant surprise when he saw the gun, the comical squelching of his organs that could be heard in the silence immediately after the popping report of the weapon, and the hilariously melancholic look in his eyes when he crumpled down onto the floor – like he'd just lost a valuable commission rather than his life – was too humorous to be true. He died like the entitled bourgeois snob that he was, and we found it gut-bustingly funny. Raucously, carelessly, triumphantly, we cackled and shrieked our way to a bar, where we sat and had a hand-steadier.

Whether no one heard or no one cared, we couldn't tell, but it seemed that none of Elitto's neighbours took the trouble to call in any help for quite some time. It was twenty minutes or so before we heard a siren go whizzing past. We laughed again and had another drink. Job done.

This time, POW claimed the credit. Oh boy, did we claim the credit. We couldn't wait to let the world know that we'd taken the gloves off. More than anything, we wanted the assholes who thought that they could prosecute wars without ever seeing a speck of blood know that their cocoon was being broken wide open. We wanted them to be shocked and afraid, and we wanted them to wonder if we were coming for them.

If I hadn't already known it – let's face it, the thug in the car was an accident and as unexpected for me as it was for him – I learned that night that assassination is easy and fun. If you hate the person enough, and you've convinced yourself that he deserves to die, his death is a lark. A spit in the eye and a punch on the arm, as if to say, 'gotcha', with a wink and a giggle.

I also learned that you don't even have to be the one pulling the trigger to get the benefit out of killing. It's almost enough just to be there, to watch and enjoy the show without the attendant stress of thinking, 'What if I miss? What if he has a gun and he shoots back?' You get to see it from a different angle, and it seems to take more time, which extends the entertainment of it all.

If circumstances had been otherwise, I would naturally have loved to have been the one taking the shot. Nothing beats that. The surge of supremacy that seizes your every cell and electrifies your mind when you pull the trigger is like nothing else. Seriously, I recommend that everyone should kill someone at least once in their lives. Good luck stopping at one, though. Once you figure out how agreeable it is, how very therapeutic it is to see another die in their own goo and gore, and to know that you've rid the world of a nasty bacterium, you'll want to do it again and again. Pretty soon, everyone that annoys you will be lined up in your imaginary sights, and you'll fantasise about sending them to the hell they deserve for doing something as minor as taking your parking space.

I must go on, but before I do, one more thing. It's a bit personal, a bit embarrassing, but here goes. I found out that night that a killer is a sexy, sexy being. The kill itself is one of those whole of body experiences that kind of echoes an orgasm, and as a spectator one comes away wanting terribly to have boisterous, brutish sex with the perpetrator – in this case our dear Bev. I could just about have jumped his bones when we were walking down the street, and that's one of the reasons I needed those drinks in that bar, to settle down my quivering need. Which was only partially successful.

I know that Abby felt it too, because that night she threw Bev another bone, so to speak, and while they were moaning and carrying on in the next room, I was masturbating myself to a feverish climax. For a little while, I considered bursting in there and turning Bev's accomplishment into what probably would have been his lifelong dream, but I stayed where I was. I didn't need awkward conversations afterwards. Where Abby can just get up and carry on as if nothing has happened, I get weird and my weirdness somehow transmits to the other party, and the whole thing gets creepier and creepier the further it is in the past. I've been known to ruin great friendships that way.

Maybe that's why I've been celibate for so long; I just don't need the shit my own mind does to me, and I often have trouble facing the people I've slept with. Does that make me odd?

Anyway, I digress, and the big moment is upon us.

21. Beach party

Oh, wait. Before I get onto what happened at Ruben Vega's place, I should fill you in on the reaction to the assassination of Alvarez Elitto. This marked a pretty major departure from our previous stance, in which we admitted that we'd regrettably been compelled to wreak a little havoc here and there, to break a few things and to make a bit of a mess in order to press our point, but had steadfastly maintained that we were against killing or even hurting anyone.

You already know our philosophical rationale for turning into cold-blooded executioners – the business about bringing the war home to the warmakers – so I won't replay it for you. It was, however, very well received by our community. Not one word of admonishment was raised against us by our own. Rather, they cheered us for at last adopting the enemy's tactics against him, praised us for ridding the world of that preening deadshit Elitto, and encouraged us to expand our operations in that direction. I began to wonder whether any of our supporters had ever really been pacifists at all. They took to the idea of killing and death with astonishing alacrity – almost as easily as we did.

The opposition, of course, had a few bad things to say about us. They called us hypocrites and murderers and all those other offensive terms, but we laughed publicly and unashamedly in their faces. We dug deep into our arsenal of annoying axioms, tossing out epigrams like, 'there's the biter bit' and 'sauce for the goose is sauce for the gander'. Abby's favourite, 'hoist with his own petard', got another run, and we told them straight out that they should expect more, not less, terror (and clichés) from us. It infuriated them, which was terrific, and boosted our profile tremendously. We were a genuine force to be reckoned with at last, and even though the bastards that ran PIVOT and its supporters in and out of government never even looked like backing off from their plan to invade Venezuela and steal its riches, there was a growing awareness of their evil. Along with an increasing tolerance, or at least understanding, of ours.

We wanted to strike again quickly to maintain momentum, but we had to wait at least a week or two to allow our ally, complacency, to sneak back into the lives of our suddenly jittery foe. This was frustrating, because all of a sudden, our adversaries were making rapid inroads in their own program.

The Teterboro arson had inconvenienced PIVOT and friends a bit, but they quickly recovered and got a new 'care' package full of humanitarian armaments down to Caracas. The 'protests' had now become vicious riots, and all the violence was being blamed on the government and police force. It was said that the paid protestors and agents provocateurs using the goodies from the new shipment of nasty stuff were simply defending themselves, even though proof, which never quite made it to the mainstream media, continually emerged of their actions triggering the trouble.

In the midst of all this, somehow the Teterboro job became seamlessly transformed from being portrayed as an accidental gas and paint explosion to being characterised as an act of terror carried out by 'covert pro-government' forces who had made their way from Venezuela to blow up a warehouse supposedly full of t-shirts and first aid kits. Without so much as a blush over changing their story so radically, the media morphed the former accident into an international act of war, and much of the public bought it wholesale. This irritated the fuck out of us because our act of resistance and assistance had been turned against the people we were trying to assist.

Yet again, our president had declared Venezuela a national threat, and spoke of creating a 'no-fly zone' over it, or perhaps even sending troops there to 'restore order'. Like she would be doing the people there a favour by bombing and shooting them. This invasion would be conducted under executive order, so there would be no need for Congress to interrupt its usual work – debating the acceptability of what people do in the privacy of their own homes or with their own bodies, and passing laws to eliminate the last vestiges of privacy.

We spent a week or two furiously condemning the actions, plans of PIVOT and its partners in war crime, warning our readers that yet another Nuremberg-level war crime was being planned. But it felt weak and ineffectual, and we were getting very itchy trigger fingers.

In my mind and in my heart, the lust for death had taken root. The idea of shooting people, exploding their heads and busting open their guts, was always on my mind, and at times it was like a physical need. I'm sure Abby felt that way too, and as we plotted our next job we became increasingly keyed up.

Lucas and Nevin, who thus far had been shielded from any real action – they'd been on the scene when I shot the bagman from the restaurant job, and had been shot at by that security guard, but they had yet to take a shot in anger themselves – were champing at the bit. True to Chekov's formula, we'd introduced those AR-15s to the boys in a previous act, and now it was time to make them go off. They wanted blood, and there was only one place we all wanted it to come from. We had to strike at the heart of PIVOT.

Our next target could only be the exceedingly rich and egregiously ugly Ruben Vega – Arky Zenstl's replacement and the new president of the organisation. This little piggy had a little more of the veneer of respectability than the previous incumbent: he was at least nominally Venezuelan, and it had been a long time since the Vega family had soiled their hands doing something as grubby as using a second-rate restaurant to launder cash. Vega was a one percenter all the way, and he lived the life associated with that tiny group of bloodsuckers. This made researching how to kill him all the easier.

Nevin got hold of a copy of the episode of *Lifestyles of the Nauseatingly Wealthy*, or whatever it was called, where they had profiled Vega and his horribly skinny, Botoxed-to-bejesus wife. The main focus of the program was the Vegas' mega mansion in the Hamptons. The producers had even thoughtfully pinned the house location on Google Earth for the star-struck viewers, presumably on the assumption that none of them would ever see the Hamptons, let alone be able to locate the house. Just half an hour's viewing told us where this pig-pen was, and what times of the year the head hog himself could be expected to be there. We also learned that he loved to entertain on hot Friday evenings, and that a crowd of his closest hangers on and their associated pimples would flock to these hyperindulgent soirées. Honestly, could these vain dolts make it any easier? It was like they'd sent us an invitation. We made a decision to attend one of Ruben's do's and liven it up a touch.

We made up a couple of very cheap looking signs that said Sagg Security to camouflage the van, which Bevan brought around to our front door in Devoe Street so we could load up the semiautomatics. We wrapped them in towels and blankets and took them out at intervals, along with what we called our diversionary surprise. I kept watch the whole time to ensure that no one was lurking to see what was going on or, worse, casing the van with a view to making off with it.

We all dressed in newly purchased black clothing – from the secondhand store as usual – put ski masks in our pockets, and at about 9 p.m. crowded excitedly into the van for the long, uncomfortable drive to the Hamptons. On the drive, Abby reiterated the plan over and over, and we each repeated our understanding of the parts we had to play. The mood was serious but there was an undercurrent of exhilaration. We were all stretched like piano wire; taut and fine, and ready to cut through anything that got in our way.

Bevan drove sedately, we talked quietly, and the journey seemed to take forever. At a quiet point on the Montauk Highway we stopped and Abby fixed the crude decoy signs to the sides of the van while we stifled giggles inside. As the van crept down Ocean Road to Surfside Drive in serene Sagaponack, Abby issued final instructions.

'There is certain to be additional security on-site following the demise of the late, unlamented Mr Elitto. So the first thing, we deal with them. There may be a few of them stationed around the property, and they need to be eliminated quietly. Bevan and I will take care of that, and it may take some time. You need to wait patiently and quietly in the van. Weapons at the ready, safeties on until you exit the van; it wouldn't be a good look if one of you shot each other up just getting out. Bev or I will signal you when it's go time, and you know what to do – silent as cats through the sand dune scrub to the beach; Jayney on the northern end, then Lucas, Nevin, Bevan and me, just outside the light from the deck. On the signal, we all step into the light and open fire. You wait until that signal from me. Our primary target, Mr Vega, must be front and centre in the line of fire, and we all concentrate our fire on him to start with. Once he is confirmed down, spread that lead, ladies. Lay 'em all down. No witnesses.'

We nodded, scared, pumped and ready. The plan was beautiful in its simplicity.

'Remember, the United States government designates every military age male in a blast zone radius as a combatant when they bomb gatherings like this in other countries. These people are all combatants, and they deserve to die. There may be one or two innocents among them – collateral damage, as it were, but that's part of the point of this exercise. We need to show these fuckers that in a war, innocent people get fucked up, too. Ready?'

We all nodded again, wide-eyed and straining to get into action. I could almost smell the blood and hear the screams, and it was delicious. I had to put those electrifying images out of my mind – I needed to concentrate.

Bevan parked the van at the very end of Surfside Drive; it was fortunate for us that the Vega house was the last one on the long drive, and where the road ended, a sandy track to the beach began. There were no other lights on anywhere but the Vega house, where true to tradition a noisy party seemed to be in full swing. There was a gatehouse in which two squint-eyed guards were riveted to their phones, but no sign of any other security. The driveway was littered with Bentleys, Porsches, Maseratis and Mercedes Benz sports models, but there was no activity going on there – everything seemed to be focused on the ocean side of the house, as we'd guessed it would be.

Bev and Abby got out of the van, and as she approached the gatehouse I could see the glitter of polished steel in her hand: the blade of a long knife reflecting, in pointed shards, what little light there was. They didn't put their ski masks on – that would have been a dead giveaway to the guards – but sauntered up casually, as if they thought they were expected.

We couldn't see what happened, but Abby and Bev explained it to us later in sweetly sickening detail. Abbs had gone in first and was pretty much inside the gatehouse before either of those dimwits even looked up from their glowing screens. I can just imagine it – they look up and there is this sexy, sinuous woman with short, close-cropped black hair and diamond eyes slinking towards them like Lara Croft. They must have thought their games had come to life before them.

'Can I help you?' asked one.

'I'm here to relieve you,' Abby answered coolly.

'What do you mean?' said the guard, still unsuspecting and puffing himself up to look manly for the babe.

'I mean this,' said Abby. She lunged at the guy and sank her blade into his neck all the way up to the hilt. He never had a chance to utter even a sound but for the soft gurgling that came from his throat. Before number two could react, Bevan's strong hands were around his throat and his neck had been snapped like a twig.

A quick look around showed that there were no CCTV screens and no walkie-talkies around, which suggested fairly strongly that there were no other guards around the place. Still, to be sure, they dragged the two bodies all the way into the gatehouse – the encounter had begun in the doorway – closed the door, then conducted a covert tour of the property's perimeter. They found no guards and no security measures, just dumb bunnies drinking up a storm and listening to bad jazz.

They came back to the van and silently signalled to the three of us in the back of the vehicle. Cramped and dying of tension, we all filed out. As noiselessly as we could, we walked down the sandy track to the beach and set up our diversionary surprise. When that was done, we lined up in the prearranged order, weapons at the ready.

There were a few glamorous gluttons drinking, dancing and chatting on the deck overlooking the sea, but a lot of the guests were inside the house behind a wall of glass. The night sea air was a trifle chilly, I guess, although under my ski mask I had begun to feel hot, and my breathing was constricted.

At a nod from Abby, Bev got the distraction going, setting off a pile of fireworks that boomed and lit up the sky in a series of gorgeous colours and starbursts. On cue, the guests started rushing out of the house onto the deck to watch the dazzling display. The grossly rotund figure of Ruben Vega, clad in an expensive tuxedo that hugged his ball-like figure, pushed to the front of the crowd, his pudgy hand gripping that of his emaciated wife. He looked at her in pleased surprise, and she returned the look, each obviously thinking that the other had organised the display. It was a touching last moment.

Abby waved, and we stepped out of the shadows – in truth, the glow of the fireworks should have given our positions away but those dumb fucks were too dim to look anywhere but up – and in a beautifully choreographed movement we lifted our guns and started shooting for all we were worth. The fireworks kept exploding, and heads and hearts were suddenly bursting and erupting on the deck too, in a cacophony of splendorous booms, bangs and thuds. Vega was riddled with bullets in less than a second, almost cut in half, so we waved our guns around like we were watering the garden, spreading death and mayhem everywhere. Each of us had a thirty-round clip in our AR-15, and when all that lead had blasted through bodies and heads and windows and walls, we all very professionally and calmly reloaded with a second magazine of the same size, and started shooting again. The whole process took well under a minute, but it felt more like an hour, and it engulfed my whole life. My past, my present, my future were all joined together and I was the universe. It was sublime. It was pure, artistic, graceful and magnificent.

Then, one by one, the guns fell silent, and although a few fireworks still shot up into the air and bathed the scene in eerie blue, green and red light, the comparative silence was suddenly deafening, and my ears rang like a thousand bells. I was spell-bound by the exquisite annihilation we had wrought. Then the sounds of moans and cries started filtering through, and I was back in my body, looking at the carnage. There was blood and human detritus everywhere, broken glass and shattered lives, the sounds of deepest horror coming from the mangled and confused survivors.

I turned my head and looked at Abby. She was waving me away, and the boys were already on the move. I ran into the darkness, leaving that consummate hell behind me and struggling to contain the blind revelry in my soul. It was the high point of my life. An overpowering achievement and an irresistible experience. God, I wish I could do it again tonight. If every person could just once feel that control, that raw domination over existence... I know, I've said this all before, but this was the peak, the most transcendent feeling of them all, the superlative moment of my entire existence. I tried to get that sublime image out of my head and concentrate on running through the soft sand. We had to get away!

There had, of course, been people who had not come out onto the deck in the house – some guests and the service staff – but their thoughts were not with us. The last thing they wanted to do was to see or in any way deal with us. They were rushing around in helpless shock, trying to revive the dead and comfort the mutilated, slipping in the lakes of blood and gore, no doubt adding to the slapstick of the scene. So we got back in the van and drove off down the road, doffing ski masks and staring in blank joy at each other in the blurry dark of the van. There was no traffic on Surfside Drive or even on Ocean Road, and before we knew it we were back on Montauk Highway without encountering a single witness.

It was then that the hollering, the hugging and the back-slapping began, although it seemed to me that in the back of the van, at least, it was a little forced. I hadn't watched Nevin and Lucas during the shooting, but later, I heard that they both acted as automatons, and Lucas at least testified that he had been horrified by what he had done, and that he was sure Nevin had felt the same.

That night, I guessed the enormity of what we had done was on their minds. This was no graffiti job, or even a good old-fashioned robbery. This was industrial scale killing. Slaughter most primeval, most palpable and three dimensional. Even as we drove through the night, there were survivors trying to come to grips with the unadulterated violence and terror that we had dealt them. People who had watched loved ones cut to pieces by bullets, their guts and brains spread all over the deck, what they'd had for lunch mingling with what used to hold their thoughts and dreams and memories. People who would be crippled and broken for the rest of their lives by what we had done, for no other reason than that they had accepted an invitation to have cocktails with a fat man and his skinny wife.

I had to banish from my thoughts the idea that some of our victims may not have been to blame. They were all guilty by association, if not directly accused, like Arthur Scarde, who we later found was among the victims. For the rest, well they were happy to partake in the spoils of Ruben Vega's war, so why shouldn't they suffer its consequences?

In the back of the van, after the initial outburst, Lucas and Nevin went quiet and seemed shaken. Once the adrenaline wore off, I could see that they were frightened and appalled at what they had done. In the front, Abby and Bevan were as chirpy as primary school kids, chatting away with innocent happiness and laughing at everything. I wasn't quite tuned in, but I gathered that they were congratulating each other for their performance in the hand to hand combat phase of the operation, in which they had despatched the security guards with cruel enthusiasm. Later, Abby said to me, 'Jayney, you have to look them in the eyes when you're killing them. That's the ultimate high. The otherwise unreachable pinnacle.'

'I don't know, Abbs,' I said. 'I'm not sure there's anything that could top the feeling of just standing there with a semi-automatic cutting people down like twigs. It's so fundamental, so satisfyingly predatory.'

'Just wait; one day you'll look someone in the eyes as you kill them,' she said. 'Then you'll know.'

I thought of the wheel man around the corner from Arky Zenstl's restaurant. For a millisecond, we'd looked into each other's eyes, but in that instant I could see that he thought he was going to kill me, and frankly, I thought so, too. So I was seeing it from the reverse angle that Abby was talking about, I guess. He'd thought he was looking into the eyes of his victim, and he was not going to show any mercy. That was what had helped me pull the trigger.

Bevan pulled off the road in a quiet, dark spot out by the Shinnecock Hills Golf Club so Abby could get our silly little signs off the side of the van and retrieve the fake licence plates. When Abby got back in the cab, she was grave.

'The back number plate is missing,' she said. Her voice was as taut as her face.

'Shit,' said Bevan.

It was the first breach of hygiene we'd ever had, and it was potentially a serious one. We were all quiet for a long time, but eventually Abby – who else? – broke the gloom.

'It's probably somewhere on the highway,' she said. 'They'll never connect it to Vega's house or to us.'

'You're right, Abby,' I said. 'What are the chances it fell off on Surfside?' I was trying to make light of it, but I could tell I sounded scared.

'Nah, wouldn't have happened,' said Bev. 'Remember we hit that bump around Amityville on the way in? Probably fell off there.'

'Yeah, right,' agreed Abby.

'Should we go back and look for it?' asked Lucas, his voice tremulous.

'No.' Abby was short, definite. 'That would be worse. Just forget about it, and we'll go home. We've got a bit of work to do, getting these weapons inside, cleaning them and storing them. Don't worry about the plate; it's a fake anyway.'

But worrying about the plate was exactly what we were all doing.

22. 'Not right? How so?'

By the time the guns were cleaned and stashed, the clothes and props destroyed, and our work finally done for the night, it was well into the early morning. Nobody felt like having a drink, and we were all strangely quiet. Perhaps it was just tiredness, maybe it was the missing licence plate, and possibly it was the knowledge that POW had fully, irretrievably entered the war by committing what many would quite reasonably call an outrage.

Abby didn't come to bed with me; she went with Bevan. Of all of us, they seemed the least affected by the magnitude of what we'd done. They were obviously worried about the licence plate, but they were clearly happy with what they had done and with each other.

I wasn't jealous. I was too tired for that, and I could see how they had bonded over their shared kills. Good luck to both of them, I thought wearily as my head hit the pillow.

By the time I emerged late-ish next morning, the story had taken over the media, as was to be expected. All the television channels were covering the attack without a break, and there was near universal condemnation of our act of 'terrorism'. The storm of disgust at the killing of these people – every one of whom was deemed by the media and commentators to be an absolutely innocent victim – was almost comical.

Abby was livid. 'Fucking innocent?' she fumed. 'There's no way that fat, lying, thieving warmonger or any of his friends were innocent. And if they were, then that would be the point anyway – people have to learn that innocents die in war too. In fact, they're the fucking main victims!'

So she went onto our POW social media and pointed out that we had, reluctantly, been given no option but to bring the horrors of war home to those who would make it happen in faraway lands. We didn't want to kill, you understand, but we had to. And if there was unfortunate collateral damage, well, that was one of the unavoidable costs of war that those who champion it are forever telling us is worth it. She said it was funny how they changed their tune when it was them, their families and friends on the receiving end.

We lost some followers out of it, and gained some as well, some of them possibly not the kind that we actively sought. Oddly, a lot of veterans were on our side. They thought it was about time that the warmakers got the salty taste of blood in mouths usually filled with caviar and champagne, and tears in eyes more accustomed to glowing at the number of zeroes on their bank statements.

We were front page news worldwide, roundly detested as abominable terrorists. While it was infuriating that the over-whelming majority refused to see the very point that we were trying to make, it was also kind of cool. We were mad, bad and dangerous to know, and there was a certain amount of cachet that went with that. So we plied our side of the story as widely as we could and hoped that someone, somewhere, got it. I'm pretty sure the schemers at PIVOT understood our message – we rammed home to them the notion that as long as they planned war on Venezuela, they would have one in America.

On the home front, things weren't going quite as Abby would have liked. We were all stalked by the fear of exposure thanks to the lost licence plate, and acutely aware of the penalties we would now face if we were caught. Lucas and Nevin were also less than impressed with Abby and Bevan's new arrangement. I think both of them knew they'd never stood a chance with Abby, but while she wasn't attached to anyone but me there was still always the possibility, however remote, that one day she would wake up, see one of them as her true love and run to him with open arms. It's remarkable how powerful and persistent a delusion can be among men. They really are such children.

Three days after the Surfside Massacre, as the media tagged it – everything needs a catchy title – Lucas and Nevin crept into the front room, where Abby and I were chilling in front of the television, watching the last of the dwindling coverage. Outrage and compassion have very short use-by dates, and even the media could see that tears over a bunch of indulgent parasites who pretty much got what they deserved wouldn't play well to the plebs for long.

'Abby, we need to talk,' began Nevin in an uncertain tone. Lucas looked sheepish, and his eyes darted around the room, no doubt checking for Bevan's shadow, even though the big guy was off at work. Here it comes, I thought. Abby looked unsurprised but mildly annoyed, as though she'd been waiting for it but dealing with it was still distasteful.

'Ah.'

'Lucas and I, we don't want to do this anymore. POW, I mean,' said Nevin. Lucas studied the flyspecks on the wall, and Nevin, having glanced at Abby, searched for imaginary dirt on his fingernails.

'Oh?' Abby affected concerned dismay. 'Truly? Is there any particular reason why?'

'It's, well, it's not right, Abbs,' said Nevin. There was a note of hope in his voice; he hadn't expected her to be so reasonable. Poor sap: he should have known it was a trap.

'Not right? How so?' She was still sweetness itself, but I could see that the fuse was burning down quickly. I suspect Lucas could, too, but he didn't make any moves to help his hapless friend.

'Well, the killing. It's just not us. It's too much.'

'Too much?' said Abby, beginning to get a little warmth in her voice. 'Too much?' she said again. 'And it's not too much for the United States to be sending guns and bombs down to Venezuela to kill little kids? It's not too much for our friends at PIVOT to be planning to rape an entire country? It's not too much for you chickenshit motherfuckers to spend your days and nights playing at war, but when the fucking moment of truth comes, when you need to stand up and be counted, when you need to have the courage of your convictions, then it's too much? Christ all fucking mighty!' She had detonated properly at last. 'This is not a game. It's not one of those things where you have a safe word, and you can say it and the bad stuff stops. This is a fucking war, and you're already in it. You don't get to just pull out and go home. You stay till we win or die!'

'But Abby, it's not right.'

'Of course it's not right!' She was shrieking now. 'It's hard and repulsive and dangerous and grim. Because it's a fucking war! And now it's all too hard for you soft-hearted dears, you've decided you want to desert. Well you know what we do to deserters in this country? We shoot them. And make no mistake, I will fucking shoot you. You know far too much, and you're the kind of weak-minded dipshits who'd piss your pants and spill the beans at the first hard question. So you stay the course, or I fucking kill you now.'

She was wild-eyed, in mortal earnest and as agitated as I have ever seen her. The boys were completely terrorised; they knew she meant every word.

'Here's the deal,' she said more calmly. 'No more weapons. No more killing for you namby-pamby pussy boys. You're strictly support. You get to watch while the real heroes do the work, and you get to keep your prissy little hands clean. You gutless shits: every single night you sit here and watch your fucking cop shows and your war shows and your torture shows and you love it, but then when it comes to the real thing you don't have the stomach for it. Fine; you can do it all vicariously for the rest of your days, and never go near another weapon or pull a true revolutionary act. See if I fucking care.

'But I swear, you put a single foot wrong, you look sideways at the wrong time, I will mow you down with an AR-15. And if you ever, ever breathe a word about quitting again, or if you just happen to forget to come home one night and run to your mammies, I will hunt you down and I won't even do you the kindness of shooting you. I'll cut your fucking throats. Understood?'

Tears were standing in Lucas' eyes, and Nevin was literally cowering and shaking.

'Understood?' thundered Abby.

'Understood,' they both mumbled to the floor.

'Now get the fuck out of here.'

They shuffled up the stairs as fast as their trembling legs would carry them. I was stunned, but I kept my composure. Abby had become something I couldn't really recognise. But then again, I was also disgusted at the boys. I was appalled that they could be so cowardly and weak as to want to opt out now that it was actually getting properly exciting. Abby was right – all their lives they'd been seduced by the violence and carnage on their television screens, but when it all got real, it frightened and overwhelmed them. I felt a little bit sorry for them, but I also backed Abby. I just wasn't sure that she had a grip.

'Sorry about that, sweetie,' she said. 'I couldn't let that one slip. If we discussed it reasonably now, they'd never shut up about it. So I just needed to lay down the law. Not too over the top, was it?'

'Umm, no, Abbs. Very commanding, but very reasonable.' I was lying.

'I thought so,' she said. 'And I don't think we'll have any more trouble from them. But just in case, let's keep an eye on them. And let's keep our glocks loaded and handy, shall we?'

There was a sinister menace about her smile this time, and I knew that the chances of all of us getting out of this alive were suddenly seriously diminished. I foresaw trouble, but I had come too far to back out. Not that Abby would have let me.

If there had been tension in the house before, the next few days were traumatic. Lucas and Nevin avoided Abby, Bevan and me, and they spent a lot of time whispering in the kitchen. Abby wore it for a while, but eventually she called a house meeting.

Lucas and Nevin turned up looking vaguely defiant, but they were on time, buttoned down and subdued. Abby, her short black hair glistening and her eyes shining ice blue, was pleasant, accommodating and reasonable.

'Look, I know I was a bit hard on you the other day,' she began with a disarming smile. 'But let's put that behind us. We're all on the same side, and we've all committed some very serious crimes, so we need to stay together, and we need to trust each other. If we fracture now, someone could do something stupid and quite possibly cost all of us our lives or our freedom. We don't want that, do we?'

'Of course not, Abby,' said Nevin. He was the braver of the two. 'And that's not what we meant the other day...'

'I know you didn't,' she replied. Her smile seemed frozen on her face, and for that reason it was all the more frightening. 'And it's quite possible that I overreacted. But you must understand, we've come so far together that any talk of dissent or discord makes me very nervous. We've got to have each other's backs.'

'But we don't think killing people is the right way,' said Lucas. I was impressed by his gumption.

'I know it's hard,' said Abby. 'I don't want to kill people any more than you do.'

'Liar,' I thought to myself. I couldn't wait to kill someone else, and I was certain she felt the same way.

'But somehow, we found ourselves in this war, and we can't just walk away from it,' she said. 'If we do, they will kill thousands and thousands of innocent people. I know it seems counterintuitive, but if we kill a few bad people, we save a lot of good, or at least a lot of innocent, people.'

Lucas took a breath as if he was about to say something, but stayed silent.

'How about this,' said Abby. 'For the time being, we put a moratorium on killing? Hmmmm? We go back to burglary and all the other fun stuff, but we won't hurt anyone, okay? I really want us all to be friends again.'

This cheered the boys up a little bit, although I could see they weren't truly convinced – but they were truly cornered. And despite the niceness that was now pervading the room, the threats that Abby had issued a few days previously still hung in the air like a blood red cloud.

'Hey!' Abby said suddenly, as if struck by a new thought. 'Diego has some excellent buds. How about Jayney and me go down to the bodega and score some weed and beer, and we just forget about all this shit?'

I leaped out of my chair and threw a huge grin at the boys.

'I think that's a great idea, Abbs,' I said. 'I think we could all use a break from POW, and put these disruptive arguments behind us.'

'Agreed,' said Bev. He had, as usual, been a silent spectator with an inscrutable expression. I am sure he was aware that jealousy over his intimacy with Abby – irregular as it was – was behind at least some of the antagonism, and he was keen to smooth things over.

'Sure,' said Nevin. He nudged Lucas, who nodded.

On the way to the bodega, Abby said to me, 'If those two fuck things up, I will kill them.'

'Oh, I know you will,' I said with a wary sideways glance. She looked magnificent, and terrifying.

When we got back with booze and drugs, Bevan had gone off to work, and we had a cosy party of four. Abby lavished attention, praise and affection on Nevin and Lucas, even throwing in a couple of trivial criticisms of Bev, and of course the boys lapped it up. In half an hour she had them laughing and cooching up to her, vying for her responses and generally being clueless boys. She was on fire, flashing her eyes, hunching her shoulders to make her boobs look bigger in that awfully tight sweater, licking her lips often and slowly, and lightly touching them on the arm when she was talking to them, or stroking cheeks, or mussing hair. Once or twice she forgot her own hair had been cropped short, and tried to throw it back or to gather it up in a ponytail. The boys didn't notice this, but I quietly thought it hilarious. More than once, she rolled her eyes at me as if to emphasise how easy it was to manipulate them, and I chuckled and joined in the fun.

For a few weeks, we kept our POW activity to a dull minimum, just working the social media, pushing out blog posts and looking for easy targets for some boredom-reducing vandalism and theft. Abby made contact with the producers of the Tanner French television show, hoping to once again appear as Eirene and explain why we'd killed and maimed all those people, but they weren't interested. The feeling was that they might be seen to be condoning terrorism, and even though Abby suggested that she submit to hostile questioning, they declined. It was good to know we were dangerous enough to completely avoid, and we took the rejection with cheerful insouciance. It was worth a shot.

Then, one day at college we signed up to a short course in which a guest lecturer was to deliver three lectures on 'the impact of modern war'. And that gave us the idea for our next operation. It would be risky, exciting and new, so it ticked all our boxes, but nobody would be badly injured, maimed or killed in its execution. At least, we didn't think so.

23. Stockholm

The deal was this. Richard White was a journalist or, rather, a cowardly stenographer for the government. A cheerleader for multiple wars and a veteran of none, the closest White had ever come to seeing action was arguing over a cab on Eighth Avenue. The reality of war was as far removed from his experience as the reality of hunger. Or integrity, for that matter.

He was one of an ever-widening group of 'journalists' who were privileged to be the mouthpieces for various anonymous officials – the kind who lay the allegations on with a trowel and back them up with evidence you couldn't find under a scanning electron microscope. No government spook ever told him anything he didn't believe, and questioning his sources was naturally out of the question. The way he looked at it, if he didn't explicitly trust and print everything he was told, no matter how deeply it offended credibility or ignored actuality, his nameless, faceless informants might withdraw the privilege of spreading their bullshit to the world. It wouldn't be more than a passing nuisance for them to find another willing puppet up whose ass they could stick their hands, all the way to the elbow. So rather than risk losing their confidence, he wrote whatever fiction they told him to write.

We knew White's history well. He'd parroted a colourful array of lies and accusations over the years, and he could be relied on to wave the flag for every planned action, incursion, invasion or 'humanitarian intervention'. Before the attack on Iran, he had penned a series that went into convincing depth on the country's nuclear program. He'd named names, cited geographic locations, exhaustively listed the components and materials that were stored in these locations, right down to the numbers on the doors of each building, and stated categorically that his sources were unimpeachable.

When, following the invasion of Iran, not even one of these locations was found to house anything like the stuff he'd guaranteed was there – in fact it became obvious that not one of his stories had contained a single shred of truth – and as the attack became a quagmire (funnily enough, the Iranians had suspected an assault was in the works when the US and NATO had signed an agreement with them in 2015, and had prepared accordingly), he was unabashed.

'It was the best intelligence we had at the time,' he said. Shame he never thought to ask even a single probing question or check a single one of the 'facts' fed to him by government shadows.

In the run up to the US instigated Potato Revolution and subsequent flirtation with nuclear war on Russia, White had led the chorus of government shills accusing the Russian government of running massive concentration camps where dissidents were tortured, beaten and enslaved. After the failure of the revolution, the world learned that these facilities were refugee camps where hundreds of thousands of Ukrainians who'd fled following the complete collapse of that country's economy (thanks to a US sponsored fascist coup back in 2014), were housed, fed and clothed by the Russians. White's newspaper never retracted its wild allegations about concentration camps, and still referred to the neo-Nazi-backed totalitarian government in Kiev as 'the legitimate government' – even as Ukrainian security forces tightened their grip so hard it began to look like our own police state.

At the time he came to deliver the first of his three-lecture series to our history class, White had for some time been the media poster boy for the campaign to demonise the democratically elected government in Caracas. White and his confederates were peddling a story that government death squads were roaming the Venezuelan countryside, shooting, hanging, gassing and bombing any brave freedom-lover who dared to stand up for the poor, marginalised capitalists and those friends of the people, the oil companies.

In reality, the complete opposite was true: there were death squads, but they had been bought, paid for, armed and trained by the CIA, and they were making a bloody mess of anyone who voiced support for the government. The trouble was that support was so widespread and vociferous, these CIA plants didn't know who to kill next. The thing was turning into a bloodbath that was getting more and more difficult to hide. And yet, the perpetrators remained absolutely deadpan as they blamed the government for their wetwork, and sang the old familiar refrain of the need for a humanitarian bombing.

We hated Richard White, everyone like him and every-thing they stood for. So we decided to make friends with him.

The idea was simple, and deliciously diabolical in intent. We would kidnap Mr White and ensconce him in our base-ment, and over a period of a week or three – hell, why not a couple of months? – *Stockholm* him. That is, induce *Stockholm* syndrome in him and turn him to our way of thinking, then set him loose. He would be a celebrity; as a freed hostage, he would be all over the media, and the establishment wouldn't know what to do with him when he started speaking against them. His inside knowledge on how the grand deception works would be invaluable, and his turncoat status would create talking points that could drag out for weeks or months.

Of course, during that first lecture – sadly, he missed his subsequent dates – White spoke a lot of drivel. Although the topic was the impact of modern war, what he actually did was try to sell us on the administration's most recent and current wars by painting a picture of a world that inexplicably hated the United States, and needed to be taught to love us through the frequent and lavish use of ordnance. The role of the media in 'shaping the truth' (yes, he actually used those words, which I found distasteful – as if the truth could be shaped) was of course of vital importance, and working closely with the administration etc. etc. etc. blah blah blah. The whole thing was one giant emetic concocted of lies, self-deception and unbelievable conceit. He was nothing but a con artist, and a self-satisfied, delusional one at that.

Sitting in the front row, Abby and I appeared to lap it up. She, in particular, was shameless in her giddy appreciation of everything White said. Acting as though every word was a pearl of wisdom she must carefully gather so she could create a string of glittering White truths, she made copious notes, looked up at him adoringly as often as she could, and constantly adopted the beatific expression of one in the midst of an epiphany.

At the end of the lecture, we hit on White like giggling groupies, and Abby mercilessly stroked his ego while patting his arm and batting her lashes. He bought the whole farcical performance eagerly, strutting and preening like a peacock.

'I just think the way you invent the truth … it's so masterful,' she burbled as he grinned. 'It's like you don't even need to fact-check; you just know all this stuff.' He wasn't listening to her actual words; he was so taken with her pawing and gushing obeisance he assumed she was complimenting him.

'It's no wonder all those government types trust you to deliver their stories,' she said. 'You do it with such imagination. You're wonderfully creative, you know.'

I had to keep my mouth shut or I would've laughed out loud, but I couldn't compete with Abby's catty compliments anyway. She was beautifully backhanded.

He lapped it up, that lying sack of shit, and even though he wore a wedding ring, he was obviously getting all worked up by Abby's physical approach. Typical – a scumbag in one area of life is so often a douchebag in every other.

'I'd love to pick your brains some more,' said Abby. She was actually running her fingers though his hair. *I'd love to pick your brains too*, I thought – *off our basement floor in a dustpan*.

'Can we meet, somewhere away from all this?'

He didn't even have to think about it. Before she'd finished the sentence, he was nodding and saying that getting together would be a marvellous idea.

'Hellsinki on Ninth, in Hell's Kitchen,' she said. 'Do you know it?'

'No, I don't, but I'll find it,' he said.

'It's a little bit punky,' Abby cooed. 'A little bit dive bar. Perfect for someone like you.'

'I'll be there at eight tomorrow night.'

'I can't wait,' said Abby. With a suggestive twinkle in her eye, she rubbed half her body up against him yet again.

He was delirious. Unwillingly and apologetically, he extricated himself from her grasp and slithered away. Only when he was well out of the room and couldn't possibly see or hear us did Abby break character.

'What a cunt,' she said. She was so right. Neither of us ever really used that word, but in this case, there was no other that would do the job. I looked forward to breaking him.

That night, we shared the Stockholm plan with Lucas and Nevin. Bev was already onboard – he and Abby had obviously discussed it in one of their private moments, which I'd noted were becoming fewer and further between. I guessed that the sexual fire ignited by acts of extreme violence would need further stoking if it was to be fanned to its former ardour. Most nights, Abby was back with me, a return I accepted with a superior inward smile.

Lucas and Nevin, predictably, did not embrace the idea with enthusiasm, but neither did they object. Abby explained that this was a way of turning the tide of public opinion back in our favour, that it didn't involve any but the most low-level force, that it was a newsworthy event that we could capitalise on and, crucially, that they didn't have to dirty their pretty little hands – she and I would work the whole operation.

Things had been much more temperate and less fractious in recent weeks, so there was little of the remnant tension that had characterised the early days after the beach party. But I could see that the boys were still nervous, and they were afraid that if they objected, or even questioned the plan, Abby would turn on them with the ferocity she'd shown after the Surfside job. And they did not want to be on the receiving end of that again. They agreed to the plan and shuffled off to mope some more. I'm sure they were relieved they wouldn't have to take any active part in it, and with luck wouldn't even see the prisoner when he was transferred to our cellar for re-education.

The idea of kidnapping Richard White had awakened my sense of adventure and got my trigger finger itching again. I wanted action, and I wanted to see blood. I hoped we would get into a situation where we would have to defend ourselves while the abduction was being carried out, just so I could shoot someone. Preferably Richard White. I really wanted to hurt him.

Steamy late summer heat rose from the street in Hell's Kitchen, and there were a lot of people around at eight the next night. We parked in West Forty-Fourth Street, and Bev and I waited in the van while Abby went to meet with her beau.

'I hope she doesn't go too far,' Bev said as Abby sashayed down the street in a tight pair of black jeans and what appeared to be a painted-on t-shirt. I couldn't tell precisely what he meant, whether going too far meant fucking Richard White or killing him, but I assumed he would much rather she kill the bastard. He was so sweet.

The atmosphere between us was kind of awkward and our conversation stilted. Neither of us wanted to talk about what was on both our minds – Abby and him, Abby and me, and where we both stood in relation to that – so we sat in strangely companionable, watchful silence.

It was funny, the way Bev had changed. Since he'd become strong, self-sufficient and better at everything – even better looking – he'd become less open. That old goofy over-enthusiasm had disappeared, and in its place was this enigmatic coolness that made him more profound, but less accessible. I missed the old Bev, and for a short few minutes in the van, the awkwardness between us brought a shade of him back. I've already confessed to a brief moment or three in which I entertained the idea of having sex with Bev, so you know I was periodically susceptible to his developing charms, but right then, in the back of the van, he was just my old and brotherly friend, and I wished we could talk to each other without the spectre of Abby between us. Even though that spectre was what brought the old him back, and probably the old me as well. I'm not sure I'm making sense here, but I'm being as honest as I can. Try to understand: we had a bond and a barrier between us, and Abby was both.

Looking back over what I now think of as the POW Progression, I can see how it all evolved, and how the quest for new levels of stimulation led to some instances of excess. I can easily see how I was consumed by bloodlust, how Abby – I am being as candid as I can here – turned into a bit of a psychopath, and how Lucas and Nevin had their romantic ideals of violence, as nurtured by TV, films and games, violated by the animal reality of it all. But I can't trace the change in Bev, at least not the mental change, because I have no idea what he was thinking, what motivated him or why he did any of what he did. As we all became more of what had been lurking inside us, he became less. We transformed into amplifications and distortions of what we were underneath, but he seemed to shrink and become more shadowy, like he had a mirror, but it darkened and reflected less and less.

Anyway, I am rambling. Luckily for Bev, and for you, Abby and White weren't long inside Hellsinki. They'd met on the street and gone in for a drink, but before the cocktail glasses had sat on the bar long enough to create condensation rings, they were out again.

'I'm so glad you came to meet me, Richard,' Abby had murmured in that husky undertone of hers.

'Dick,' he said.

'Dick,' she repeated. 'Funny, that's exactly what I want in my mouth right now.' She could be saucy when she wanted to.

'Where?' He was not new to this game.

'My van, outside. Now.'

He'd almost fallen off his stool in anticipation. So in a matter of minutes they were striding towards the van, she in front with an evil grin and he behind looking like a dog about to be given a bone. Abby threw the door open and stood back.

'Get in,' she commanded, and he was swift to comply.

As he did so, I coldcocked him on the head with the butt of my pistol, and he slumped to the floor like the sack of shit he was. We dragged his body in, and hauled ass out of there. Less than a block down the road, Abby had reached a gloved hand into his jacket, found his cell phone and tossed it out the window. They wouldn't be finding him that way. And it was doubtful that he'd told anybody where he was going, seeing as how he was a married man on his way to initiate an illicit affair.

Pulling up in Devoe Street, Bev double-parked out the front of our house, and we wrangled the still inert form of Mr Richard White out onto the road. In spite of our promises that they'd be hands-off on this crime, I'd called Nevin, and he and Lucas were there to help. They got in grabbed Dick White, and dragged him into the house while Abby and I loudly talked about how we didn't know how our friend had got so drunk so quickly. Bev sped off to park the van elsewhere.

By the time White woke up, he was tied to a chair secured to a brick pillar in our basement. Abby and I were watching him, waiting for him to regain consciousness. It took a long time, so it may be that I'd hit him a bit too hard with my pistol. Oops.

When he did open his eyes, he was groggy; it was clear that his head hurt even though we had cleaned up the blood that had been spilled, and dressed the wound. If he hadn't been the cause of much, much worse violence happening to thousands of innocent people, I may even have felt sorry for him.

'Oh, sorry,' said Abby as he began to focus a little bit, a confused wrinkle on his brow. 'Did I forget to give you a head job?' Her tone was sugary, and she affected a little girly pose, which I think only confused him more. He wasn't quite with it, and I guessed it could be a day or two before we would get a lot of sense out of him.

After her syrupy start, Abby turned suddenly feral. 'You fucking idiot! As if I would ever go near you, you repulsive reptilian slime.' She slapped him hard on the face. 'That's for your wife, you fucker.'

White hung his head and said nothing for a while. What could he say? At last he lifted his head and looked Abby in the eye. I gave him points for bravery, and also for stupidity. She was not in the sort of mood where it was safe to challenge her.

'Why am I here?'

Abby reverted to sweetness. If she was playing the role of a med-less schizophrenic, she was doing a stand-up job.

'You're here to help us,' she said with the solicitousness of a nurse comforting a patient. 'We're going to teach you how to be a real human being, and you're going to go back into the world and use your position to teach others the same thing.'

'Oh, god,' White said. I couldn't tell if it was relief that he wasn't going to be killed, or derision at the plan.

'Have you heard of the Stockholm syndrome?' Abby asked, fondling his face gently. He groaned. 'Well over the next few weeks, you're going to become its next victim. Sorry, graduate. We are going to be so nice to you, and sometimes so nasty to you, just to keep you on your toes, that by the end of our time together, you'll be devoted to us both, and you'll do anything to further our cause. You'll believe in it, and you'll be ready, if necessary, to die for it.'

'You're going to try and brainwash me?' His voice was laced with contempt. I thought Abby would snap again, but she remained calm.

'My dear Mr White,' she said. 'Don't for a moment think that yours is the kind of mind that will be able to resist what's coming. Your colleagues and friends at the State Department may tell you that you're some sort of superstar, but you are a weak, desiccated little man whose pathetic excuse for a brain will be putty in our hands in just a few days. And if by chance you should prove capable of resisting our conditioning, your brain will actually be paste on our walls. Understood?'

He said nothing. I think the conversation was tiring him. I made a mental note to dial back on the force next time I needed to knock someone out with a pistol butt.

'Sleep now, my pretty prey,' said Abby, stroking his cheek as his head drooped toward his chest. 'Tomorrow, we begin classes. It'll be so exciting. We'll start with all the deaths your inane jottings have helped to cause, and move on from there.'

He was dropping off as she spoke, so we started walking away, but as we got to the bottom stair out of the basement, she stopped and called loudly to him. He jerked his head up.

'Careful you don't soil yourself, Dick,' she said. 'There's a tasty punishment for that.'

We actually did have an extensive plan worked out for Richard White. A lengthy series of intensive lectures, videos that he must watch, and performances that we would carry out. These included 'good cop, bad cop' turns, 'secret' meetings in which one or the other of us would come down alone and whisper that she was falling in love with him, and that soon she would save him and they would run away together. We planned a few sly psychological tricks like doing strip shows to drive him wild, giving him massages and sponge baths, and occasionally beating him for minor transgressions.

We figured that after a couple of weeks of this regime, he would be so dependent on us that we could loosen the restraints a bit, and maybe even offer little strolls in the backyard in return for good behaviour. It was all going to be so much fun.

In that first twenty-four hours, Lucas and Nevin affected not to even know that there was a kidnap victim in the cellar. They ignored our comings and goings from the basement, acting as though it had nothing to do with them, even though we had to walk right through the lounge room to get to the basement stairs. Their reaction was correct and even helpful to an extent. It wasn't yet an avowed POW operation – that would only come out after his release – so it was all on the down-low.

Relations with the boys lacked sparkle, I guess, but there was much less of the sullen waywardness that had pervaded after the Surfside massacre, which, let's face it, had really only been a few weeks earlier. I know the way I'm recounting it makes it seem like all these things happened over a long span of time, but the reality was all very intensely packed together, and the atmosphere, interactions and affiliations could change almost hourly within those fraught, stressful days. Still, every day without a killing seemed to settle the boys more, and to make Abby and I more edgy. Bevan remained on the periphery, noncommittal as to whether he wanted to kill or didn't. He would have just done whatever Abby wanted him to, I suppose.

Anyway, Abby and I went to bed that night sober and straight, needing to be fully in possession of our faculties for the next day. The education of Richard White was to commence in earnest, and we were also working on ways of bringing Lucas and Nevin back into the fold. This involved giving them a couple of little jobs to do without any direct supervision or accompaniment. They could go out and trash a store, steal a few trinkets or bust up a couple of offices, and it would make them feel tough, useful and trusted. It seemed like a good plan, and we had high hopes for the future.

But the future never happens the way you want it to, and the next day, everything changed.

24. The end

An odd clicking sound in the backyard startled me out of a light, troubled sleep. I'd been dozing for a couple of hours, thinking about our guest downstairs. Had we been seen abducting him? Had he told anyone where he was going? Would he start screaming the house down to draw attention to us? Could Richard White be our downfall?

For the last three quarters of an hour I'd been toying with the idea of going down and putting some tape across his mouth. He'd been quiet so far, but how long could that last? Maybe he was dead? Should I go and check on him?

Then that click, or clunk, or clatter, in the backyard. Christ, what if he had slipped his moorings and gotten out? My 'nine', as I called it – the 9mm pistol I had grown inordinately fond of in the recent past – was within arm's reach of my bedside, so I grabbed it, shaking Abby with my free hand as I did so. I got out of bed.

'What?' she said. There was sleep in her eyes and but her mind was sharp. I put a finger to my lips and she stopped to listen. There was definitely something going on outside in the predawn twilight. Putting her hands swiftly on her own nine, Abby got out of bed and we crept towards the window overlooking the yard. There were several dark-suited figures sneaking around out there. Armed, dark-suited figures. Shit.

We opened the bedroom door and stepped into the hallway. Bevan was already standing there holding an AR-15, and he motioned to the back door, then to the front door.

Running to the front lounge room carrying our pistols, we instinctively split – Abby went upstairs to rouse Lucas and Nevin, and I went down to the basement to get the other guns and check on our guest. I was shaking and I had an ugly feeling of doom, but I knew I had to do what must be done. *So this is where it all ends*, I said to myself.

When I got down into the basement and switched on the light, I could see that Richard White was still securely tied to his chair, and the light shook him out of a doze. He must have had a shocking night's sleep, sitting up that way. It's strange what goes through your mind, even at a time like that. I remember thinking it was a miracle he hadn't peed his pants; he'd been down there for almost twelve hours.

He lifted his head and looked at me. I stared back and said with as much menace as I could muster, 'Keep your mouth shut.' The gun I was waving spoke more eloquently than I could.

I wondered how Bev had come and got an AR-15 and not woken White up, and asked myself how bad his concussion was. It would be a shame if I'd rendered him brain damaged and immune to conditioning. And why hadn't Bev got more guns out? I resolved to take him to task over that, once the shooting was over.

White watched me get the guns out of their stash spot, and his eyes widened. With my pistol jammed into the elastic waistband of my pyjama pants and an armload of high velocity weapons, I must have looked like a bizarrely threatening figure.

I ran up the stairs as stealthily as I could, emerging into the lounge to find Abby with the two boys, and guessed that Bevan was guarding the back door. Peeling back the curtain with visible trepidation, Abby looked out onto the street. She turned to us with horror in her eyes. She whispered that there was a large, militarised gang out there and it looked like they were preparing to mount an assault. Fuck! They hadn't come to make an arrest, but to close the case. Typical law enforcement.

Lucas and Nevin took the weapons I shoved at them with some reluctance, and I handed one to Abby. She absently flicked the safety and checked the magazine while peering out the window. The incursion seemed imminent. At that moment, an insane wailing arose from the basement. I had left the door open, and the sound of Richard White screaming shocked the hell out of all of us.

'Go down there and kill that fucker,' said Abby to me. Her lips were tight but her voice was steady.

I didn't hesitate. I put my rifle down on the couch and got my pistol back in my hands, ready to shut that bastard up for good. I was looking forward to it.

I raced down the stairs, the frantic yelling and howling that came from down there terrifying and at the same time steeling me. He stopped when he saw me and realised just how I planned to quieten him down.

'You motherfucker,' I hissed.

Instantly he began to whine and to cry. Yes, to cry like a baby. That pussy.

'Time for you to die,' I said.

'But I haven't done anything wrong.' He was sincere. And possessed of a very bad memory.

'Remember Russia?' I said. 'The concentration camps that were refugee camps? Remember Iran? The nuclear facilities that weren't, which you and your friends used to start yet another war? Remember Venezuela and the death squads you lied about?'

He was shaking his head and tears were running down his face. I think he was seriously trying to deny that any of it was his fault. He didn't plan any of it and he didn't take part, but he sold a gullible public on the 'need' for it all to happen, so he was as guilty as fucking hell as far as I was concerned.

'Remember Iraq?' I said. 'Remember the weapons of mass destruction you swore would be found on day one of the campaign, but that didn't exist? Well guess what. I found your weapon of mass destruction. It's in here.' I tapped his forehead with the barrel of my nine. 'Only this time, it's real, and I am going to deal with it.'

'Oh God please no,' he snivelled. 'My wife...'

'Your wife?' I was appalled. It riled me that he had the temerity to bring up the wife he'd been only too pleased to cheat on less than twelve hours earlier. 'You heartless, faithless, gutless motherfucker. She'll be much better off without you.'

I pulled the trigger, and in a flash his brains were a pink smear on the pillar behind him and on the wall behind that, and partially sprayed on me too. I laughed grimly at his desperate, tearfully miserable death, and for a split second I felt an echo of the surge I'd been looking for. But it wasn't as passionate and as fulfilling as I'd imagined it would be; there was something empty and even pedestrian in it, even though I'd looked into his eyes as I killed him. I knew I'd have to find a new level.

Just then, a loud, rumbling explosion shook the house, followed immediately by a second boom from a different part of the house, and then there was a crunch of splintering wood, the shriek of shattering glass, the drumroll thunder of running boots, and the popping clash of firing weapons. I ran up the stairs to enter the battle and most likely join my friends in a dashing, desperate death. I was ready, because I knew I'd never find that new level anyway. Once you get over the thrill of killing, there's nothing left.

Flash grenade smoke was filtering down the stairs, people were yelling and guns kept firing as I ran, regretting the fact that I'd left my semiautomatic upstairs – I would have preferred to come out shooting. And then, above it all, I heard Abby scream, a terrible, guttural cry of anguish and pain that rose to a desolate crescendo, then faded like a ghost, and I knew in my heart that she was gone.

My life, my soul and my joy ended with that sound, and I was left only with rage and determination. I cocked my pistol as I approached the door; at least I would take one or two of the bastards with me.

As I stepped out of the basement doorway, the butt of a very large rifle crunched my cheekbone and almost snapped my neck, and everything went black for a long time.

I never saw the carnage in our living room, the scene of so many wonderful bacchanals and boisterous celebrations, but I have heard about it often since. Abby was dead, shot through the head and chest. It was amazing that she had the strength left to utter the scream that still haunts my dreams every night.

Nevin was dead too; having faced and killed the man who'd shot Abby, he'd been cut down in a brutal storm of lead. Bevan had taken several slugs to his upper body while defending the hallway and he was injured but not too badly, considering. Lucas had somehow emerged unscathed, having been found cowering behind the couch. His gun hadn't even been fired.

Lucas cut a plea deal, and he gave away a lot of POW's secrets. We were tried separately and I have never seen either of them again. I was not allowed to see Abby's body to say goodbye, and as far as I know she was cremated without any ceremony at all, except for a couple of distraught family members standing by to make sure she was gone. Bevan is in Terre Haute, Indiana, awaiting execution, and Lucas is in Fort Leavenworth for the rest of his wretched days. So much for cutting a deal.

25. I still love you, Abby

So now what? The light went out of my life the instant Abby died, and I had already recognised that I had passed my peak as a human being, so I was ready to die that day the cops stormed the house. Those cruel fuckers cheated me of that. So I sit here waiting to die, reliving my memories and missing Abby.

I think about what happened to us, how we began with such promise and became the antithesis of what we thought we were. The answer is too easy – it's the same thing that happened to America. Violence corrupted us. I found out – as did Abby and Bev – that with violence and death come power and ascendancy and, for a while at least, a sense of satisfaction. That magnificent elevation doesn't last, but it does start a hunger for more that is never sated.

We discovered, each in our own way, that violence is sexual. It starts out being seductive, but then it becomes addictive, all-consuming, enlightening, enlivening and irreplaceable. Once it makes its insidious way into your life, violence becomes indispensable. It's like a benefactor that gives you independence, insight and dominion, as long as you feed it and as long as you worship it in return.

The lead-up to an attack becomes a period of intense, euphoric self-belief. You're supercharged, primed, explosively confident and exquisitely aware. You're ready to take on any challenge and not just beat it but smash it. Grind its bloodied face into the dirt like a worm, and move onto the next target. You're indomitable and invincible.

The time between episodes of violence becomes a time of waiting. You're chafing, aching for the surge of omnipotence it brings and the flood of release it incites. Listless, empty, you wait. You pine and fret, hoping that something, anything, will happen to set you off.

Then, an idea arises. A plan crystallises, and the blood begins to pump more freely in your veins. It gets hotter and faster until you pick up the gun, or the axe, or the knife – anything at all that you can use to crush, brutalise and obliterate your victim. And then you feel that rush of holy authority, a surge of vitality and lust, and you know you're truly alive because you're killing something else.

I can see now why violence persists in this world. It's too thrilling, voluptuous and viscerally fulfilling, too primitively motivating and ultimately rewarding to ever disappear. Once it has you, nothing else comes close to its ability to captivate, awaken and gratify you.

Funnily enough, I remain a pacifist. I still find war a stupid, wasteful, tyrannical burden. A frustratingly blunt instrument wielded by unimaginative weaklings whose only answer to a myriad of problems is to devastate the lives of others.

The difference is, now I would happily kill to persuade others of the righteousness of my cause. The only thing wrong with pacifism is that there's so little killing in it.

At the trial, it emerged that the lost licence plate had been found outside the Vega residence in the Hamptons, and Bevan's fingerprints were lifted off it. His prints were on file because he worked in the security industry. If I could, I would apologise to Lucas for suspecting him of being a snitch. I was sure it was him, especially when he walked away from the siege untouched.

I was convicted of the Surfside massacre and the murder of Richard White, in addition to a catalogue of break-ins and burglaries, petty vandalism, and being an accessory to the assassination of Alvarez Elitto.

Because the massacre was a federal crime, being a terrorist act, I was sentenced to death. So was Bevan, as noted above. I guess there will also be a trial or something over Zenstl's driver, and probably the Teterboro barbecue. I don't care – what are they going to do, execute me twice?

The saddest, maddest and most soul-destroying part of it is that although we slowed down PIVOT just a fraction, we didn't stop them. Even as I write, bombs are falling on Caracas and several other Venezuelan cities and towns, in the name of 'humanitarian intervention'. It makes me so fucking mad I could just cry. But I never do. I've lost my tears. I knew I had when I didn't even cry over Abby. I miss her terribly, and I always will, and I'll always have electric memories of our lives together, but I can't cry for her, and so I can't cry for anyone.

I know Abby went more than a little bit crazy. It's easy to see that in time's rearview mirror. But she will always be in my mind and my memories the same funny, sweet, beautiful and smart friend who was there for almost every good thing in my life. We shared our whole lives together; there isn't a moment that I would replace or remove, or a second I wouldn't relive if I could. So what if she was a little bit irrational at the end? That's not the way I think of her. I see warmth, generosity, spirit and intellect, and I feel her lying next to me in my hard prison bed. She is still, and will always be, the love of my life.

And my future, such as it is? I guess I sit here on death row for a few years while appeals are exhausted and the state does whatever it can to prolong my agony. Then, one day, they will come along to take me out and kill me for the crime of killing. And no one but me will see the irony.

Until then, I'll have to find something to do. Writing this has been fun, and it certainly brought back a lot of wonderful, warm and gratuitously violent memories, so I think I'll give it a rest for a few weeks, then pick up the pen again. I have an idea for a lovely story about a family of Venezuelan refugees who find peace and tranquillity among the tall trees and rugged lands of Oregon. I've never been there, but I can picture it in my mind.

To my parents and family, I am sorry for putting you through all this, although I hope that in some ways you can be proud of me. I helped Abby and Bevan show the world that war in any form is ugly and that at the end, its usefulness is limited if not nonexistent.

My parting statement to you, my reader, is this: war makes murderers, liars, whores and animals of us all sooner or later, and as humans our only way forward is to kill war or it will kill us. We won't even see what we've become until it's too late.

Women's Federal Correctional Facility, Fort Worth, Texas

The Cat Man
A tragicomic love triangle set in a crazy cat cult.
by
Nick Bruechle

"An enthralling, frightening and satirical study of cult leadership, dynamics and behaviour. " Online Book Club Review

The Cat Man is a funny, cynical and sometimes brutal love story of life, love, gullibility and manipulation.

Loving, loyal Rex is a dog person dealing with the catty people in his life – Chloe (his obsession), Casper (the Cat Man) and his feline-loving cult members.

Will he bring the cult down, and win Chloe's heart?

The Cat Man is now available at nickbruechle.com

The Psyman
by
Nick Bruechle

We make the reality here.

In our oxygen-soaked future, the three F's of Fear, Freedom and Fame reign supreme, surveillance is a way of life, and the Gobblers are tightly controlled by the Sharps.

In this dystopian, post-apocalyptic world, Necker experiences a war like no other, Bock lives through the peaks and troughs of transient fame and becomes a revolutionary, and Biz is drafted into the ranks of the Sharps, destined to rule.

But Biz is different to the other Sharps, and when he learns why, he also learns the key to restoring true Freedom to the people. Will he liberate the minds and change the lives of the Gobblers, or does fate have something else in store for him?

Nick Bruechle's dark vision of a fame-obsessed society wreathed in war and propaganda is by turns wry, terrifying and sad. His world is beautifully realised, chillingly authentic, and far too close to our own reality for comfort. *The Psyman* will have you questioning the nature of freedom, the art of propaganda and the dangerous distraction of fame.

The Psyman is now available at nickbruechle.com

The Reprint
by
Nick Bruechle

Who is Jakob Petersson? He wants to be the man his ex fell in love with, rather than the easygoing stoner his friends prefer. But right now he is neither.

And wait – did he commit a brutal crime last night?

Jakob's search for identity, meaning and the truth will reveal the dark secret of the deceptively idyllic city of New Elysium, and for that he will pay the ultimate price.

The Reprint is a thought provoking exploration of personality, a desolate portrayal of depression and drug addiction, and a mysterious adventure in a dystopian future.

The Reprint is now available at nickbruechle.com